The Scandinavian War Bride

Désirée Ohrbeck

Copyright © 2026 by Désirée Ohrbeck

All rights reserved.

No part of this book may be reproduced in any form or by any electronic or mechanical means, including information storage and retrieval systems, without written permission from the author, except for the use of brief quotations in a book review.

Cover and interior design by Covered by Kerry LLC
www.coveredbykerry.com

ISBN (Paperback): 979-8-9943110-0-4
ISBN (Hardcover): 979-8-9943110-1-1
ISBN (Ebook): 979-8-9943110-2-8

Published by Embarkation Books

"In life's crossroads, opt for the path requiring the greatest sacrifice."

– Simone Weil

In loving memory of my Danish grandmother and the thousands of women who, like her, took a leap of faith into the unknown and trusted their hearts, leaving everything they held dear behind.

Inspired by both the joyful and heartbreaking events that shaped my family.

Any similarities between the names, events, and locations in this work and those in real life are coincidental and used for creative purposes only.

COPENHAGEN
1938–1947

November 10, 1938
Kirsten

Kirsten is frozen in place, too scared to move. At her feet, splinters of glass are scattered across the dining room floor. One wrong move and her world shatters.

"Oh, for crying out loud, child!"

The whoosh of her father's blow sweeps past her temple, but she is prepared and ducks just in time. The smell of sour tobacco and scorched metal hits her nose. The next blow from his rough worker's fist lands squarely on her jaw. The force snaps her head to the side. A burning sensation shoots up her spine before settling as a nauseating ache in her stomach.

AT TEN YEARS OLD, KIRSTEN UNDERSTANDS WHEN adults discuss serious matters, though she doesn't fully grasp their meaning. Her parents' arguments and worries mostly center on money matters and a situation in Germany. A dangerous man named Hitler and his National Socialists, who are not the benevolent type of socialists, are causing trouble. Otherwise, her parents mostly talk about food prices and unemployment.

"Little pitchers have big ears," her mother usually says, before shooing Kirsten away. But she forgot to do that tonight.

˷

MOMENTS BEFORE, KIRSTEN HAD BEEN SITTING AT the dinner table, carefully finishing the last detail of an 'E' in her red notebook, hoping for her teacher's approval. Just as she was about to blow the ink dry, her parents' conversation shifted. This evening, the usual concerns — Copenhagen's unrest, her older brothers, and their ongoing money troubles — were put aside. They were talking about something that happened down in Germany.

Shattered windows, people beaten and shot, women and children driven away in trucks. Kirsten didn't want to linger and listen. Yet she sat immobile. A drop of dark ink dripped from the tip of her pen and landed between two lines of her letters. Tears welled in her eyes as her careful work was ruined. Watching the ink bleed, she imagined brown-shirted men running through shattered glass with clubs, smashing shopfronts and windows.

"Will I have to stay home from school tomorrow?" she asked. She was supposed to play hopscotch and marbles with the girls from her class; they had agreed on it.

Her mother folded her arms across her chest. "Do you think I want you under my feet all day?" she said in a voice that suggested everything was perfectly fine, "Of course you're going to school, you little fool."

A waft of her father's sweat, combined with the smell of cooked potatoes, filled Kirsten's nostrils. She took one last swig of milk before heading to her room, but in her haste, the glass slipped and broke.

⁂

KIRSTEN IS REELING FROM THE BLOW. SHE BREAKS her fall, landing hard on her hands and knees. When she looks up, she catches her father's eyes over the box of paper dolls on the dining table. His expression makes her think of bugs being crushed beneath a heel and she wants to flee; to disappear under the floorboards.

At the corner of her vision, the glass shards glint. White drops, like glistening pearls of snow, sway gently on the sharp edges. Kirsten swallows hard, twisting a strand of hair around her finger. With a tiny popping sound, a strand pulls from her scalp. *Everything is my fault*, she thinks. *The shattered glass. Father's rage. What he will do to Mother later.*

Kirsten's mother looks up from the table where she is stacking plates after dinner. "Karl, that's enough now."

"Oh, shut up, Edith! Can't a man get two minutes of peace in this house?"

Kirsten's knee feels as if it is on fire.

"Get up off the floor, child. Don't just lie there," her mother sighs.

The searing pain in Kirsten's knee is drowned out by a throbbing ache in her palm. As she lifts her hand, a bloody streak appears between her fingers, making her lightheaded.

"I'm sorry, Dad." Kirsten slowly rises, a tingling sensation running down her shin as another trickle of blood flows.

"You scoundrel!" Snorting, her father picks up the latest

Danish newspaper, *Socialdemokraten*, from the pile and goes to his armchair by the stove.

Kirsten sways. *One, two, three*, she counts to herself before pulling up her knee-high socks. As she does, a surge of anger hits her. Gone is the pain in her knee and palm. The hatred feels white-hot. If she dared, she would ask, "Why do you get so angry at me, Dad? Why am I always afraid around you?" Instead, she tiptoes out of the living room, carefully avoiding the broken glass as she goes to fetch a bucket and cloth from the kitchen.

As she sweeps up the glittering shards onto yesterday's newspaper, she overhears fragments of her parents' discussion.

"Thousands of storefront windows smashed... Jews driven away... concentration camps... synagogues set on fire."

"Who did this?" Kirsten's mother sets down the stack of dirty plates with a forceful thud. Hoping for a treat, Spot sits beside her, fixated on her every move.

Even before her father answers, Kirsten recognizes his sigh, as if the answer to her mother's question is obvious. "Goebbels."

Kirsten rubs the cloth against the diamonds on the floor. Her parents' conversation continues. "Brownshirts... Swastikas... Communists..."

With each word, Kirsten's chest tightens, and she swallows hard to keep the sob lodged high in her throat from escaping.

She glances up, noticing the way her mother's shoulders hunch up to her ears as she slowly moves around the table, gathering the dirty cutlery. "He doesn't even remotely resemble their image of an ideal Aryan. Far from their notion of a perfect human," she says.

"Work rumors have it they released prisoners and put them in uniforms. Murderers, rapists, and psychopaths turned into Brownshirts." Her dad coughs. "They have no moral compass and will do anything for their superiors."

"Imagine just standing idly by." With a sigh, Kirsten's mother wipes her hands on her apron, the fabric stretched across her pregnant belly. "Germans used to be such fine people." Her movements are jerky as she wipes the dining table with a grayish rag.

"Do you think things would be any better up here?" Kirsten's father snorts. The newspaper snaps as he turns a page. "No one stands up for those the majority tramples on."

"Hopefully we won't see Jewish people wandering north after this." With a sweep of the rag, Kirsten's mother gathers a few crumbs in her palm.

"Those in power will never truly understand the life of ordinary people." A sound like a whip crack fills the room as he flips another page. "We must tread carefully to avoid creating an 'us versus them' mentality." He picks up his pipe and singes the top of the tobacco. "Together we are stronger."

Kirsten presses down on the rag, watching the soapy water streak across the floor. The fireplace crackles. Her father takes his time holding the flame above the tobacco pipe, charring and puffing.

"Denmark's National Socialist Workers' Party has five thousand members. Maybe the Nazis will get seats in Parliament here after the next election."

Kirsten's mother picks at a corner of her apron. "It's probably just a temporary craze in Germany. The Danish people won't fall for that."

From behind the newspaper, Kirsten´s father sighs. "Denmark is the country with the most Nazi parties and the fewest Nazis. People have no qualms opposing us socialists in whatever way they can." Scowling, he continues, "Watching them march through the streets making those ridiculous salutes, looking for trouble — it makes me sick to my stomach."

"Don't you think our boys will straighten them out?" Her mother glances toward the end of the dining table where Kirsten's older brothers usually sit.

Does that explain why Laust, Martin, and Knud often get home late? Kirsten thinks to herself. *Is that why her mother tells them that "mad cats get their skin torn" as she gently dabs their grazed cheekbones?*

After checking the floor twice, Kirsten wraps the shards in newspaper, tucking in the ends to prevent any from slipping loose, before dropping the bundle into the kitchen bin.

In her cloth shoes, she tiptoes into the bedroom she shares with Martha and little Ingrid. Martha is out enjoying herself again. She's allowed much more freedom since her confirmation. Ingrid is, doing the dishes in the kitchen — standing on her stool so she can better reach. Playing school, her voice carries through the house, with Ingrid as the teacher. Kirsten smiles. Her younger sister is so eager to begin school next summer.

Her father's voice carries from the living room, too. Kirsten hears him say something about giving someone a thrashing and feels her throat getting dry. If the men in brown shirts ever felt her father's fists, they'd quickly come to understand the meaning of behaving.

꒰

KIRSTEN SIGHS AS SHE UNDRESSES. SHE TRIES SO hard. But it always goes wrong somehow. The memory of her father's blows makes her back muscles tense. His presence always puts her on high alert. How do Martha and Ingrid avoid his anger when she can't? Climbing into bed, Kirsten folds her hands above the blanket. *Dear God, make me good. Amen.*

She finds a good strand of hair and wraps it around her index finger, twisting until she reaches the root. Then she pulls. When she opens her hand, a chestnut-brown curl unfolds.

It's all my fault. I talk too much and I'm not cautious enough.

Kirsten places the strand of hair over the cut on her palm and presses down with her thumb. It pulses, warm and tender. Then she scrapes a fingernail across the raw, throbbing wound on her knee. Tears well in her eyes at the pain, but the burning ache sends her thoughts fleeing. Turning onto her side, she folds her hands again and whispers: *One day you'll be free of me. Then you won't have to deal with my cheekiness, Dad. And you will no longer have to endure my difficult nature, Mom.*

Dr Hansen
Kirsten

"Speak up so I can understand you, child!" exclaims Kirsten's mother, hands on her hips, a frown furrowing her brow. "It's time to take you to Dr Hansen. This can't go on any longer."

When Kirsten presses the top of her throat with her fingers, she can feel two swollen, tender lumps. They remind her of the area above Spot's eyes.

"You sound like you have porridge in your throat." Her mother quickly brushes Kirsten's hair with her hands.

"I don't want to go to the doctor. I want to go to school."

Mom sighs. "Yes, you're a little bookworm."

Kirsten imagines herself as a greenish-brown larva, gnawing her way through a book — emerging on one page and disappearing on another. She smiles at the image then shakes her head. Her mother is right. Sometimes at school, small white lumps rise from her throat. When her teacher has her back turned to class, writing on the chalkboard with her squeaky chalk, Kirsten surreptitiously smears the lumps under her school desk.

"In my skirt pocket lies your will!" The furrow on her mother's forehead is back. Kirsten ducks just in time to see the dishcloth whizz past her cheek.

*

Kirsten kicks her legs back and forth. *Now I can see my right foot, now I can see my left foot. Right foot. Left foot. Right. Foot. Left. Foot. Right. Left. Foot. Foot.*

At Dr Hansen's office, you must always wait. *One-two-three. Four-five-six. One-two-three.* Kirsten counts to herself, creating an inner melody with her swinging legs as the rhythm.

"Be still, child!" Her mother's elbow jabs into her ribs.

It's so hard to stay still. Counting helped.

*

"The child exhibits tonsillar hypertrophy."

Kirsten knows Dr Hansen is referring to her. She looks up at her mother.

Looming over Kirsten, the doctor says, "Your tonsils are enlarged. We'll have to get rid of them."

That's old hat, let's get rid of that, Kirsten thinks.

Straightening up, Dr Hansen turns to Kirsten's mother. "My secretary can schedule an appointment for you. We can perform a tonsillectomy as early as this week." Glancing downward at his papers, he makes a note.

"How much will it cost?" Her mother's voice is barely audible, like when Kirsten's father is in one of his moods.

With a sigh, the doctor taps his golden fountain pen on the prescription pad and quotes a number. "For surgery and anesthesia."

His bushy eyebrows peek out from above his glasses. The wrinkles on his forehead look like the folds in Spot's neck.

Kirsten looks up at her mother and then down at her hand. Her mother's knuckles are white around Kirsten's squeezed fingers.

"I'll have to talk to the girl's father," she says, turning sharply toward the door.

"When you are ready, you can make the arrangements with Miss Iversen in the front office. The payment must be paid in full when you bring the girl in for surgery."

Kirsten's mother nods briefly. "Thank you, Doctor," she mutters, and hurries off with Kirsten.

Tonsils
Kirsten

Kirsten's mother ties her scarf under her chin. "I'm off," she says, slinging her bag across her shoulder. "I'm cleaning the stairs at number eighteen and then I have a shift at the cigar factory."

Reaching into her purse, she pulls out her wallet and hands Kirsten's father a bundle of tightly rolled-up bills. He is yet again without a job. This time, an argument with his foreman has left him sprawled on the sofa.

"You must give the doctor all of it when you drop her off, Karl." She glances in Kirsten's direction. "Remember what we talked about? For the girl's sake."

Kirsten's father grumbles and sits up. He takes the money, runs his thumb over the roll, and pockets the bills.

❧

"Kirsten, K-I-R-S-T-E-N," Kirsten spells out. "Marie, M-A-R-I-E."

"What a clever girl you are." The secretary adds Kirsten's name to her ledger.

"Pedersen, with a 'D'. P-E-D-E-R-S-E-N."

Kirsten
Marie
Pedersen

"Go sit over there and wait while I speak to your father." The secretary gestures toward some chairs by the wall.

With a nod, Kirsten chooses the same seat as last time.

"Are you absolutely certain, Mr. Pedersen?" Although the secretary lowers her voice, Kirsten can still hear her clearly.

Kirsten watches the secretary's face twist into a grimace, like her mother's when Kirsten's bad breath gets too near. But the secretary's gaze has something else to it, too — something sorrowful — as she looks in Kirsten's direction.

"I'll come fetch you later," Kirsten's father mumbles, his back turned, already on his way out of the waiting room. Before he leaves, Kirsten watches him stuff something into his pocket.

☽

"Now, you must be a brave little girl," Dr. Hansen says with a light tone and averted eyes. The doctor bends down toward Kirsten. In one hand, he holds a metal clamp. On his forehead is a lamp that shines so brightly she must squint to look at him.

"I have nothing you can squeeze, so hold on tightly to Miss Iversen."

The secretary places one hand on Kirsten's forehead. "Try

to lie still. That will make it less painful." She gently strokes Kirsten's arm with her free hand.

Feeling the cold steel in her mouth, Kirsten thinks of black, salty licorice and nails. A dry metallic taste spreads across her tongue as it scrapes against her molars. The rod continues down her throat, making it impossible for her to swallow.

"I've changed my mind. I don't want to do this. It doesn't even hurt anymore." The words sound as if she has a potato in her mouth, her teeth clicking against the metal.

Kirsten wants to jump up and run away. Anywhere far, far away from here.

"It will be over in no time." Blinking rapidly, the secretary seems bothered by something in her eyes.

The tightness in Kirsten's throat eases, and the stinging behind her eyelids fades.

Placing the rod on the metal tray, Dr. Hansen looks at his secretary. "Will you be able to hold her?"

Kirsten feels a firm grip on her shoulders. With a quick glance at his secretary, the doctor adjusts his headlamp and leans over Kirsten once more. In his hand is a tiny instrument resembling a doll-sized clamp. This time, as the rod travels down her throat, there is a determination in the doctor's movements.

Kirsten feels a tightening; a struggle between her muscles, wanting to both reject and embrace the foreign object. She feels the instrument ripping her throat apart, envisioning gaping red and yellow wounds screaming for help. Then follows a taste of salt and blood before she passes out.

"I'll never do that again! Ever! You should be ashamed of yourself!" Dr. Hansen towers above Kirsten's swaying father as he delivers the reprimand.

Her father coughs into his hand and wipes his nose with the back of his jacket sleeve. The familiar stench of beer, liquor, and cigarette smoke spreads through the waiting room. Kirsten feels a rising tide of nausea, her stomach churning. Unable to swallow because of the pain in her throat, saliva drips from both corners of her mouth.

"Let's go." Kirsten's father pulls her up from the waiting room chairs where she has been lying. "It's over, girl. Now you have no tonsils."

His focus swims as he attempts to look directly at her. He has that smile on his lips she knows so well: *sorry* mixed with *come on, it's not that bad, right?*

Kirsten looks away. She might have had her tonsils removed, but she now sees her father in a new light.

The Twins
Kirsten

The door to her parents' bedroom is slightly ajar. Kirsten studies the veins in the wood, letting her focus wander around the black Bakelite handle.

From the living room, she hears the familiar rustling sound of her father's newspaper. Kirsten imagines the movement as he flips a page in a jerky motion, letting the day's news fall into place. Like a tiny figure behind columns of miniature text, he sits behind his newspaper wall, half his legs sticking out below and a column of smoke rising behind the barrier. A glimpse of his face shows as the pages come together, parting once again as he opens the day's news like an embrace. As if she is standing next to him, she hears the crackle of his pipe tobacco with each puff.

Kirsten's attention returns to the bedroom. Her older sister Martha is in there. And her mother, of course. A lump forms in Kirsten's throat as Martha sings: *The angel of light walks with splendor through the gates of heaven.*

"Dear God," Kirsten whispers, "Save their souls. Drive the darkness away."

Martha's voice continues: *His gaze encompasses both the magnificent and the minuscule, as he kisses the sleeping infant.*

Kirsten pushes the bedroom door open. A wave of metallic sickness hits her. Sweat, bad breath and urine create a pungent odor that stings her nose. On the edge of her bed, their mother stares into nothingness. On the floor in front of her sits little Ingrid.

Dear God, she is so small. Only eight years old, Kirsten thinks, before glancing towards the dresser where Martha is stroking the twins' cheeks. *I must be the grown-up,* Kirsten thinks. *I am twelve now, after all.*

"Mom, please try one more time." Martha lifts a pink bundle from the dresser drawer. Kirsten's mother pulls up her blouse, ready to nurse the little one. A deep sob escapes her lips as the fabric falls and covers her flat chest. On the wall behind them, dark gray shadows move, mimicking their helplessness. Despite the drawn curtains, a beam of light shines in from the doorway and falls upon little Ingrid and the baby. The baby's face glows gray against the pink bonnet. Her eyes are shut. A faint wheezing is the only sign that she is breathing.

"It's pointless." Kirsten's mother holds the flap of skin from her chest with her index and middle fingers. A pearly drop of milk balances on the tip of the downward-facing nipple, then trembles, loses its grip, and lands on the baby's chin.

"I can ask the farm if they have milk?" Martha, already headed for the door, gathers her shawl around her shoulders.

"It's pointless," their mother repeats. She presses a finger to the baby's ashen cheeks, prying the mouth open, and places her nipple into the baby's doll-like mouth.

Kirsten's heart is racing. An impulse to run comes rushing over her. The next moment, it feels like an elephant is standing on her chest, and she gasps for air. Her legs tingle and sting, and her hands tremble as a sweat storm sweeps through her body. Intense heat gives way to an icy chill. Her head buzzing, she looks around the bedroom, momentarily seeing herself from the outside before she snaps back into the room again.

Her mother's nipple is long and spongy. Using her free hand, she cups her breast, trying to push out more drops. Bubbles of mucus form at the baby's nostrils.

"Try the other one." Hurrying over, Kirsten changes her direction and goes to lift the light blue bundle from the dresser drawer. Martha follows, taking the pink twin from her mother, and whispers softly into the girl's face. Kirsten gently places the boy in her mother's lap and watches her force his blue-gray lips apart. There's a dull emptiness in his stare. A few bluish-white drops drip onto his mouth. Kirsten feels like pumping her mother's breast until the milk flows for her baby brother. Instead, she turns away.

☽

IN THE DAYS THAT FOLLOW, KIRSTEN AND MARTHA change diapers, soothe and swaddle the babies, and tend to household chores.

When Kirsten passes the bedroom door, she can hear hollow coughs. It doesn't sound like much at first, but then comes the fever and a cold sets in. The worst part is the rattling, wheezing sound of their struggle to breathe before the coughing fit begins. In moments of silence, Kirsten quietly walks into the room and places a hand on their bodies, checking that they are still breathing.

After a few days, the fever subsides. That night, Kirsten sleeps peacefully. The next morning, the aroma of coffee greets her from the kitchen, where Martha is preparing breakfast. The conversation flows easily and the cutlery clinks in a cozy way; a brief moment of relief.

But then the twins' coughing fits return. Thick, sticky mucus oozes from their mouths and noses. Kirsten and Martha boil dirty cloth diapers while their mother rests, exhausted, on the bed. It is an endless battle against secretions and vomit. Once the twins are wiped down with a warm, damp cloth, they burp up the meagre bit of milk their mother has dripped into their mouths.

☽

KIRSTEN WAKES TO A COLD BEDROOM. FROST flowers create intricate swirling patterns on the window. She breathes on the glass and draws a circle. Outside, the frozen grass in the yard looks like tiny, sharp icicles. From the hallway, she hears Martha's soft voice: *Grant us peace and rest, Lord Jesus, as we place our trust in you; comfort the weary hearts and close the tired eyes.*

In her parents' bedroom, Kirsten hears the bed make a creaking sound as their mother gets up. "It was probably for the best," she says, loud enough that Kirsten can hear it.

The floor creaks, the curtains rustle, and the sound of the window latch clicks. Kirsten can almost feel the draft.

"Stop crying, Martha."

Martha's sobs grow in intensity. Kirsten feels her body grow heavy. Then she clenches her fists and whispers: "Where is your light, God? Why did the shadows of the night and the powers of darkness win?"

In the living room, their father's newspaper is silent. When Kirsten opens the door to her parents' bedroom, Martha and their mother glance at her. God's angel of light has passed through the room. Ingrid sits in a corner with her matchstick arms wrapped around her legs. Her right cheek is flushed with the mark of a slap. The window is ajar.

Kirsten walks over to the dresser drawer where the twins lie, resembling both porcelain dolls and old men, with tall foreheads and oversized eyes. A pale gray fist sticks up from the pink baby doll, her fingertips thin as paper.

"It's good you laid them like that, Martha," their mother sighs.

The babies' faces are turned toward each other, as if whispering a farewell before giving up.

"They entered the world together." Martha's voice breaks. She stands by the window.

Kirsten's mother sighs and lies down on the bed with her back to the dresser.

Little Ingrid rises and quietly moves to stand by the bed. Her hand creeps forward but is slapped away.

"Get out!" The voice has the hiss of a wounded animal. "Go away!"

Tears stream down Ingrid's face, yet not so much as a sniffle escapes her. At the window, Martha turns and reaches a hand out to Ingrid. Together, the three girls slip out of the room, leaving their mother behind with her twins.

IN THE KITCHEN, KIRSTEN CAN BREATHE AGAIN. She ignites the gas burner and fills the kettle with water.

"Those poor little things." Martha sighs as she fetches coffee cups from the cupboard. "I should have gone to the farm."

The cups clink as Martha sets them down. Pouring boiling water over the coffee beans in the cloth filter, Kirsten pauses, her hands trembling too much to continue. Madame Blue, the enameled coffee pot, waits patiently, her swan-like neck poised as water fills her rounded form.

"Mom wouldn't have it." Kirsten thinks her mother shouldn't have given up. Instead, she says, "She couldn't handle any more little ones."

Little Ingrid's mouth quivers. *I'm such an idiot*, Kirsten thinks. *When will I learn to keep my mouth shut?*

"They could have been mine." Martha strokes her stomach. "I could have kept them alive." Martha ruffles Ingrid's hair, giving Kirsten a long look. "Let's go for a walk. We'll pick some nice small branches and place them by the little ones."

Ingrid leaps from her chair, her eyes sparkle with excitement.

Kirsten puts the cups in the sink. "I'll join you. I need some fresh air."

Springtime
Kirsten

Kirsten sends a hateful thought to the Germans as she sits at the newspaper-covered dining table with the rest of her family. Chewing on a meatball that consists more of oatmeal than ground beef, she looks with disdain at her potato. She squashes it with her fork, swirling the mash in the meatball grease.

One year into the Nazi occupation, much is different. With a wolfish hunger, Kirsten catalogues the changes as margarine replaces butter and oats are used to stretch rationed ground meat. Now, Danish butter, cheese, milk, and bacon end up in German stomachs instead of Danish ones as coupons and rationing are introduced in Denmark.

Kirsten experiences changes to her body, too. Firm, soft lumps have developed under her tiny nipples. In the privacy of the outhouse, she notices dark hair sprouting from between her thighs. Her mood swings are as unpredictable as the German occupying forces. Thirteen is no easy age.

Sighing, Kirsten glances at the frying pan. She understands why her mother wants to reign supreme over cabbage and potatoes, and doesn't allow anyone in the kitchen when she's cooking. In a house with many mouths to feed, food waste can mean the difference between happy and hungry bellies.

On the radio, they claim Denmark isn't as severely affected as many other countries. Still, the Nazis are in complete control, and Kirsten feels like she's missing out when her growing desire for independence clashes with the occupation. She must always be careful and has learned that it's wisest to keep her head bowed and her gaze lowered.

Occupation, rationing, Dad's anger, Kirsten thinks, running her finger around the edge of the dinner plate. *I wish I could shoo you all away! I long to live life!*

❧

"Thanks for dinner, Mom," she says as she leaves the table.

In her head, Kirsten maps out how she and Martha will sneak into town once the house has gone quiet. Her body tingles with anticipation.

My sister's a scaredy-cat, so I'll have to plan our entertainment, Kirsten thinks, smiling at her own boldness. She has meticulously planned how to get into town without being caught by their father. *Go to bed in your party clothes. Remember to put your shoes and coat by the windowsill*, she silently repeats to herself.

❧

"What if he finds out?" Martha is picking at her cuticle.

"Stop being such a scared little mouse! Otherwise I won't be able to go either." Kirsten is standing in front of her older sister.

"Someday, we will be caught." Martha's cuticle is now bleeding.

"Today's not the day, agreed?" Kirsten smiles wryly.

Martha turns away as Kirsten tries to give her hands a squeeze. "The place will be brimming with Germans!" Flustered, Martha tucks a strand of hair behind her ear.

"You will handle them in your own sweet way. They never bother looking at me." Kirsten hopes her voice sounds light.

"You're getting to an age where men pay attention to you." Martha glances at the lumps under Kirsten's blouse.

Folding her arms, Kirsten rolls her eyes. "But it's so boring here!"

"One day, your reckless behavior will get you into trouble, little sister." Martha strides out of the room and slams the door behind her before Kirsten can deliver the cutting remark that's ready on her tongue.

☽

KIRSTEN USES HER FOUNTAIN PEN AND A CODE TO write in her diary about what she hopes will happen soon. Silly princess dreams that she knows belong to a little girl, mixed with what she hopes is a realistic future waiting for her. Her first crush. Holding hands. Her first kiss.

As evening falls, to ease her restlessness, she helps her mother clean up. She sweeps ash from the wood stove into the metal container. Outside, she is careful to check which direction the wind is coming from as she tips the box upside down. Then she fetches brown coal and peat, her footsteps quickening as she is looking forward to the night.

Later, the two sisters lie fully dressed in their beds. Once the house is quiet, Kirsten glances over at little Ingrid before throwing off the blanket.

"Good thing she's such a sound sleeper."

Martha puts a finger to her lips. "Maybe she's pretending."

Kirsten nudges her little sister, who smacks her lips and turns in her sleep.

At the window, she loosens the storm hook and climbs out, setting the latch so she can open it from the outside when they return. She hears Martha's stealthy footsteps following after.

Kirsten gazes at the horizon. The moon is lit up, the wind is mild: it's springtime in Denmark. A breeze caresses her skirt, carrying the scent of soft soil from the yard. Behind her, the bungalow looms like a yellow monster.

I'm no longer a child, she thinks. *Why should I be deprived of fun and vibrant colors?* She lets her fingertips run over the rough bricks. *I'm being suffocated. There's no room to move for me here! Outside our front door, Denmark is occupied, and inside the house, Dad rules us with an iron fist. No matter where I turn, I'm being controlled and watched.*

Kirsten inhales the night air and starts down the paved path. At the gate, she carefully lifts the hinge to avoid its metallic creak. Finally, she and Martha are standing on the street.

"Ready?" Kirsten looks expectantly at Martha.

With a buzzing in her ears and a lightness in her feet, Kirsten runs. Her body falls into rhythm. Her breathing and legs work in unison along the gravel roads, past the cabbage fields, toward Copenhagen. As she feels her shoulders relax, she glances at Martha and quietly sings Bing Crosby's song:

Would you like to swing on a star,
Carry moonbeams home in a jar,
And be better off than you are,
Or would you rather be a mule?

LALE ANDERSEN
KIRSTEN

One thing the German occupation has taught Kirsten is to stay alert when she's out and about.

On this early Sunday morning, Kirsten is on her way to babysit. The city is mostly still asleep, but the streets show lingering signs of last night's partying. *If you keep your eyes peeled,* she thinks to herself, *you never know what treasures you might find.*

Someone has forgotten their coat on a bench. Kirsten looks around to see if anyone is nearby. Morning sunlight glimmers on the Church of Our Savior's twisted spire. People leave the strangest things behind when they've been out partying. However, on closer inspection, that's not the case with this coat. At the collar, long, light locks of hair dance in the wind.

"Are you all right?" she asks.

A heavy wave of musky perfume, booze, and cigarettes hits Kirsten's nose as the wind carries a whiff from the bench. As Kirsten takes a step back, she hears the gravel crunch under her feet. There is no answer from the coat.

Kirsten moves closer and pulls the collar aside, revealing a woman with dark ringed circles under her eyes. Her hair is disheveled, and her lipstick smeared. Squinting, the woman brushes a strand of hair from the corner of her mouth. A smile plays in her eyes as she pushes herself upright.

The person sitting on the bench is no ordinary individual. Kirsten recognizes her immediately.

"Gut Tag," the woman says with an unmistakable German accent, close enough to the Danish "hello" that Kirsten understands.

God knows how a famous singer like Lale Andersen has ended up on a Copenhagen bench, Kirsten ponders. She's famous for singing that one song. Everyone knows *Lili Marleen*. It was originally sung by Marlene Dietrich, but she emigrated to America and has refused to return to the German Reich. Lale Andersen is now singing for the Nazis throughout Europe, lifting the spirits of the troops with her performance. It seems the tour has reached Denmark. Each night, the familiar tune of *Lili Marleen* from Radio Belgrade fills the trenches on either side of the front, providing a brief respite for both German and British soldiers. So popular is the song that for its brief radio broadcast, fighting ceases.

"Guten Tag. Hello," Kirsten says, using her most practiced school German, wondering if Lale knows exactly where she is.

Kirsten studies the celebrity's features. Like a two-part curtain, her hair frames her face. Her thin nose and delicately plucked eyebrows, arched high, give her a perpetually surprised expression. Her blasé attitude — a mixture of mystery and playful teasing — shifts as her eyes meet Kirsten's.

"Didn't you used to have a bob and dress in sailor suits

like a man?" The words leap out of Kirsten's mouth before she can catch them.

Lale raises an eyebrow. "Things change. Goebbels wants strength through joy, so that's what I´m giving him."

Kirsten recognizes the radio phrase. "Kraft durch Freude."

Lale nods in agreement.

"You almost look Danish," Kirsten says.

Lale gazes at a flock of pigeons nearby. "During my cabaret days, German audiences wanted a performer who was both androgynous and a seductress. Now that kind of woman is viewed as depraved."

"One must adapt, said the eel." Kirsten makes a wavy motion with her hand to demonstrate the saying.

With a flurry, the pigeons take off over the water.

"I don't mind being a chameleon. Back in Germany, people now believe I have Norwegian heritage."

"I hope, for your sake, you never encounter a Norwegian who can put your language skills to the test." Again, Kirsten feels like stuffing her words back into her mouth.

"You'd be surprised how much you can get away with if you keep your mouth shut." Lale winks teasingly.

With a tug, Kirsten pulls her red beret down onto her forehead.

"So, now I'm a blond, long-haired diva from Scandinavia. I hope you don't mind that I'm borrowing a bit of your Viking culture?" Kirsten shakes her head and Lale continues: "With the right Aryan background, everything is easier."

Blue embroidery adorns her dress. Images of dance halls, patterned curtains and tablecloths flit through Kirsten's mind, but before she can speak, the singer's posture shifts with a sudden jerk. Lale's head shoots up, exposing her white neck. The motion sends a shiver through Kirsten.

"We've got company," Lale whispers.

Two stout uniformed men in dark coats and wide belts approach them.

"Take these." Lale extends a hand, and Kirsten quickly accepts a pair of tickets. "I hope to see you there." Tossing her head towards the park, in the opposite direction to the men, she stands, shielding Kirsten from view.

Kirsten slides the tickets into her pocket and leaps onto the path behind the bench.

"Gentlemen! My escorts!" is the last thing Kirsten hears before sprinting away from the two Nazi soldiers.

BLACK RUDOLF
KIRSTEN

From the bar the Germans call Deutsches Eck, or German Corner, the sounds of a wheezing accordion and a hoarse singing voice carry in the breeze outside the nightclub. Once Kirsten gets used to the accent, she understands.

> *Does Black Rudolf know how to kiss?*
> *You better believe he does,*
> *'Cause she taught him how.*

The famous sea shanty, *Black Rudolf*, sung in German-Danish, features rolling 'R's and a melodic range far exceeding the subdued, flat tones of Danish.

> *Does Black Rudolf know how to make love?*
> *You better believe he does!*

Inside, people are whistling and catcalling. Kirsten

pictures what lies behind the establishment's closed doors: well-groomed Germans in olive-green uniforms, their polished boots beneath the tables in the dimly lit bar; the rich smell of velour hanging in the air as the bartender serves foamy beers. She pictures a stage: a podium hazy with swirling smoke; the thick smell of tobacco; cigarettes dangling from soldiers' lips beneath their carefully trimmed mustaches.

"I'm not sure we should go in." Martha fiddles with a button on her coat.

"We've been running as if our lives depended on it. If we're going to get a beating from Dad, no matter what, we might as well."

Martha bites her lip. "This is the last time I'm doing this."

Kirsten opens the door to a cacophony of sounds. For a moment she stands frozen as her eyes adjust to the darkness. A beer mug smashes, and roaring laughter erupts. Kirsten walks to an empty table. The hairs on the back of her neck stand up as she feels eyes creeping around her face, then senses them crawl further —gliding around her neck, lingering at her bust, settling around her hips — before finally wandering back to meet her eyes. She's confused; this kind of attention is usually directed at women older than her. She straightens her back as sweat breaks out on her palms.

⁎

WHEN LALE ANDERSEN FINISHES HER SAILOR'S song, the men jump up and stomp their feet on the floor. Smiling at each soldier, the singer lets her gaze linger on every face. Kirsten feels as though as she's being let in on something too personal. The impression leaves her with a mixture of unease, curiosity and confusion. It's as if the clientele are sharing experiences about something intimate Kirsten doesn't yet quite understand. The room radiates an energy, a common unspoken understanding that makes her feel left out. Lale's eyes meet Kirsten's, and the singer arches an eyebrow.

"Ladies, may I offer you something to drink?" As if a thread snaps, Kirsten's connection to Lale breaks at the interruption. Directly in front of her, a German soldier, fully uniformed, stands at attention. His German-accented Danish pronunciation of "drink" is marked by its characteristically harsh, over-pronounced 'R' sound.

Seeing a man in uniform sends a jolt of fear through Kirsten. Her heart pounds. Unable to move her damp fingertips from the table, she tries to control her voice. "Yes, thank you," she replies hesitantly.

There's a click as the soldier snaps his heels together. He thrusts out his chest. "Meine Damen. I'll be back in a moment."

Kirsten watches him go to the bar. "He called us 'my ladies'. I don't think anyone has ever addressed me like that." She leans towards Martha and whispers, "He's surprisingly nice, for a German."

Under the table, Martha kicks her shin.

The German comes back with two full glasses. "Now, let's 'hugge' us. Isn't that what you Danes would call it?"

Martha nods. "Yes, hygge is a term we use to describe a cozy atmosphere."

She sounds like a schoolteacher, Kirsten thinks, but smiles and nods at her sister.

"I've brought my friend," the soldier says, looking at Martha. "He's around the same age as your younger sister."

He edges his chair closer to Martha's. As he sits down, he gestures invitingly to his friend, who responds by taking a seat next to Kirsten.

The older soldier glances toward the stage. "Where did the beautiful Lale go? I hope she didn't go back to Norway," he laughs.

From the speakers, a rhythmic beat of maracas fills the room. The soft, warm sound of the wooden instrument blends with the sharper notes of a trumpet as Kirsten's foot taps along.

Drinkin' rum and Coca-Cola...

She sings along, drawing out the word "Cocaaaaa-Cola," her voice sweet and syrupy like the drink itself. *We are going to have a fun evening!* she thinks, catching Martha's eye.

Guarantee you one fine time working for
the Yankee dollaaaar.

A German soldier, his face flushed, rises shakily from another table. "Forget 'Yankee dollar' — are any of you ladies interested in working for Reichsmarks?"

Thrusting his pelvis in a controlled rhythm, he surveys the women in the room. Kirsten averts her eyes as he wipes a smear of beer foam from the corner of his mouth. Around them, laughter roars. Kirsten's nostrils twitch. There's an atmosphere of a predator stalking his prey.

"By the way, my name is Heinz, and this lion here is Rolf." Leaning over the table, Heinz gestures towards the soldier next to Kirsten.

"I'm starving," Kirsten blurts out.

"There's no free lunch in this world," Martha hisses.

"What's your beautiful sister saying?" Heinz's piercing gray eyes hold Kirsten's gaze.

"She's reminding me I was just sick." Kirsten swallows hard. "I should probably stick to water." Kirsten hopes her smile reaches her eyes. Her spine is damp with sweat.

"You have been ill, Fräulein?" Rolf furrows his brow. "Do you need some fresh air?"

Kirsten shakes her head; she's heard about that trick before. No way is she going outside with him. "Just a glass of water, thank you. I don't need anything else."

Their arms brush against each other.

"I'll be right back with a cool glass of water for you." Rolf leaps to his feet.

Perhaps Martha was right after all, Kirsten thinks. *Perhaps this was a mistake.* A shiver runs through her. It feels as if she's in open water. *If I venture farther out, am I going to sink?* she wonders, glancing over at her sister.

The sound of Rolf placing a glass in front of her jolts her back to the room.

"To my new beautiful Danish friend." He scoots his chair closer to hers. "Tell me about yourself, Fräulein."

Kirsten feels her shoulders tense. "Teach me some German instead," she replies.

"You're interested in languages, jah?"

Kirsten nods. She points: "Im Raum gibt es... um..." Suddenly, she can't remember a single German word. She closes her eyes, picturing the illustrations in her school textbook.

Eine Bühne.
Einen Sänger.
Stühle und Tische.

Kirsten feels a little embarrassed as she lists the stage, singer, and chairs around them. *How silly!* Finally, she looks back at Rolf. "Can you understand my German?"

"Jah. Well done, Kirsten." Rolf winks. "Now I have a task for you, Fräulein."

This game is surprisingly easy. Give him what he wants. Lower your gaze, encourage him to talk about himself. *Play along*, Kirsten thinks. "Yes?"

From his pocket, Rolf takes out a photograph: a younger version of himself. Frozen in time, his eyes meet hers. A gentle feeling spreads through her as she looks at the picture. A double-breasted olive-green jacket with room for stripes and medals, the shoulders of a boy, a belt at the waist, baggy trousers and long black boots. She studies his face. What does that expression conceal? Sadness? Patriotism? Hope? The downy hair on his cheeks and chin is barely visible. Kirsten looks up into the older Rolf's cool gaze. His eyes, sharp and hungry, full of self-assured confidence, cut through her. Does he sense her vulnerability? As Kirsten's fear intensifies, Rolf's expression grows increasingly entitled. The balance shifts, the power she felt when he introduced himself ebbs away. It is as if he knows how the rest of the evening will unfold. Kirsten is frozen, her breath held captive as Rolf's burning stare pins her to the chair, making time stand still. *How does innocence turn to predation?* she thinks.

Slowly, with each word enunciated clearly, Rolf asks. "What do you see, Fräulein?"

☽

EXCITEMENT HANGS IN THE AIR, THE ROOM ALIVE with a vibrant buzz of anticipation. *Something is brewing*, Kirsten thinks, sipping her water. The men glance at their watches. *What are they waiting for?* Kirsten checks her own watch: 9:55 p.m. She lets her eyes wander across the tables in the room. In the quiet, the smell of old, worn chair upholstery becomes stronger, a mixture of sweat and spilled beer heavy in the air.

At precisely 9:57 p.m., the speakers crackle. The sound of a trumpet march begins. The room is vibrating. Lale Andersen steps onto the stage with a confident stride and stands in front of her admiring audience. But a moment later, her expression shifts to confusion.

What's happening? Kirsten thinks. Lale's eyes, which moments ago sparkled with anticipation, now have a wounded expression that makes her face crumble. Suddenly, Kirsten understands the situation. The speakers aren't just playing the melody of *Lili Marleen*, but the vocals of Marlene Dietrich.

The sound of a needle scratching vinyl abruptly stops the music. *That record's ruined*, Kirsten thinks. The venue is eerily silent. There's not a single sound; no chair scraping, no beer mug clinking. Everyone is watching the brightly lit stage. And there Lale stands, alone, looking like someone who's had the feathers plucked from her swan costume. No longer a diva, but an ordinary woman someone has dressed up. Stiffly, she turns and walks toward the stage exit.

"Marlene Dietrich, you traitor!" The voice is loud enough for everyone else turn to see where the utterance came from. The man plants a foot on the floor with a stomp and a chant, and the room falls into unison: "Lale! Lale! Lale!"

Lale squares her shoulders and elongates her neck. A flicker of emotion crosses her face. Her eyelashes, like delicate butterfly wings, settle softly against her cheekbones. Stepping further onto the stage, she is illuminated by the spotlight. Slowly, she raises her arms, making the ethereal angel wings on her dress point upward. The room breathes silently. For a few more seconds, Lale has them all held captive. Then her velvety, husky voice fills the space:

> *Bei der Kaserne*
> *vor dem großen Tor...*
>
> *Wie einst Lili Marleen.*
> *Wie einst Lili Marleen.*

The men are in a state of trance. Bathed in the spotlight, in her cream-colored robe, Lale resembles a Nordic goddess. Kirsten is enraptured by her prominent cheekbones and the curve her velour lips form as the wings of her eyebrows angle teasingly at the audience. However, Kirsten has a feeling that it's not solely Lale the men are moved by. A man covers his eyes and wipes his nose with the back of his hand. A streak of snot glistens in the light as he rests his forearm back on the table. *What wartime horrors have shaped these men's reactions?* she wonders. When bullets fly past your ears in the trenches and the ache for your loved ones intensifies, what enduring scars does this harrowing experience etch onto your memory and being?

Lale's melancholic, dragging voice seems to guide the men home to their wives and girlfriends. *Perhaps the best war songs aren't about war, gunpowder, and bullets at all, but of everyday life?* Kirsten thinks. She snorts. Who would have thought that's all it took? Big, vigorous men, falling apart at the sound of a woman's voice!

The soldiers' gleaming eyes send shudders down Kirsten's spine. How come they feel so moved when all Lale's sorrowful, gray-toned voice evokes in Kirsten is a dance of death?

"Oh, how I miss my Lili Marleen! Back home, she's waiting for me by our lantern."

The man at the next table sighs and takes a long swig from his mug. "She surely knows what a man needs." A crooked grin stretches across his face as he glances at his companion, whose eyes remain fixed on the schnapps in his glass. "Marlene Dietrich can stick with her Yankees for all I care. I prefer our Lale Andersen."

Kirsten thinks of elegant, blonde Marlene Dietrich in her silent films: her top hat tilted at a rakish angle, her long legs a blur of motion. In a stunning act of defiance, the celebrated star went to America and remained there in exile, ignoring Hitler's order to return to Germany. Kirsten smirks. "Hitler's an idiot," was Dietrich's alleged response.

Kirsten sides with Dietrich, but now the Germans are here and she is determined to make the most of a difficult situation. Only time will tell who wins the war. She glances around the room. *Imagine having the nerve to refuse a request, like Marlene Dietrich did.* Her eyes fall on Rolf. *Why bother with flights of fancy? As if we mere mortals have a choice!*

She looks over at the next table, meeting the soldier's shining gaze before he pulls his cap low. "Do you guys remember the mud? Sticky, like clay. The rats? The fear? The exhaustion?" the man shouts. The others nod in agreement. "How we heard the cannons and bombs roaring around us? Hoped and prayed to our God and creator that we'd come out of it with our life and limbs intact?" he continues as the men murmur. "And then..." He looks around, "Every night at exactly 9:57 p.m., everything fell silent when we tuned in to Radio Belgrade. For three minutes, Marlene Dietrich drew us into her embrace as she sang *Lili Marleen*."

The table falls silent. Each man stares as if he were far

away, lost in his own thoughts. Kirsten thought men couldn't be afraid, yet their eyes tell a different story.

From the stage, Lale's husky voice tenderly wraps around the guests. Her sugar-sweet words envelop Kirsten like a melting piece of candy.

"Soldier, compose yourself!" Out of nowhere, a slender man in uniform appears. He's clearly of a higher rank than the others at the table; both his bearing and uniform distinguish him.

In an instant, Kirsten's body tenses. *Is trouble brewing?* She sinks deeper into her chair.

"Such language is unbecoming of a representative of the Third Reich!" The superior's mouth twists into a grimace that reminds Kirsten of her father's when beer and schnapps have taken effect.

Kirsten's eyes fix on the golden skull on the SS soldier's cap. *Not all that glitters is gold,* she thinks.

The soldier leans over his subordinate: "Are you aware that Marlene Dietrich exhibits highly immoral asexual behavior?"

Kirsten has heard the talk. Dietrich is attracted to both men and women and frequents bars for homosexuals. The thought of kissing a girl makes Kirsten's lower abdomen tingle. *What does it feel like to kiss a girl?* she wonders. Not to mention what it feels like to kiss a boy. She's not done either, yet.

In Hollywood, Dietrich has recorded anti-Nazi songs. They're meant to demoralize the German soldiers, but judging by the atmosphere here, and the Nazis' advance in Europe, Kirsten doesn't think it's working.

"Take pride in your service for Deutschland. And for heaven's sake, regain your composure, soldier!" His reprimand echoes through the room. Kirsten pretends not to have heard anything and keeps her eyes on the table in front of her.

The reprimanded soldier stands, clicks his heels together, and with an arm outstretched in the well-known Nazi salute shouts, "Heil Hitler!"

A collective sigh of relief rises from his comrades at the table, followed by an echoing "Heil Hitler!" With a smile, the soldier lifts his glass high, then turns to the establishment and nods. The performance is over.

Rolf taps Kirsten on the arm. "A toast to Copenhagen and the mild, war-anxious Danish dogs." He winks at her. "And not least to their beautiful young women."

Kirsten closes her eyes, and when she opens them, she is changed. Like stepping into an H. C. Andersen fairy tale, entering a fantastical world on the first page and leaving transformed by the time you reach the end. Kirsten has witnessed how a woman can be adored one moment, only to fall hard when she is cast aside the next. She has seen how women can be touched by hands that have engaged in violence one moment and in their lover's bed the next.

My world is no longer the same, she thinks. *Who am I now? Vulnerable to men? Powerful because of my youth? Am I reliant on them, or will I be able to navigate their world and stand on my own two feet?*

Kirsten meets Rolf's gaze. Does he sense her change, too? She sees herself from the outside. There is so much of life she wants to experience. She moistens her lips. Her head buzzes. Tonight, she could have an experience with Rolf.

In her mind's eye, she sees her mother standing with arms crossed. *I don't have the courage. Not tonight,* Kirsten thinks. *My body is calling for something my mind doesn't quite understand.* She shifts restlessly in her chair. *I must leave this place before I say or do something I'll regret.*

But before she can rise, Rolf kisses her, leaving a wet, beer-tinged mark on her lips. Kirsten recoils.

"Well, well," Rolf smiles, but something flickers in his eyes. "No need to be afraid."

The face in front of Kirsten is suddenly not Rolf's, but has bloodshot eyes and a red, puffy nose. *Dad?* she thinks for a split second before she blinks, and once again it's Rolf's face she sees.

This is not how my first kiss was supposed to be! Kirsten wants to wipe away the sloppy kiss and throw it back at him. She was supposed to be kissed by a sweet boy, not by a German who was aware of his power over her.

"Has anyone ever told you how beautiful you are, Fräulein?" With a light touch, Rolf's finger follows the path of Kirsten's blue veins, their branches clearly visible through the thin skin of her forearm. "It's this kind of porcelain skin the Führer envisions for the Aryan race."

Kirsten feels her heart pounding. At the same time, there's a swirling sensation in her abdomen as a blend of nausea and a tingling pulse rush through her body.

"Oh, you liked that!" Rolf smiles as he notices Kirsten's shivers.

Kirsten! This is going to end badly, a voice whispers in her head. A new, bubbling feeling pulls at her; the desire to step closer to something intimate. The urge to stretch time, to get a grip on her outer and inner self, moves her to take his hand.

"You have beautiful hands," she says, pretending to study them. "Slender fingers, clean nails," she stammers.

Now that she's really looking, she notices he has delicate hands. Long fingers with nail beds that don't grow out over ridged and calloused nails. Hands that don't yet bear the marks of hard, physical labor. Hands completely different from her father's and older brothers'.

Rolf looks at her curiously. Then he lights up. "No one has ever said that to me. May I use these tools you find so captivating to lead you to a dance?"

Kirsten's gaze flickers. *This one is a quick thinker*, she muses. *My boldness has brought me here, but where will it end? Why do I feel the urge to step closer to the danger while fearing where it will take me? Will I dare to follow where he wants to go? How do I know whether to follow my head or my desire?* Questions, confusion, and curiosity pull her mind in different directions. *But a dance can't hurt, can it?* Meeting Rolf's eyes, she nods.

"Time for us to leave!" As Martha pushes back her chair, the screeching sound makes Kirsten shudder. Before Kirsten can follow Rolf to the dance floor, Martha wedges herself between them. Her voice quivers sharply. "We thank you for tonight. I have a workday tomorrow." Martha takes a firm grip on Kirsten's upper arm. "And my little sister has school."

Martha grabs her coat and purse. Kirsten tries to pull free, but Martha's fingers dig in.

"You are not my mother, Martha!" Tears well up, and Kirsten barely has time to grab Rolf's picture and yank her coat from the back of the chair before her sister drags her away.

"Will I see you again?" Rolf's voice echoes behind her.

"Maybe," Kirsten whispers over her shoulder before she stumbles out into the night air, where she can finally pull away from her older sister.

"What'd you do that for?" Kirsten's eyes dart back toward the door. In there is Rolf and Lale.

"We need to leave before something bad happens."

Kirsten both understands and doesn't understand. She

feels trapped in her body and in the role of little sister. She hates Martha for humiliating her but is also grateful for her intervention. From inside, music and loud shouting in German can be heard.

Across the street, on the opposite sidewalk, a couple strolls by. Glancing at the bar with disapproval, they cross the street. They spit on the ground in front of Kirsten and Martha and give the sisters a long look before continuing.

"Why do you always have to be so boring?" Kirsten says.

OUT OF THE DARKNESS
KIRSTEN

The weekend is here again. Kirsten is peeling potatoes while her mother flips cauliflower fritters.

"Get a move on! Your dad and the boys will be here soon." Her mother casts a hurried look over her shoulder.

As Kirsten adds a potato to the pot, her thoughts drift to the way men have started glancing in her direction at city parties. Tonight, her plan is to go to Café Mokka. Martha meant it that evening with Lale when she said it was the last time she'd sneak out, but Kirsten doesn't care; she's found a routine that provides her with a feeling of freedom each weekend.

She watches as the potato sinks to the bottom of the pot, then floats back up. The dances, the glances, the music, the cigarette smoke, the bubbling atmosphere of life and lightness; it's all she thinks about during weekdays. With a final wipe of her hands on the dishcloth, she places the pot onto the stove.

The Scandinavian War Bride

With the house finally quiet, Kirsten eases open the window and creeps out onto the stone path. But as she heads for the garden gate, her father and older brothers step out of the darkness.

"You little bitch!"

Kirsten feels a tingling in her fingers. Black spots dance before her eyes. "Please, Dad! I'm sorry!"

"I'll teach you 'sorry'!"

All the air seeps out of her, like sand scattering in the wind.

Her father's bear paws strike Kirsten's temple, causing her to stagger. Although she struggles to stand upright, her older brothers emulate their father, raining down blows on her face with thunderous force.

Kirsten falls onto the stone path. Like a heavy sack of flour, her body offers a silent, soft resistance. She clenches her teeth and feels a sharp pain shooting through her jaw. The rough stones scrape against her shoulder.

How many times have she and Ingrid had to cart their father home from the bar in a wheelbarrow because he was too drunk to make the journey himself? How many times has she snatched his weekly wages from him to prevent her mother from taking extra shifts at the factory to feed her kids?

The blows continue. A numb drowsiness engulfs her. *Let me fall asleep*, she thinks. But her mind races on. She has toiled endlessly, boiling countless greasy, stained sheets and mountains of oil-stained, dusty work clothes in the cauldron, sweating over the washboard. She has cut from the soap bar, rinsed and rinsed and rinsed again under the pump's icy water, wrung out and hung to dry. She always tried her best.

How many buckets of potatoes has she dug up? At the dinner table, her older brothers devour the freshly peeled summer delights one after the other without thinking about how long it took her to dig, scrub, and peel them. Not a single black spot, not a piece of peel was left in the pot. So why does she yearn for a love from them that will never be hers? The tip of a shoe hits her stomach, causing a bitter taste to rise in her throat and bringing tears to the corners of her eyes.

One day I'll leave, Kirsten thinks. *America is my dream. A place far away from the family I've been given. One day my fear will disappear, and I'll never again have to lower my gaze. I won't look back as I walk out of the house.* Kirsten sees herself passing through the kitchen and the living room in her mind; hears the birds chirping outside. *I'll leave the front door open behind me, walk down the stone path, and slam the garden gate shut behind me. Until then, I'll pretend to live by their rules.* A groan escapes Kirsten's lips as the thought results in another painful kick to her stomach.

"Karl!" Kirsten hears her mother's voice. "You're chasing your children away!"

"Shut up, Edith," her father slurs, gasping for breath.

Kirsten feels the closeness of another body. The scent of her mother. Then the familiar smell of alcohol returns.

"God help you if you ever try something like that again!"

Kirsten feels drops of spit on her cheek before everything swirls warm and black.

Springtime
Martha

It's been almost a year since the liberation, and the atmosphere is still jubilant. After five dark years of Nazi occupation, light has finally returned to Denmark.

Martha breathes in Copenhagen's spring air. A wave of dampness, the sharp sting of car exhaust, and the comforting aroma of freshly baked bread from down the street wash over her. Her body hums with youthful energy and anticipation.

Is it about to happen — true love? It's about time for me to meet 'the one', she thinks. She is twenty-one and fears she'll soon become an old maid. The Germans occupied her country all throughout her youth, and the time wasn't right for romance and relationships. At least not in Martha's opinion.

The British are everywhere in the city. Whenever Martha passes an Allied uniform, she smiles and says, "Thank you." She's grown accustomed to seeing them in the Copenhagen streets. After Germany was divided into British, French, American, and Russian zones, the British and Americans travel to Denmark whenever they're on leave from their postings in Germany. To ensure the best experience for the liberators, Danish tourist bureaus organize guided tours for the soldiers to visit the royal regalia at Castle Kronborg, the old-world architecture amusement park Tivoli, and other Danish landmarks. Spending their eight days of leave on holiday in Denmark has become so popular that buses run regularly between Germany and Copenhagen. Everywhere, Martha sees soldiers tilting their heads back to admire the old buildings. Everywhere, they take pictures: of the City Hall Square, of voluminous flower boxes outside shops, and of the bustling life happening in the streets. Copenhagen, compared to impoverished Germany, is brimming with optimism.

Martha has encountered many of the British soldiers known as Tommies. But although their conversations flow easily and spark laughter, none has yet stirred a flutter in her heart. Recently, American soldiers — GIs — have also arrived. They're on leave from Bremen and the American zone in southern Germany. Compared to the British, Americans are more relaxed, outgoing, and less serious. Their approach to dating is more casual. But Martha desires something deeper and more committed than just a short-term fling. Chatting with them is one thing; getting involved is quite another matter altogether. She knows that to the soldiers, her demeanor might come across as too reserved, or even boring. But she prefers that to giving the impression that she's only looking to have a few days of fun with a soldier on leave.

Still, she's drawn to the charming and boisterous American soldiers.

Other young Danish women often throw themselves at the GIs to get their hands on much-desired chocolate, tobacco, and nylon stockings, or to walk arm in arm with the representatives of freedom and victory. Martha, however, is patiently waiting for '*the one*'.

AND THEN ONE DAY, SHE LITERALLY BUMPS INTO him. Riding home on her bicycle, she passes Tivoli gardens and out of nowhere a tall man in uniform steps backwards into the street, forcing Martha to step on her coaster brake.

Losing control, Martha hits the curb with the front wheel. She lands on the sidewalk before she can process what's happened.

"I'm so sorry, miss. Please let me help you." His voice is thick with a drawl, each vowel a long, slow sound.

Strong hands grasp beneath her arms, hoisting her upwards. Dazed, she takes a step back from her rescuer, wincing quietly from the pain, and adjusts her hair before looking up. *He's tall*, she thinks, *taller than me*. His eyes have the color of golden amber and almost turn translucent when they light up with a smile, crow's feet fanning out like the tips of a bird's wings.

"Thank you," she says as she picks up her bike, her voice trembling slightly from the fall. Miss Iversen's English lessons have proven useful since the Allies started appearing in the streets.

"Are you all right?" he asks.

Martha nods and winces again when the movement sends a searing pain from her neck to her lower back.

"I'm not used to bicycles." He points to the street. "Where I come from, we have cars." He extends his hand. "I'm Forest. Forest Edgar Rhodes."

"Martha," she replies, perplexed, as she feels his warm, firm handshake.

"Let me make up for my clumsiness by inviting you out to dinner. Tonight?"

Martha studies him. There's something about his confidence that draws her in. His hair is raven-black, his shoulders broad. *And those smile lines!*

"I don't know," she says, aware that she must wake up before the crack of dawn to make it to work the next morning.

He smiles at her again. Sunlight illuminates his face, making his amber eyes glow warmly. There's something both boyish and manly about him.

"At least let me walk with you, pushing your bike for a bit." He positions himself in front of her, seizing control of the handlebars.

༃

As they walk, Forest smiles and talks and laughs constantly. Martha gestures silently when he needs to make a turn. *That's how most Americans are*, she thinks to herself, *always talking*. They lack the Danish reserve. In Denmark, people only speak when they need to communicate something specific, either by initiating a conversation or responding to someone who has spoken to them. Otherwise, they stay silent.

The arrival of American GIs in Copenhagen meant Martha had to get accustomed to their unusual, energetic ways. Initially, she found it challenging to keep up with their rapid-fire conversation and respond accordingly. She smiles to herself, almost forgetting that she's still in pain from the fall. *Perhaps*, she muses, *their mannerisms are a way to fill the awkward gaps in conversation between people unfamiliar with one another. Maybe it helps ease discomfort for everyone, especially Danish girls with limited English.*

"From Germany's ruins, we've arrived in your impressively organized Nordic nation," he says.

Hearing her country praised, Martha's posture straightens with pride. Forest explains that his eight-day trip to Copenhagen cost him forty-five dollars.

"Here, the houses have roofs, windows have glass, and there are potted plants on the windowsills. People bike on the roads and the sidewalks are walkable," Forest says, gesturing with a sweep of his arm. Martha smiles and nods. "Towers and spires rise toward the sky — and bridges only come apart by design," he laughs, nudging her lightly. Martha looks at him and blushes when his eyes meet hers.

"Where in America do the soldiers that visit Copenhagen on the buses come from?" she asks, mostly to get him to tell her where he is from.

"North Carolina, Minnesota, Illinois, North Dakota, New York," he lists, while Martha enjoys his melodic accent. An image of golden fields, sun-kissed skin, and a dry wind flickers in her mind every time he opens his mouth.

"From all over America," he continues. "I, myself, am from the greatest state there is! And, dear Miss Martha, can you guess what state that might be?" He turns to her with a cheeky raised eyebrow.

Martha shakes her head and smiles.

"TEXAS, of course!" he shouts, a grin illuminating his face.

And then he tells her all about Texas, and the first American airbase in Germany, and that he's stationed in Wiesbaden.

"Texas," he says, "has vast, golden plains that stretch endlessly under the wide-open sky." Martha nods encouragingly, urging him to continue. "The nature is wild, beautiful and untouched." He looks at her, but his mind seems to be far away. "Ever since the oil started flowing, the contrast between the traditional, rural way of life and the rapid change in the cities has become as stark as the difference between two entirely separate planets."

Floating oil, progress, and nature. Martha can't quite piece the images together in her mind. As if Forest has read her thoughts, he explains: "After the war, Texas is booming." He makes a high humming sound. "The sound of oil drills is everywhere."

Martha can't picture the oil boom either. Instead, she imagines the sound of wind from an open kitchen window, tall grass rustling gently in the breeze, the sway of old oak trees, and the clatter of horse hooves. She sees a flowered cotton apron, cinched at the waist, and busy arms working purposefully. She peers over the woman's shoulder and follows the rhythmic movements of her hands as she kneads dough upon a flour-dusted table, a nearby pie dish awaiting filling.

Caring for others, that's what I was born to do, she thinks. Shyly, she looks down at her shoelaces. *What greater, silent expression of a woman's most important responsibility is there?*

As if through a funnel, she hears Forest's voice beside her. His soft, deep laugh makes her look up. *To have a life where one's path is set,* she thinks, *where the day's tasks are performed wearing an apron, making the ordinary feel special. That's the purpose of life on God's green earth.*

Though the images of America are strong in her mind, Martha knows she must soon break off the conversation and say goodbye. She turns to him, wanting to be reserved toward this stranger, but her heart skips as she looks into his face, and she feels a smile on her lips.

"Thank you for your help." She shakes his hand, and again her body tingles at his touch. "I can ride home from here."

She needs to consider her reputation. Remaining in the

company of a man for an extended period is ill-advised, particularly in public spaces during daylight hours. Taking the handlebars from him, Martha readies herself to mount the bicycle and resume her ride.

"I'd like to take you out." With his arms outstretched, Forest resembles a small child who has been unjustly deprived of a cherished toy. He offers her a wry smile.

"I don't think so," Martha replies, thinking: *There's no future in that. He is stationed all the way down in Germany.* And before Forest can react, she hops on her bike and waves over her shoulder. *I need to leave before I get confused*, she thinks, and pedals away. *What would I do with a man who lives on the other side of the world?*

But butterflies flutter and tickle in her stomach as she practically flies over the bridge towards home.

FOREST DOESN'T GIVE UP SO EASILY. The following day he is waiting in front of Tivoli as Martha passes on her bike.

"Martha!" He steps out into the street, forcing her to stop.

She can't help but feel flattered by his attention. How long has he been standing there waiting? Just like the day before, they walk together until she says goodbye, gets on her bike, and pedals home. This continues for the rest of the week until one afternoon Forest says:

"I'm returning to my base tomorrow. May I write to you?"

He's not a skilled writer. Still, Martha looks forward to his letters with their sparse descriptions and handwriting that resembles a child's. Every week, a letter from Germany lands in her mailbox, and every week Martha feels chosen as she opens the envelope with its foreign stamps. Gradually, she forms an image of a man from a humble background; a man with integrity and principles she respects. In the letters, he reflects on the qualities he values in a woman. As she reads, Martha blushes, sensing his implication that she embodies the characteristics he desires in a future spouse and mother to his children. Modest, hardworking, caring, skilled in the kitchen; all virtues Martha takes pride in possessing. When it's time for his next period of leave, she meets him at the bus stop as he arrives in Copenhagen.

This time, Martha allows Forest to take her out. He escorts her to the Dagmar cinema to watch a movie by the famous film director Dreyer. Martha doesn't tell Forest that during the occupation the Nazis used to beat and torture their prisoners in the basement.

On another day, he invites her to Tivoli. Again, Martha is overcome with memories from the occupation as she remembers how the rollercoaster was severely damaged when Nazi sympathizers snuck into the park and planted incendiary bombs, destroying the Copenhageners' beloved park. As they pass the Concert Hall, the Glass Hall, the Arena Theatre, she remembers the colossal damage from the explosions that resulted in Tivoli closing for two weeks. Martha doesn't share this with him either, as his shining eyes admire the rebuilt park. She can't bring herself to burden his leave with descriptions of the scars the war has left on the city and in her mind. She has learned that as time passes, some wounds heal. When Martha hears low-flying planes, she no longer waits for the air-raid siren. She no longer thinks: *Is it the enemy?* But instead: *Is it the British or the Americans?*

☽

ONE EVENING, FOREST WALKS HER HOME AFTER A night out dancing. Outside a stairwell, he stops and leans in for a kiss.

"Forest, no," Martha says firmly, placing a hand on his chest. "I will only do that if you're serious about us."

Forest, as if jolted, stares at her with a puzzled expression. Finally, he straightens and says, "You're an honorable woman, Martha. Let me sleep on it."

When they part outside her parents' house, Martha doesn't know if she'll ever see him again. Overcome with sadness, tears sting her eyes. It surprises her how quickly her heart has made room for Forest. She's glad, though, that she held her ground and didn't compromise her principles. Being a respectable woman takes priority over the attraction that's been growing over the last few months.

By the next morning, she has his response. He waits at the garden gate, his eyes fixed on her as she walks toward him. She stops when she reaches the end of the path, nervously looking for signs of emotion on his face.

"Martha Pedersen," he says, "will you marry me?"

Martha's Fiancé
Kirsten

Kirsten is hiding away in her room with a book to avoid the household chores.

Today, Martha is introducing her fiancé. Everything has happened so quickly with them. They've only known each other for about six months. Forest Edgar Rhodes. *It doesn't get more American-sounding than that,* Kirsten thinks. She can almost hear a "yeehaw!" in her mind. What does her father think of him? She wonders. How does he feel about Forest leaving for America with Martha when his deployment ends? And what about Kirsten herself? How does she feel about her older sister sailing off to America and maybe never returning home to Denmark again? Martha has always been such a cautious type. Now she is running off with a cowboy from Texas, following him to the end of the world.

Everything Kirsten has ever dreamed of is happening right under her nose. The more she thinks about it, the less inclined she feels to help in the kitchen to show her support for the newly engaged couple. Kirsten sighs and turns another page in her book. But the words on the pages won't stick in her mind. A little green worm of jealousy gnaws at her insides. She twists a strand of hair around her finger, but before she reaches the root and feels the familiar pain, her mother calls from the kitchen:

"Kirsten, are you twiddling your thumbs in there?"

Kirsten sighs and puts the book down. Before she goes into the kitchen, she wraps a scarf around her head to keep her curls in place.

THE KITCHEN IS IN COMPLETE CHAOS. ON THE stovetop, pots and pans are bubbling and boiling, and by the sink, glasses and jars without lids stand ready next to serving bowls. Her mother and Ingrid are bent over the kitchen table, busy chopping and slicing toppings for the open-faced rye bread sandwiches.

"You'd think the king himself was coming to visit." Kirsten checks that the scarf fully covers her hair with her fingertips. She's well aware of her mother's efforts and knows that she's traded goods with the neighbors and worked extra shifts to make the feast possible.

"Drain the water from those potatoes, Kirsten!" her mother says breathlessly from the cutting board.

Kirsten removes the pot of boiling water from the stovetop and pours it out. A soft, hollow clatter echoes as the water hits the bottom of the sink.

"If they're starchy, they'll be impossible to slice," her mother says with a sigh.

Kirsten fetches the jug of cold water and pours it over the steaming potatoes. "Want me to get some chives from the garden? I can refill the jug on the way." *Just two minutes away from this chaos will do me good,* Kirsten thinks.

With a nod, her mother uses two fingers to extract a couple of home-pickled beets from a jar, carefully placing them onto a serving dish.

☽

IT REQUIRES A CERTAIN TECHNIQUE TO REMOVE curlers without ending up with hair that's static. Satisfied with her reflection, Kirsten smiles at herself in the mirror. Her curls have just the right springy bounce, making them dance at the slightest movement.

She walks into the living room, where the table is set. The aprons are hanging on the hook in the kitchen. Now they wait.

What is Martha's fiancé like? Kirsten wonders. She won't be able to stand it if Martha turns into a giggling girl when she's with him. Her older sister has already changed so much since she met Forest. She moves about with such deliberation; it is as if she's practicing being the perfect American wife already.

In fact, Kirsten thinks, *Martha can't talk about much else but him. I'll never be like that. No man is going to change me, no matter what.*

☽

THEY MUST BE ON THEIR WAY, BUT EXACTLY WHEN they'll arrive is hard to say. It's a long drive from the new airbase in Fürstenfeldbruck.

Shortly after their engagement and Forest's transfer, he landed Martha one of those coveted jobs with the Americans. He lives in barracks with other soldiers; she rents a room in a boarding house. Each week, Martha dutifully writes a letter to her family, though the contents offer little more than a confirmation of her contentment as she patiently awaits their departure for America.

Kirsten hears the garden gate open, and even before Martha and Forest reach the front door she can hear a deep voice with a foreign accent.

"Finally, I get to see your childhood home, hon." The smooth tone of an American bass is followed by Martha's bright reply, disappearing in the wind.

Then they're at the door. Kirsten hears confident knuckles on the front door. Her father grunts and gets up from his seat by the fireplace. He folds his newspaper neatly and places it on the seat of his chair before walking through the living room to the front door. *Cologne, shaving foam, and razor,* Kirsten thinks as he walks past her.

☽

THERE HE IS, MARTHA'S FIANCÉ, FOREST EDGAR Rhodes. He must duck to get his tall build safely through the front door. *Stilts,* Kirsten thinks at the sight of his lamppost-like legs, ending in two shoes the size of which Kirsten has never seen in her life. Inside, he kicks off his violin cases with his heel and parks them against the baseboards. As he bends down, Kirsten notices his hair, slicked back with pomade, lying in shiny streaks that are evenly spaced like the teeth of a comb. Images of glowing amber and fresh breezes flicker in Kirsten's mind as he straightens up and meets her gaze.

"After you, Daisy." Forest extends his arm, letting Martha walk into the living room first. *Daisy,* he calls her, because: "You're as fine, slim, and beautiful as a daisy," he apparently once told her. When Kirsten read Forest's words in one of Martha's letters, she had to look away, blushing. *What a strange way to express oneself!*

In the living room, Martha turns and looks intensely at Forest. She's flushing to her neck, and her dimples are deep in her cheeks.

Their father seems confident as he greets the American, but Kirsten knows better. His voice is pitched higher than usual. And then there's his smile, which makes her think of a cattle show. She turns to look at her older brothers. Laust fumbles with his tie and discreetly wipes his palms on his trousers before extending his hand to their guest. Kirsten bites her cheek and looks down at the floor to keep from bursting into laughter at the absurdity of the situation. Her brothers are wearing their mother's homemade striped sweaters; their adult physiques having surpassed the limitations of their childhood Sunday best attire. Laust's suit is so ill-fitting that it is too short around the wrists and ankles.

Kirsten wears a long, smooth skirt and a blouse with a white collar, her chestnut-colored hair curled and styled according to the latest fashion. Her hands fumble over the buttons on her blouse. She feels as though she's in some kind of in-between state; her thoughts never quite fitting right in her sometimes child-like, sometimes adult mind. She's seventeen years old — far from a child, but not yet a fully grown woman either. Not confident, but certain that life has experiences beyond the ordinary waiting for her. Her hands move from the buttons to a strand of hair at the back of her neck but stop mid-motion. Here, where everyone can see her, she must keep up appearances. Looking down to keep her expression neutral, she tries to rid herself of the uncertainty, ushering it out of her body to disappear into a crack between the floorboards. She inhales and puts on her armor, so no one can see how she is really feeling.

The price she pays for the effort of sitting through a family lunch with no mishaps is familiar to her. Now, if she takes off her mask, the last bit of energy will seep out of her, leaving her drained and exhausted, mentally and physically. But not yet. If you didn't know better, you might think she was in her element.

When Forest is done greeting her older brothers and Ingrid, he turns to shake Kirsten's hand.

"I'm the raisin at the end of the sausage," she says with a smile.

Forest looks confused, seeking help from Martha.

"It's a Danish expression. She's trying to say she's the last one to greet you," Martha explains, shaking her head at Kirsten in exasperation.

"In Denmark, we have a lot of expressions that have to do with pigs," Kirsten adds.

Forest looks even more confused, then he throws his head back and roars with laughter. "Your sister has a funny bone, hon," he says to Martha and wipes his eyes.

˜

AT THE DINNER TABLE, KIRSTEN SECRETLY observes the newly engaged couple. Martha is radiant. Her gaze frequently drifts toward their father, and whenever it does, her shoulders rise to her ears — until she turns her eyes back to Forest and her shoulders fall back to their natural position.

"Call me Dusty. Forest is fine too," he says whenever someone addresses him by his last name. Kirsten smiles as she translates his name in her mind. *Dusty forest. Dusty woods.*

It has an almost poetic feel to it. But when she looks at him, with his cowboy-military appearance, she feels conflicted. In full uniform, in a small Danish living room, he is eating open-faced sandwiches with an array of condiments Kirsten has never seen combined before. Occasionally, he runs his fingers over the sleeves of his jacket. "The United States Air Force got new uniforms last year." He stands up to show them.

Kirsten forgets to look at the uniform, unable to take her eyes off his long legs. She forces her gaze upward. The suspenders give him a boyish, vulnerable appearance.

He points at the insignia: "Our uniforms are finally different from the US Army's."

While the rest of the family is preoccupied watching Forest, Kirsten stuffs her face with liver pâté and jelly. She pretends to wipe her mouth with the napkin as she chews the bread, letting the congealed meat juice and fatty taste of the pâté melt together.

"Dark blue wool," he continues proudly.

To Kirsten, the uniform doesn't look much different from the one the German Nazi soldiers wore. Theirs also had lapels, four pockets, and four buttons. The only differences are the belt and the color. And the quality, of course. Kirsten bites into a beetroot.

Forest turns and extends an arm, encouraging Kirsten to feel the fabric. Her fingers, on their way to the sleeve, brush against his hand.

"Impressive. Different from the coarse ones we saw during the occupation." She sends Martha an apologetic glance. The touch of Forest's hand felt intimately inappropriate. "You Americans certainly don't lack anything."

The wool has weight to it yet feels soft against her fingertips. Straight machine-stitched seams, so precise that even her mother or Martha wouldn't be able to match them, adorn the pockets. The jacket fits like a glove at the shoulders and chest. Rounded corners add softness to the lapels. Two breast pockets and two larger ones at hip height. Sparkling golden decorative buttons embellish the breast pockets and shoulders.

"Ingrid, come and feel," Kirsten urges.

Ingrid touches the lapel near the shirt collar, then looks up at Forest. "I like the symmetry. The number four repeats on your uniform."

Forest laughs. "Your sister is funny," he says to Martha.

"My sister loves patterns," Martha explains.

Kirsten pictures the German soldiers. A year ago, they fled the Danish streets they had controlled for years. *It's not the design that separates the winning and losing sides. It's the ability to think freely*, she thinks.

Wedding Day
Martha

Martha hears three quick, happy raps on her boarding house door. "One moment," she calls over her shoulder as she carefully releases a curl from her hair. She sprinkles it with sugar water before turning from the mirror.

A messenger is waiting outside. "Miss Martha Pedersen?" the young man asks. His red cheeks and shortness of breath suggest a hurried run from the florist's shop. Martha nods, her eyes fixed on the flowers in his arms. Carnations, lilies of the valley, and roses adorned with greenery. *Simple and elegant, just as it should be,* Martha thinks. He did well. She smiles and sends a grateful thought Forest's way.

"There's also a card for you," the messenger informs her, handing over a small pink envelope.

Martha takes it and thanks the young boy before closing the door.

Inside her room, Martha gently puts the flowers on the dresser beneath the mirror. She studies her reflection. Red spots bloom on her cheeks, even though she hasn't applied makeup yet. Martha swallows nervously. *I am so happy;* she thinks. *Today, I am getting married!* Her dimples are nestled deep in her cheeks.

She turns away from the mirror and looks over at the bed. Her ivory dress awaits, spread out like an angel with long arms. The color reminds her of thick, fresh, smooth cream. *Refined but modest,* she thinks as she studies the simple figure-hugging gown with its high neckline. She fingers the delicate lace with a light touch. *So fine and dainty, like a newborn.* She opens the envelope and unfolds the card.

You are the best woman in the world.
Your Forest.

Martha smiles. *He has indeed traveled far and wide in the world to find me,* she thinks, placing the card on the nightstand. Then she turns and looks back at the bed. *What will our intimate life be like? Will I experience his gentle or wild side in the bedroom?* Embarrassed by her thoughts, Martha tucks a stray lock of hair behind her ear. He has a wildness in him she doesn't recognize in herself. Hopefully, he is right when he says her gentle temperament has a calming effect on him. *We will have a good life together,* she thinks. *I know my role and will embrace it with joy. A wife follows her husband, and I will do everything in my power to create a safe home for us.*

Martha recalls their many walks through Copenhagen while getting to know him. It took time to get used to his foreign ways. *It will probably be the same in America,* she thinks, *but when you love each other, everything will work out.* She applies her lipstick with small dabs. *It might be difficult for both of us at first; he hasn't been in his homeland for several years, and for me, everything there will be new and foreign. But together we will overcome any challenges that may come.* Exhaling sharply, she blows her worried thoughts away. One thing is certain: *a gentle approach achieves the most.*

Martha checks her reflection in the mirror and smiles again before focusing on removing the rest of the hairpins. Her curls turned out well. Last night, she dampened her hair, wrapped strands around her finger, and secured the twists with bobby pins. She lets her thoughts flow as she releases another curl. *We have so much in common.* The glass clinks as she drops the pins into the bowl on the dresser. *Forest grew up in a family with a temperamental father, and so did I.*

"I will never be like my father," Forest assured her one evening.

"Or like mine," Martha smiled and kissed him on the forehead.

Forest's father has passed, and perhaps that's just as well. At any rate, he sounded like quite a character. "In Germany, the memories of my childhood were kept at a physical distance," Forest confided in her. The feeling of liberation is something that Martha readily recognizes. *In America, we can become who we want to be,* she thinks. *I will continue to be careful, cautious, and loyal.*

Martha considers her hair, which still needs styling. Gently, she runs her fingers through it, allowing the soft curls to cascade around her face before her attention returns to the wedding dress. *Today marks the start of my unwavering daily commitment to Forest.*

THE KISSING BENCH
INGRID

Ingrid hurries down the gravel path. Her body wants to twirl, as if there's sunshine waiting to burst forth from within. But that's not something she can do at her age. Only small children let loose when they feel bubbly inside. Once you've been confirmed in church, you're considered an adult. And she's a year older than that. Fifteen is halfway to being a middle-aged thirty-year-old.

Above her, she hears the squeals of people on the roller coaster. The smell of popcorn hangs in the air, and couples stroll past, arm in arm. Although she'd rather stand, Ingrid sits down on their bench. *It's ours — mine and Erik's,* she thinks, letting her fingertips dance over the armrest.

The first time she sat here, Forest had invited her and Martha to Tivoli. Ingrid waited on the bench while Forest and Martha left to buy ice cream. And then suddenly Erik stood in front of her. The first thing she noticed was his crooked smile.

"May I sit down?"

She sized him up. His crooked smile tipped the scales. "It's a free country."

"Yes, finally." He pulled a half-empty cigarette pack from his inner pocket and lit up, shielding the flame with his hand. Between each drag, he held the cigarette in his palm.

"What a peculiar way to smoke," she said with a smile, mostly to start a conversation. There was something warm about his presence that drew her in.

"When you smoke like this, no one can see the glow of the cigarette." He took a drag, demonstrating his point.

"Are you hiding that you are smoking?"

He met her gaze, "Not anymore," and extended his free hand. "Erik Lund."

The handshake was warm and firm. He smelled of oil, spring breezes, and the cigarette he was smoking. The scent reminded her of her father's, but Erik's was softer and warmer in a way that made her cheeks flush.

"Ingrid Pedersen."

He held her hand longer than was appropriate between two strangers.

By the time Forest and Martha returned with the ice cream, Erik had asked for her address, and they had agreed to meet again.

That's how the bench in Tivoli became theirs, and since then, they have met for many rendezvous, here in Tivoli and around Copenhagen. They also meet at Erik's rented room in a dodgy part of the city. Not the nicest place, but it's private and his rent there is cheap.

Ingrid looks down the gravel path. Still no sign of him.

SHE BRUSHES AN INVISIBLE SPECK OF DUST FROM her coat sleeve. How many times has she dressed up discreetly, so her mother won't suspect anything, folding the wrap-around dress around her body? Thanks to Martha's skillful hands with needle and thread, no one notices that the dress is made from old curtains.

"Put a sweater over that dress," her mother says, pinning a brooch to Ingrid's V-neck. Ingrid lifts her chin, so it doesn't prick her skin.

"You don't want to be mistaken for the girls you can buy for money," her father's voice bellows from the living room.

Ingrid pictures him in his armchair. When he sits and grumbles like that, there's no danger. She uses the voice she knows he has a soft spot for: "That's the fashion of today, Dad." But even as she strives to keep her voice carefree, her heart beats fast, and she maintains her distance, just in case.

Her parents don't understand fashion, so she takes off the sweater and hides the brooch when she's out of their sight.

Ingrid smooths the fabric down from her waist to her lap. Did her mother's clothing once cling to a slender waist, too? Now, her body is marked by childbirth as she sways and swells around the kitchen, her skin bearing the strains of stretching and tightening. *It doesn't help that she dresses like a peasant woman*, Ingrid thinks, shooing away a fly. Her mother is from a time of practical skirts, wool socks, and shawls.

"SO FINE, SO UTTERLY PERFECT," ERIK WHISPERED the last time they were in his room.

Ingrid found him both frightening and alluring. His eyes had something milky about them. He'd snuck her into his room without the landlord noticing.

She crosses her legs, and squints up at the sun, letting her breathing settle. Their meeting spot by the roller coaster is ideal; the noise prevents anyone from overhearing their conversations. Ingrid leans her head back and looks up. Rhythmic metallic sounds from the rollercoaster cars and shrill screams circle above her. When she and Erik sit together, sometimes their faces are so close that his lips brush her cheek. She wants to turn so their lips meet, but of course that's unthinkable to do in public. Instead, she lets her breathing become a part of his.

Their rendezvous has become a ritual. Before heading out to meet him, she meticulously prepares at home, brushing her teeth and washing her private parts thoroughly, as well as her underarms. She selects her finest underwear and finally wraps herself in her dress. Then she's ready.

They've done the forbidden thing many times. Afterward, she walks home with swollen lips and a warm lap, silently cursing her own foolishness and regretting her choices. *Next time, there will be no fooling around*, she tells herself. Dizzy and disoriented with anxiety, she spends the following weeks waiting for her period, terrified that this time it won't show up. But her fear lasts only until the bleeding comes, or the next time she and Erik meet.

What if I never see him again? She thinks. *I would wither as quickly as the roadside flowers do when I put them in a vase on the windowsill in my bedroom.* The thought makes her eyes burn.

"Being in love is a sort of madness," her mother often says. *The secret thing Erik and I do together in bed*, Ingrid thinks, *is like a fire I run away from, but always come back to.*

The tips of her shoes are worn, she notices, as she swings her legs back and forth on the bench. Ingrid looks at her hands. She loves placing her palm against Erik's. "It's bad luck," Kirsten always says. "You must never compare hands!"

But when Ingrid sees her slender hand against Erik's rough one, she knows he can protect her against anything.

One day we'll marry. Ingrid smiles. *We'll have a house and a yard, and children playing while I prepare dinner for when he returns home from a long day at work.*

A whiff of cologne hits her nose, but Ingrid doesn't need to look up to know it's not Erik's. His scent makes her want to nestle into him like a baby bird. Yes, she's younger than he is, so what? Love has no age. She read that in a magazine, and she believes it. But it's still a good thing her father doesn't know that she has a boyfriend. She'd get so many beatings if he knew what she's been up to.

Working hard to push that thought out of her mind, Ingrid fixes her gaze on a wall on the other side of the gravel pathway. Unable to focus, she tears her eyes away. In Tivoli, many Danish women are in relationships with British or American soldiers. Never in her life has Ingrid seen so many people chewing gum, so many shiny stockinged legs. From every direction, she can hear the metallic sound of flicking lighters.

Ingrid pulls an apple out of her bag. The skin is wrinkled but otherwise fine. She wipes it on her coat sleeve. There aren't many edible apples left in the garden shed from the last harvest. Her teeth pierce the apple's skin, but the inside is dry; none of its crisp juiciness remains. She chews on the mealy piece, using her saliva to bring out the flavor. Then she almost chokes on it as she remembers something Erik said the last time they were in his room.

"Tangy, juicy, and sweet. Like a Danish fall apple. That's how you taste," he said, coming up from the foot of the bed.

Ingrid greedily takes two big bites, all the way around the apple's core.

The Outhouse
Ingrid

The latch is on. Ingrid looks down between her legs, presses again. Not a drop of blood comes out. She clutches the linen cloth she's prepared. Twenty-nine days usually pass between each bleeding, but it's been weeks since she stopped counting days. It's far past that time. Lately, a thick whitish discharge leaves a residue in her undergarment, and she's had absolutely no cramps. She shudders at the thought of what her father will do to her if he finds out and kicks her heel against the barrel in frustration.

Time is quickly approaching when she must decide whether to get rid of it, yet she's unsure what to do. Who would she turn to? How much will it cost? How will she get the money to pay for it? Will she be able to walk home by herself afterward? Do quack doctors really use knitting needles when they do the thing they do? What if something goes wrong, and she bleeds to death in a stairwell, like she's heard happens to some girls? Could her shame end up driving her to her death? And what about school and, worst of all, her father? Involving Erik is out of the question. She'll have to manage this herself.

The light outside is dimming through the cracks in the wooden door. Was that a twinge in her lower abdomen she felt just now? She was thirteen the first time dark, gloopy blood seeped out with her urine. The metallic smell didn't scare her; she simply wiped the slimy substance away from her pubic hair and thighs. Even though no one talks about such things, she knew very well what had just happened to her. She has helped her mother wash the monthly cloths and knitted pads since she was old enough to stand on a stool and stir the washing stick in the boiler. Now, at fifteen, she's had two years to get to know her cycle. Counting days is her starting point. Then, before her period starts, she finds and folds the old cloths before finally enduring cramps and sweats as her blood flows. After the last day of menstruation, the dirty brownish cloths must be boiled and dried before they are stacked, ready for next month's bleeding.

Once a month, her mother's voice becomes gentle. "No, little one this time," she says and heads to the outhouse. Ingrid watches her mother's movements take on a lightness, and as night falls she usually calls from the kitchen: "Oatmeal balls for everyone tonight." Watching her mother hum to herself while working in the kitchen is one of Ingrid's favorite memories.

HER MOTHER MUST HAVE A SIXTH SENSE, BECAUSE since Ingrid began seeing Erik, she's started delivering warnings, her finger pointing at Ingrid like a pistol: "You mustn't end up like me!" she says, making a sweeping gesture over her body, "Do you think I've always looked like this?" And when it's not her index finger she's pointing, Ingrid's mother waves a ladle in the air: "Don't start with that sort of thing."

Her father is gruffer when the topic turns to men. "No one brings shame to my house!" he thunders. "None of my girls will come running home with a child. Only bad girls do that sort of thing," Ingrid's father concludes before lighting his pipe, and the topic is settled.

Just the thought of what might happen if her parents find out about her condition makes her determined to take care of the situation by herself. Better to keep quiet and find a solution involving no one.

꒰

IN THE SCHOOLYARD, SOMEONE ONCE SAID YOU could get pregnant if you kissed a boy. Ingrid was terrified the first time Erik planted his lips on hers. But no belly grew, and so she became bolder.

Ingrid sighs and looks down at the space between her thighs. She wraps a strand of pubic hair around her index finger and only let's go when her eyes sting. How do you stop fooling around before it's too late, when your body feels so good entangled with someone else's? Besides, Erik gets so happy when she gives in and lets him go all the way.

"When will you be done?"

Ingrid startles at the hammering on the wooden door.

"The rest of us also need to use the privy."

Ingrid uses newspapers to wipe herself. Its rough surface scratches against her soft skin. With a tug, she adjusts her underwear and blouse, then lifts the latch.

The Quack
Ingrid

Folding her hands over her stomach, Ingrid's mother positions herself so she blocks the way, forcing Ingrid to stop in front of her. Ingrid feels her jaw muscles tighten.

"I know what's going on with you," her mother whispers.

Panicking, Ingrid's heart pounds in her ears. Her mother's disappointment is painted all over her face. But Ingrid sees more than just disappointment. Is there any trace of sorrow? Of despair? Her mother tosses her head, signaling without words that she should follow her into the kitchen. Ingrid bows her head.

In the kitchen, her mother quietly closes the door behind them, opens the cupboard and fetches the weekly newspaper, *Amager Bladet*, from behind the plates. Ingrid's gaze falls on an advertisement: "Housekeeping and help wanted for a single man." That kind of 'help' is something one should stay away from, as it has nothing to do with cleaning and cooking. On the second-to-last page, Ingrid's mother finds what she's looking for.

"This is where you need to go." She looks at Ingrid for a long second and points to a notice offering help to women in need. Ingrid nods, understanding. She lets her fingertips brush the back of her mother's hand as she reaches for the newspaper.

"Take care of it sooner rather than later. Your father doesn't need to know anything about this," her mother says, turning her back to do the dishes.

THE NEXT MORNING, INGRID IS UP EARLY AND OUT the door before the rest of the family wakes up. After a brisk walk, she crosses the bridge to Copenhagen and heads for the Vesterbro neighborhood.

Her destination is the dreaded Istedgade. In her head, she crosses off the first two-way markers on her internal route. Now she just needs to remember the rest. Put one foot in front of the other. *Like a math problem*, she tells herself. *It all adds up if I execute each step correctly. But am I doing the right thing, or should I turn back?* As if some force is answering her question, a cool wind pushes her forward, making her pick up the pace.

Large letters on a storefront announce: *Exchange center for children's clothing*. The Single Mothers' Outreach Inc., Mødrehjælpen, is known for helping women in need. *If I don't go to the quack doctor, I'll become one of those women who need help*, Ingrid thinks. *I don't want to scrape by in life, worrying about where my next meal will come from. I don't want to beg for alms and worry whether I can afford clothes for my child.*

Her feet move on their own until she is at her destination. *I just need to get it over with*, she thinks, before stepping into the back alley.

The Scandinavian War Bride

Thousands of feet have worn the stairway's steps smooth. The smell of boiled cabbage makes Ingrid's stomach turn. Notes of mold, dust, and greasy, metallic oil overwhelm her. Ingrid recognizes the stench; it's the same smell that clings to her father and older brothers' work clothes after a long week of labor. A few floors up, she hears a child cry, followed by a slap, before the stairwell again falls silent. Ingrid grips the banister firmly, stepping carefully out of fear of slipping on the rounded edges.

How will I get back down these narrow stairs when 'it's' over? Ingrid thinks in terror. At the landing, she lets her knuckles brush against the door, so only a small, bony sound is audible. Her breathing sounds hollow in the stairwell. With a shiver, she pulls her coat tighter around her body. On the way here, she pulled Erik's sixpence up over her head to make it easier to walk through the streets of Copenhagen with her burning shame. But when she reached the Vesterbro neighborhood, she felt people's gazes on her. Did they somehow know where she was headed?

"Will you go with me?" Ingrid had asked Kirsten as they lay in bed last night.

"Absolutely not!"

Kirsten's answer stung.

"You made your bed, now lie in it!" Kirsten snapped angrily, turning away with a jerk, her back as hard as flint.

Could it just as well have been Kirsten and not me who got into this sort of trouble? Ingrid wonders.

There's a shuffling at the door on the floor above. Ingrid feels a tightness in her lower abdomen, as if her skin is giving way from the inside — a tender mix of menstrual cramps and a stretch in the pit of her stomach.

They weren't supposed to go as far as they did, she and Erik. Every time they met, they agreed just to kiss. "Only that," she made him promise. But then he kissed her cheek, then her mouth; kissed her deeper and longer each time. When Erik's hand searched under her clothes, her heart beat faster. Her mind said stop, but desire won, and reason was kicked away along with socks and shoes.

Afterward, she was ashamed. Until the next time, when the whole thing repeated itself. *Contraceptives! Where was I supposed to get them?* Ingrid sighs. And now she finds herself here in a back alley outside a quack's door.

Why isn't anyone opening the door? Ingrid's heart is in her throat. Is she waiting in vain? What if a neighbor comes out and asks what she's doing here? What will she say? As if the entire building doesn't know what's going on behind this closed door.

Again, there's a shuffling behind the door, and Ingrid suppresses a hysterical laugh. Uncontrollable laughter has always been her reaction when she's scared or nervous. Then there's a click and the door opens. A man extends his hand. As Ingrid shakes it, he says: "Discretion is of the utmost importance. You understand that don't you?"

Ingrid nods, and the man pulls her into the apartment. In the hallway, he releases her hand, and she follows his gesture into the living room. Behind her, she hears a click as the door closes.

"I know Jonathan Høeg Leunbach, so you do not need to worry."

"The Jew?" Ingrid bites her lip.

Everyone knows that Jonathan Høeg Leunbach is Jewish, and that he's known for talking about private and forbidden topics. Ingrid seems to recall that Leunbach has been in prison, too. But that was so long ago, at least before the war.

He is trying to let me know he knows what he's doing, Ingrid thinks. Still, she is scared. She's heard many stories about girls who bled to death after an abortion. Ingrid straightens up, feeling the stretch under her ribs. She exhales the dark thoughts away. *I'm sure we only ever hear the horror stories, and not about the girls who continue their lives afterwards as if it's nothing,* she thinks to herself. *Besides, what other option do I have?*

It would be better if the procedure were done at a hospital, but since she's too afraid to go to Dr. Hansen, this is the way it has to be. Ingrid watches the dust motes dance in the stripe of gray light that falls through the living room window. She's in the second back alley, where only a little sunlight filters down on the building. The ceiling creaks as someone walks through the apartment above.

"When was your last period?" the man asks her, drawing her attention back to him.

Ingrid's mind goes blank. It was after New Year's but before Kirsten's birthday, which is at the end of February.

"Uh, in January, I think."

His eyebrows shoot up, settling like withered bushes over his glasses. "That means you must be around twenty or twenty-two weeks along." He rubs his brow. "If you could open your coat for me..."

Ingrid turns to the side, beginning with the top button.

The man sighs. "I'm not seeing anything you haven't shown others." His gaze lingers in the area between her breasts and her lap. Ingrid wraps her arms around herself and looks down at the floor. When she looks up, a wrinkle appears on his forehead. "Lie down." He nods toward the examination table and disappears out of the room.

Ingrid hears running water, splashing, and scrubbing noises, like when someone is being thorough with the soap bar. She walks toward the wooden table that stands against the wall in the corner furthest from the window. The table's corners are worn smooth, the outlines of women's bodies visible in the wood's surface. Ingrid shakes her head and blinks away the imprints of rounded shapes formed by other women's heads, hips, and buttocks. She climbs up and feels the coolness of the wood against her body as she lies down.

Is it happening now? Here? A sour taste at the back of her mouth spreads along the sides of her tongue. Then the man is back, pulling up her woolen sweater. Ingrid lets herself be handled, floats away, becomes a lump of flesh without feelings or thoughts. She watches indifferently as a frown divides his forehead in two and he feels her stomach with practiced movements.

"You knew how things could end up when you started your foolishness."

Ingrid blinks. His hands wander under her ribs and press their way toward her pelvis. The pressure becomes harder, the jabs in her lower abdomen deeper and more violent. She focuses on the yellowish spot on the ceiling as tears run down her cheeks, then squeezes her eyes shut.

The pain in her stomach ebbs away as he straightens up and removes his hands from her body. "You're too far along." He turns away.

What does he mean? Will she have to keep the baby after all?

He turns back to face her: "I can't perform the procedure here. If you still wish to end the pregnancy, you'll need to go to a different address."

Ingrid feels her mouth go dry.

"Put your coat on."

Getting down from the table seems impossible. Her legs feel like lead. She wants to run far away, but her body cannot move. Even though she knows she's lying still, she feels as if she's falling. The man's outlines blur, the contours of his face wavering indistinctly before her eyes. Behind a veil of dissociation, she feels his hands grip her shoulders as he shakes her.

"I'm expecting another guest soon." He snaps his fingers in front of her face as he leans over her.

I can't get up, a voice in her head says. Followed by another commanding echo: *Get up!* Mustering strength she didn't know she had; Ingrid slowly rises onto her elbows.

A few minutes later, her coat is buttoned, and her beret pushed down on her forehead.

"If you wish to go through with this, you must return to this address exactly one week from now. A driver will pick you up outside the alley." His voice is barely audible whispers as he continues. To hear what he's saying, she must lean closer. "Five thousand in cash."

Ingrid feels dizzy.

"Bring a scarf that's large enough to cover your eyes."

Oh God, what have I done? Instinct makes her search for a corner to hide.

"Bring clean underwear and plenty of boiled cloths. And towels, if you have them."

Ingrid nods.

"The money must be in bills," he says, pushing her out into the hallway. She hears the soft click as the door closes behind her, the sound of a lock turning like a distant echo.

⁂

IT'S NOT UNTIL SHE'S HALFWAY HOME THAT SHE comes to her senses. The rain lashes against her neck and back.

She didn't get to ask him how much she would bleed

afterward, if she could walk home by herself, or when she could return to school. In the apartment, her thoughts were like slippery soap, too hard to hold on to. One moment she was at the beach with Erik, the sound of the waves merging with the noise in her ears. Next, she was in the apartment with the man with the rough hands. How could she ask questions with him looming over her and her mind in flight?

Ingrid's Letter
Ingrid

Ingrid hasn't been herself since that day in the back alley.

"Get your head out of your ass, girl!" Ingrid ducks just in time to avoid her father's arm shooting through the air. "Are you even listening to what your mother is saying?"

No, she has heard nothing. Does her mother need help in the kitchen? Did she ask her something? Ingrid's eyes search her mother's back for answers.

If his children don't respond when spoken to, her father loses it. Usually he targets Kirsten, but apparently something has changed and now it's Ingrid who is on the receiving end of his anger.

"I'm sorry, Dad."

He grumbles as she folds a blanket over his legs.

I must get a message to Erik, she thinks. *There's no way I can come up with that much money by myself.* She groans inwardly. Having to ask him for help is deeply against her nature. Five thousand kroner! She calculates in her head. A loaf of rye bread costs fifty øre, so if she has five thousand kroner, how many loaves of rye bread can she buy? She counts on her fingers. In the world of mathematics, it's as if everything else disappears. Erik earns three kroner an hour. How many hours does he have to work to pay five thousand kroner? If she has ten pieces of candy...

Ingrid comes up with one calculation after another. Concentrating intently on calculations, her mind momentarily stills. Still, it's hard to see the logic in the astronomical amount she must pay the quack. A table in a back-alley apartment where no decent girls want to set foot wasn't exactly the fanciest hotel in town. What will happen at the secret address that justifies such a high price?

⁕

INGRID WIPES HER HANDS ON THE DISHCLOTH. THE dishes are clean; her father is sitting in his chair with his blanket and the newspaper. Now she can sneak off to her room.

She finds her pen and paper. She must write now, so Postman Hansen can take the letter on his first round tomorrow. How will she make Erik understand the situation?

Dear Erik,

The Russians were supposed to arrive in December. But January went by, and so did February...

How much is a life worth in rubles? Some say: five thousand. Legitimate or not, what's the difference?

> The Russians will not be coming. Time is of the essence...
>
> Meet me at the bench?

Ingrid looks at the letter. What nonsense. Maybe she should just crumple it up? But what other options does she have than to involve him in this? Will he understand the meaning? As if of its own accord, the pen draws a doll and a pram. And in front of it: a girl with a teddy bear dangling from her hand.

If he thinks about it, he will figure out what she means. Ingrid kisses the letter, folds it, and places it in the envelope.

The Envelope
Ingrid

Above Ingrid's head, the roller coaster whirs. She swallows as nausea rises in her throat. The light between the clouds feels like piercing arrows. She removes a strand of hair from her coat, and her hand brushes the roundness of her belly. Quickly, she straightens her back, making the bulge disappear.

She massages her temples to rid herself of the headache throbbing behind her eyelids. Just a few months ago, the light feeling from hearing the laughter and chatter of lovers in Tivoli was like pastel-colored cotton candy. Now, it feels like wrapping the cottony sugar cloud around a finger and watching it turn into a sticky thread. The smell of popcorn makes her jaw muscles tingle.

She sees Erik before he sees her. He saunters along the gravel path with a cigarette dangling from the corner of his mouth. He is still too far away for her to smell him or hear the crunch of gravel under his soles, yet her body reacts, and she breathes more freely. His left hand is buried in his trouser pocket. Tears well up in Ingrid's eyes as she sees the way his posture changes when he spots her. *Like a pocketknife,* she thinks. His body rounds, his gait becomes more tentative, and his gaze flickers as it briefly meets hers. He reaches the bench and pulls her to her feet without a word.

Ingrid leans into him: "I felt so dirty."

She can feel his breathing through the wool of his coat. His chest rises against her face, his heart pounds hard. *Is he as scared as I am?* She thinks and leans into the hand that cups her neck.

"We'll keep the baby!" he says optimistically and hugs her. "I'll soon be done with my apprenticeship. We'll make it work."

I love you for what you are saying, Ingrid thinks, halfway between love and despair. Over his shoulder, she watches the balloon swings rise. After a while, Ingrid stops crying. Her snot and tears have dampened Erik's coat. Then she pulls away, avoiding his gaze.

As they stroll along Tivoli's Garden paths, the sound of people screaming in fear and delight surrounds them. *A short time ago that was me,* Ingrid thinks. *Completely unaware of how the world can change from one moment to the next.* She kicks at the gravel. *How stupid and naïve I was!*

They walk in silence a while longer. Finally, Ingrid says, "I'm too young."

I must be sensible, she thinks. *It's time to tuck away my childish dreams and help Erik decide.* His small income and poor living conditions won't sustain them. She knows what she must do.

She hears him exhale beside her. Is it relief or frustration? "I'll get the money," he says, stopping on the path. As he takes her hands, Ingrid feels her cold fingertips against his warm palms.

"My father is going to kill you." She looks out at the lake, at the people in the small boats.

Erik ducks his head, looking like someone who thinks her father has every right to give him a beating. With his eyes on the boats, he says: "There's something fishy about the whole thing," before he half-turns and glances at her.

"I don't want to talk about it!" Ingrid holds her hand up to her mouth in shock, surprised by her outburst and the shrillness in her voice.

As if she had slapped him, his gaze flickers. The conversation dies.

Before they part, he whispers: "I'll get the money."

᠌

THAT PROMISE HE KEEPS. WHEN INGRID STUMBLES into the garden the next morning, she finds an envelope in the agreed-upon spot. Back in her room, she pulls the envelope from the lining of her coat where she has hidden it. The bundles of bills are neatly divided into stacks of hundreds. Fifty bundles of varying thickness. Her hands shake as she spreads the bills out on the bed. Never has she seen that much cash in one place. She pictures the man from the apartment. Then she lies down under the covers, sinks into the mattress, and hopes she never wakes up again.

Asphalt Cowboys
Ingrid

An ambulance siren cuts through the sounds of the morning. For the second time, Ingrid finds herself in the dodgy neighborhood of Vesterbro. *Where the prostitutes and pickpockets live*, as her father would say. *And those with belly bumps who have no choice but to live in this dark and dirty part of town in barely habitable apartments*, Ingrid thinks.

Cyclists on their way to work toss cheerful comments in her direction. A few weeks ago, she would have smiled at the asphalt cowboys, but now all she feels is exhaustion. What good does it do to avert her eyes? Being here on this street means she's on display.

Waiting outside the alley, where the light from the gas lamps cannot reach her, brings her some comfort. Three ancient reliefs of gray-white angels watch from the walls. Are they harbingers of misfortune, or do they bring encouragement?

A cargo bike rattles over the cobblestones. All around her, cellars and makeshift shacks are various shades of gray. Even the street urchins, who follow her every move with their eyes as they lean against the walls and smoke, bear the color of fall rain.

She kicks a stone with the toe of her shoe. Eight days have passed. One hundred and ninety-two hours. A week. It doesn't sound like much. But if she converts it to seconds, it seems larger. Eleven thousand, five hundred and twenty seconds. Seconds that count down while a young girl turns into a bitter woman.

"It'll be all right," her mother said last night.

But Ingrid saw the darkness in her eyes as she said it.

"When it's over, Kirsten will have tidied up for you at home." Water ran between her mother's fingers as she wrung out the dishcloth. "I won't be here. I must go to work," she said with her back turned as she hung the cloth over the cabinet door.

Ingrid looks up at the sky. The colors of morning slowly conquer the remnants of night. Until now, she's been afraid that her father had an inkling about her situation. Now, she no longer cares.

Ingrid has only a vague sense of what awaits her. Her mother must know something about the procedure. Don't mothers talk to each other, just like girls in the schoolyard do? But her mother has avoided Ingrid as if she had a contagious virus.

"Wear dark clothes," is the only advice her mother gave her last night. Ingrid steps closer to the wall; she wants to melt into the stone and vanish.

"Are you lonely, Miss?"

Ingrid startles at the touch on her shoulder.

"How much?"

She looks away. The man catches the hint and continues strolling down the street, completely unaware of the shame he leaves her with. *This is what it has come to*, she thinks. *I could be mistaken for one of the street girls.* Ingrid pulls Erik's sixpence cap further down on her forehead.

A car stops outside the alley. The passenger door opens. "Ingrid Pedersen?"

Ingrid nods.

"Get in."

She stumbles into the back seat, tightening her fingers around the scarf she was told to bring.

"Tie the scarf over your eyes."

Ingrid does as she's told, and they drive off in silence. Her stomach twists as the man speeds up. Uneasy, she sinks back into her seat and rests her neck against the backrest. The man drives on, brakes hard, and takes a sharp turn. Exhaustion wraps Ingrid's brain in dullness. She loses her bearings and gives up trying to keep track of the direction the car is heading.

She could have counted the seconds, so she would have a sense of how far from Copenhagen she was. Why didn't she do that? *How can I be sure the driver wants to help me?* She thinks, shifting uneasily. *What if he's kidnapping me! Mom!*

"This is the way we have to do it," he says curtly from the front, "for everyone's safety and protection."

Ingrid wants to put her head between her knees. Instead, in her mind, she flies away — up and up and up, like the pigeons on City Hall Square. She hears her own breathing, twisting her face from shoulder to shoulder.

"Stop drawing attention to yourself!" There is a warning in his voice. Then everything becomes a murmur beneath the darkness of the scarf, and she falls into a deep sleep that carries her far away from the situation she is trapped in. Like a baby overwhelmed by the world, her system shuts down, and Ingrid gratefully surrenders.

Window Washing
Kirsten

When Kirsten is working with a bucket and cloth in hand, only thoughts of cleaning exist. Nothing else matters; not even what's going on in her family. As her body moves in determined motions, a strand of hair wiggles its way out from under her scarf and sways in front of her left eye. She pushes the curl back into place with her thumb. The gentle touch across her forehead reminds her of how a certain man treated her at the last party she went to. A warm sensation in her lower abdomen makes her stroke her midriff as she reaches for the cigarette on the windowsill.

Outside, she hears the metallic sound of the gate's hinges. She mimics the former Social Democratic Prime Minister Stauning's worried side glance in the poster above her father's armchair, turning away from the window. The handle of the zinc cleaning bucket slips from her hand. As it lands on the wooden floor, Kirsten folds the cloth and drops it onto the edge of the bucket before running toward the front door.

Before she reaches the garden gate, she hears the screech of bike brakes. Her mother throws the bike against the hedge, running up the stone path as fast as her arthritis-plagued legs can carry her.

"Ingrid?" Kirsten clenches one hand in the other.

"They'll bring her back later today once they've removed it." Her mother's gaze drifts to the side and lands somewhere behind Kirsten's shoulder. "I need to run again." She smooths her hair. "Need to wash the stairs in the apartment building. You'll have to take care of her when they bring her home."

Kirsten walks back to the house, picks up the cloth and wrings it out. She wipes the window with long, anxious drags. Using a dry cloth, she follows the window frame into the corners before smoothing over the surface. "Water, cloth, glide," she whispers.

Shortly after, she tosses the damp cloth onto the back of a chair. Just as she was finding her rhythm, the cleaning cloth began to leave dirty streaks on the window. She turns to find a dry one in the stack of torn sheets and pillowcases. Her frantic movements cause the pile to topple over in a soft, slow-motion way. Kirsten digs her nails into her palms. *Calm down*, she tells herself, trying to relax her muscles. Once she has control of her breathing, she kneels and begins folding.

Normally, keeping her hands busy helps when she's nervous, but not today. *Things have to go right with Ingrid*, Kirsten thinks.

Everyone knows the gruesome stories; has heard about how the procedures are done. Hemorrhages and clots in the toilet, sometimes with a fatal outcome. At school, she once heard rumors about a girl who filled a bucket with blood every morning after going to a quack. With trembling hands, Kirsten mechanically sorts the stack of cloths.

"Will you go with me?" Ingrid had asked her the week before.

Kirsten regrets her harshness: "I will not! You made your bed, so you'll have to lie in it."

Kirsten places the folded cloths on the shelf. Erik is probably hanging out with his resistance friends from Holger Danske right this minute. If it weren't for him, Ingrid wouldn't be in this mess. Men are never judged, while girls' swollen bellies invite scorn and contempt. Kirsten takes a cloth from the pile and blows her nose.

"You can't ever trust men!" she whispers.

Armed with a stack of pillowcase cloths, she turns and walks back to the living room. For a moment she is lost, forgetting what she was about to do. But then she snaps out of it and is back in the room, along with her senses. *I must get the bedroom ready before Ingrid comes home,* she thinks and turns to hurry there, leaving the bucket in the middle of the living room floor.

༄

HOW DO YOU READY YOUR SISTER'S BEDROOM AFTER she's been to a quack? *Do I place a glass of water by her bedside?* Kirsten wonders. Will Ingrid be hungry, or only feel like having a small bite to eat, like a biscuit? Will her body be tired, the same way it feels after having the flu? Will she want a cup of hot tea with honey instead of a glass of water? Or will she not be able to keep anything down, sick as a dog? *Do I put a bucket on the floor by her bed, so she has a place to vomit or bleed, or does that seem too dramatic?* Kirsten shakes her head as she works her way around the bedroom.

"There, Ingrid! Now there's clean bedding ready for you."

Kirsten's voice is a couple of octaves higher than usual. "And I've tucked a surprise under your pillow."

Today is the right day to let her have Tove Ditlevsen's book. Kirsten knows the best passages by heart and whispers to herself:

> *Oh, let me be a child again*
> *and sleep safe and thoughtless*
> *with mom and dad,*
> *before fear existed,*
> *and the night became my enemy.*

She fluffs the pillow and smooths the blanket over the duvet. The bedroom window is ajar, leaving the air inside the room crisp. Kirsten scans the room, goes to the window, and adjusts the curtain. Everything is ready for her younger sister. *Please return safely soon, Ingrid. Rest and wake up as good as new.*

Back in the living room, the bucket is waiting for her on the floor. Kirsten wrings out the cloth, hearing her father's voice in her head. He's always thundering and raging. The older Kirsten gets, the more his outbursts seem to her like expressions of insecurity. She glances at the poster above his chair and hurries past the fireplace, looking the Social Democrat straight in the eye: "You and my father with your accusing gazes!" Cloth in hand, the work continues. *Water, cloth, glide.*

As she cleans, she lifts her eyes to look toward the yard. *If only Martha were here, my nerves wouldn't be so on edge,* she thinks. But her older sister is busy living her life in Munich, waiting for Forest to get off work so they can meet at a café for coffee, donuts, and cigarettes. As she digs her index finger into the corner between the pane and the window frame, wiping the edge, Kirsten snorts. "Sergeant Forest Edgar Rhodes." She pronounces her brother-in-law's name aloud with an American accent. *There, you've scored big time, sister.* She glances toward her father's chair. *Even if Forest shares our father's love of liquor. That's how most men are. You must just learn to live with that. A beer or two doesn't hurt anybody if the habit doesn't get out of hand.*

Her father's cornflower-blue eyes bear no resemblance to the beer he downs. But the whiskey Forest enjoys drinking has the same deep brown color as his eyes. When he swirls the glass's contents, a soft aroma spreads through the room. The sensation of burning warmth in the mouth and body feels like the afterglow on bare shoulders on a hot summer day. But the liquid leaves a look in Forest's eyes that is just as recognizable as her father's.

In one last smooth stroke, Kirsten catches a wet streak before it runs and ruins the mirror-like surface of the window. Then she grabs the bucket and goes out into the backyard to pour the soapy water over the vegetables. As she admires the gleaming windows, she softly sings the familiar tune from The Mills Brothers:

> *You always hurt the one you love,*
> *The one you shouldn't hurt at all.*
> *You always take the sweetest rose*
> *And crush it till the petals fall,*
> *You always break the kindest heart*
> *With a hasty word you can't recall,*
> *So, if I broke your heart last night*
> *It's because I love you most of all.*

The Curtain
Ingrid

The car comes to a stop. Ingrid's hands fumble for the scarf.

"Leave it on!" the driver barks.

Her hands react as if they've been shocked by electricity. She hears a metallic click as the driver opens his door. Then, a few seconds later, another click, followed by fresh air on her cheeks. A grip on her arm pulls her up and out of the car. The sound of gravel crunching under her shoes echoes as he guides her forward. He moves too fast, and she stumbles over the edge of the pavement. A firmer grip prevents her from falling.

"One..." He squeezes her arm, and she takes a step up. "Two..." Another squeeze. By the time his fingertips prepare to squeeze again, Ingrid gets the message and takes a step. The man grunts in satisfaction.

Beneath her feet, Ingrid feels a transition threshold. The shift in sound from outside to inside is hollow. *I'm in an entryway,* she thinks, before the front door closes behind her. Warm, dry air from a stove meets her nose, with notes of peat and pipe tobacco. For a moment, she sees her father in the armchair. Then her arm is squeezed again, and she is led to the right.

"Now it's all right for you to remove the scarf."

Her eyes hurt as darkness turns to light. Ingrid looks around. At the far end of the room, panoramic windows with velvet curtains make it impossible to see out — or in. In her peripheral view, another curtain appears. A dining table covered with a sheet sits in the middle of the room. A shiver runs through her body, making her tighten her pelvic floor. Next to the table is a trolley with gauze, cotton, and metal instruments. Behind her, Ingrid hears footsteps.

"Let's get the practicalities over with." The voice is firm, his eyes pin her. From the bottom of her purse, Ingrid fetches the envelope and hands it to the man she recognizes from the apartment in Copenhagen. He pries the envelope open and counts aloud: "Fifteen hundred, sixteen hundred, seventeen hundred…"

When he's done counting, he looks up and points to a narrow wooden door: "Use the bathroom before we get started."

꙲

IN THE BATHROOM, INGRID TAKES THE TIME SHE needs to catch her breath. Once she's composed herself, she pulls the chain flush hanging from the cistern and avoids looking at herself in the mirror above the sink. Then she takes a deep breath and returns to the living room.

"Change into the clothing on the stool behind the curtain."

As she reaches out to pull the fabric aside, her thoughts tumble back to the fitting room in the fancy Copenhagen mall, Magasin. She and Erik had been strolling, and Erik got the idea to go inside Magasin du Nord on The King's Square.

"Find some dresses you like," he said when they reached the floor with women's clothing.

With each new dress, Ingrid would show him an arm, a tease before she revealed herself fully by drawing back the curtain.

On the other side of the curtain, the man coughs, and Ingrid is back in the room. How did she end up here, in this situation? At an unknown address, fumbling with her clothes? The faded green curtain has nothing in common with the Bordeaux-red velvet curtain at Magasin. Ingrid looks down at her body. *That's what you get for messing around.* The wrap dress has changed along with her body's transformation. Her hips are fuller now than they were a few months back. Her nipples no longer resemble small peas but are swollen and tender, like raisins. Ingrid cups her right breast. The glands have grown, and a yellowish-white fluid regularly seeps from them. Fortunately, her breasts don't resemble her mother's, which hang sideways with downward-pointing nipples. Ingrid turns her gaze to the ceiling and changes into the gown and tight stockings.

When she pulls the curtain aside, the man points to the table. Metal leg clamps are attached at one end. At the opposite end lies an embroidered cushion. *It could just as well have come from the linen closet at home,* Ingrid thinks. In a flash, she sees the baby twins in their drawer, and she is suddenly a little girl again, feeling the warmth of Kirsten's back as she snuggled up against her. Ingrid shakes off the flood of images. The instruments on the steel table shine in the light from the teardrop prisms of the ceiling lamp.

She climbs up onto the table and lies down.

"You'll feel a sting," the quack says, holding a needle in his hand.

Ingrid looks up at the ceiling, tracing the round stucco around the lamp.

"Three... two..." His breath reeks of tobacco and coffee.

Ingrid imagines her head resting softly in her mother's lap as she leaves the room on a cloud, her conscience fading away. A blissful indifference spreads through her body. She embraces the feeling and lets herself fall.

FÜRSTENFELDBRUCK AIR BASE

Fly Boy
Kirsten

Every day, on her way to work, Kirsten is met by the GIs' open gazes and confident postures. "Good morning, sweetheart," they say, their voices full of a warmth that makes her cheeks flush. She loves being on their territory, reaping their approving glances, bolstering her self-esteem with their comments.

"Hi darlin'." A new uniform tips his cap as he passes her.

Kirsten straightens her back and continues with a sway in her hips. Behind her, she hears the soldier whistle.

When the uniforms aren't busy falling into line and obeying orders, they rush to hold doors and offer a light the instant she reaches for a cigarette — before she even touches the handle or lifts the cigarette to her lips. At the boarding house, her suitcase is full of chewing gum, cigarettes, and nylon stockings. One long look at a soldier and the contents of their weekly rations are readily available to her.

It turned out to be easy to get the job, wave goodbye to home, and head down to join Martha in Germany. After Forest was transferred to the new Fürstenfeldbruck Air Base, everything fell into place.

"I'll help you find a boarding house," Martha said and kissed Kirsten gently on the forehead. She was home for the weekend and, as always, brought a touch of the outside world with her.

"Working in a place with homesick men is no place for a young woman," their father snorted.

"And so far away, too," their mother chimed in.

Martha assured their parents that she would look after Kirsten. In fact, she was so convincing that Kirsten became unsure whether she was going from one form of supervision to another, but fortunately Martha knew the difference between what to say at home and the reality of life on the base.

With a glance around the base's grounds, Kirsten sends her older sister a grateful thought.

In the weeks leading up to her departure, Kirsten saw her surroundings with a new set of eyes. Only now did she notice that the bricks on her parents' house were faded and the puddles on the gravel road by the gate were greenish brown. Suddenly, the trees in the garden seemed stunted. Once everything about her departure was planned and arranged, she couldn't wait to leave.

In the evenings, she would lie in bed and fantasize about parties, chocolate, coffee from real coffee beans, dresses, work suits, and leather shoes with matching purses. But most of all, her thoughts wandered to the men she had yet to meet. Then she placed a hand on her pubic bone and fantasized about being pressed into the mattress, caressing a nipple with her free hand before sliding it further down to her warm, secret place.

※

KIRSTEN HAS BECOME FAMILIAR WITH A WORLD dominated by rough voices, the clank of machinery, the chemical smell of pressed uniforms, sweat, and the scent of Old Spice. She no longer shudders when she hears the crunch of boots on gravel or sees the uniforms straighten their backs, pull their shoulders back, stiffen their gazes and bark: "YES, SIR!"

Outside the military base, the sound of Munich is different. There, no orders are shouted, no heels click on gravel. Instead, the hollow sound of bricks being pulled free and added to the mountain of rubble is omnipresent. While the military base is enveloped in shouts, clanking tools, and the smells of donuts and cigarettes, Munich smells of coal dust, people in need of a bath, and the perpetual scraping of stone.

There is a shortage of food and clothing on both sides of the English Channel. In Munich and Manchester, women stand in line for hours to redeem their rations of sugar, coffee, cheese, and meat. The Germans prefer gouda, the English, cheddar.

German women and children are left to fend for themselves, not unlike the Jews they wanted to rid themselves of so recently. Those who have lost their husbands on the front must scrape by as best they can. Three years after the war, dirty children still rummage through the ruins. Politicians talk of a massive aid package from America to Europe, but no one has seen any sign of it yet.

A woman's shoes reflect both her personal circumstances

and the state of her nation. The fashion remains unchanged from the pre-war era: Mary Janes, ankle-strapped, with sturdy block heels. But the women of Munich wear their shoes until they are worn down and the heels loosen. As they wait in the queues, the wear and tear on their bodies is visible in the continual shifting and rolling of painful knees and shoulders.

"Miss, show mercy. I have children. We are hungry."

It was bitingly cold on Marienplatz the last time Kirsten was in Munich. The voice had come from a wrinkled face. From under a greasy cap, his gaze had met hers. The man stood in the rays of the spring sun, which only reached a street level in glimpses through the gaping holes of the facades.

"THAT'S HOW IT WAS FOR MY FAMILY, TOO, DURING your insane war," she said. The anger felt like a frostbite. "Now you're paying for your madness!"

At first, she felt a sense of vengeance and superiority spread through her body. She no longer needed to lower her gaze. But the victory came too easily. *Fight like a man!* She thought as he cowered.

Usually, there's a satisfaction to delivering one of her verbal uppercuts; a tingling in her chest. But something has changed inside her. She's away from home, the war is over, life lies ahead. The anger is harder to hold on to than it was during the long, evil years of German occupation.

Kirsten shudders at the memory but is brought back to the base when she hears an airplane in the distance. She steps around a puddle. That day, the outburst didn't feel good. *A pitiful German begging for food for his family! I should have been above that,* she thinks.

"Good morning, princess." A soldier holds the door to the office building.

Kirsten smiles at him — and at herself. She belongs to no one. *Youth is fleeting*, she thinks, holding the soldier's gaze, elongating her neck, and feeling her pupils dilate.

"Good morning, fly boy."

Experiences
Kirsten

Kirsten is enjoying herself at a café, smoking a cigarette and drinking a cup of coffee, reflecting on what she has learned while working for the Americans at the base. Most importantly, you must always have a plan to get away. That has been a fundamental lesson since she moved here.

Whenever she talks to a new soldier, she asks him to tell her about his hometown and his state. *Michigan*, she thinks, sipping her coffee. *I could thrive there. Imagine living in a state shaped like a mitten. Living near one of the many lakes in a flat landscape where cows graze by the thousands — to always have butter and cheese! Being half a world away from Scandinavia but with winters like I remember them back home.* A breeze caresses her cheek. *To live a life in cold, clear air with an open view as far as the eye can see, wouldn't that be something?*

Conversations with men on the airbase have taught her which questions bring life to their eyes and which ones to avoid. It's a bad idea to ask what they miss. Then their gaze becomes distant, wet, or even hard. There is never much fun to be had from that. Asking them about their favorite holiday is also best avoided, because then they'll talk about some uncle or aunt, cousin or niece, or that 'Thanksgiving' thing she still doesn't understand.

Talking about how she feels about the war is out of the question, even if they ask. "The knot in my stomach when my older brothers didn't come home before curfew," she answered them in the beginning, when she was first asked about war memories. Or: "If I see one more cabbage fritter, I'll throw up!"

The soldiers have heard about the living conditions during the war, but they haven't experienced them. And when it comes down to it, they'd rather not know anything specific, even though Kirsten would sometimes like to share. To explain, for example, the reasons behind her reaction to the Red Cross parties' overflowing buffet tables, where she piles much more food onto her plate than she can eat.

"It's over now. Let's party!" was the most common response, before they pulled her onto the dance floor. So now Kirsten gives them the answers they expect and says something about ersatz coffee.

She envies the soldiers; their carefree attitudes, their ability to shrug off heavy topics like a coat that's no longer needed when spring announces its arrival. When *Boogie Woogie Bugle Boy* breaks through her thoughts, she needs something to calm her nerves to be in two different moods at once.

What always has a positive outcome, however, is when she asks them to say the famous Danish tongue twister, "Rødgrød med fløde." Their hopeless attempts to mimic her pronunciation make her double over with laughter.

Their articulation of the soft Danish 'D' is also funny. "How do you say, 'my name is' in Danish?" they ask.

Kirsten enunciates the words slowly: "Jeg hedder."

"Jaaa heller," they slur.

And then Kirsten bursts out laughing again. "Not 'L'. Stick your tongue out of your mouth. Like this," she says, over-exaggerating the movement.

The guttural 'R's aren't as funny, because the Americans' pronunciation takes on a harshness that resembles German a bit too much. But their facial expressions are spot on. Apparently, Danish must be pronounced with wide eyes and pursed lips.

Kirsten has learned that her Scandinavian language is the perfect entry into conversations that start with a laugh: "I can't believe how you can twist your tongue into a pretzel like that!" And sometimes end with: "Do you want to go home with me?"

She removes a piece of tobacco from her tongue. Practice makes perfect. Now she has a polished version of herself and her family, and has learned which portrayal elicits certain reactions. One evening, her father is a fervent socialist; another, a domestic tyrant. One evening, Kirsten says she dreams of a husband and children; another, she will say her dream is to seek adventures far from small-minded Denmark.

At first, she found the game — and the endless stream of new men — entertaining. Now, she's run out of new facets to add to her stories. Like a record stuck in its groove, she reuses her answers and bores herself as the words mechanically fall out of her mouth.

Kirsten stubs out her cigarette and fetches a new one from her case.

And then there are the experiences that have taught her to always have an escape plan. For example, you should never go to the movies with someone you don't know, as she did with the man who lectured her about which types of work were beneficial to society and which were not. Apparently, her work fell into a category he could see the necessity of. But in the end, she was so irritated by his know-it-all manner that she couldn't sit still. For two unbearably long hours, she sat far too close to a man she wanted to get away from as quickly as possible. When he asked after the movie if they should grab a bite to eat, she took off with an excuse about not being hungry.

And then there was the one with the hands — who taught her to always carry cash, because a man's ego can quickly turn petty. He invited her to lunch, placed his hands on her side of the table, and got upset when she kept hers in her lap. Afterward, he insisted she pay half the bill. Things turned comical because she didn't have cash on her, and so he followed her to the bank so she could withdraw what she owed him.

Experiences under the covers are part of the adventure, too — some are pleasant, some less so. *You must take the bitter with the sweet,* she thinks, tossing a few coins on the table before slinging her purse over her shoulder and leaving the café.

Dreaming of San Antonio
Kirsten

Martha and Forest are talking about their departure to America. It's Sunday, and as always, Kirsten meets up with them after partying the day before. She washes down cake with coffee and lights a cigarette before Forest can click his lighter open for her.

"Blah, blah, blah, you two," says Kirsten.

Out of the corner of her eye, she sees him place his arm on the back of her chair. Kirsten's involvement in the conversation has mostly been to complain about the lack and level of men suited for marriage.

"You're too picky, little finch. What if you are so selective you miss out on *'the one'*?" says Forest.

"There are plenty of fish in the sea." Kirsten grinds out her cigarette and looks at Martha. "Like my dear sister, I'll find a decent cod one of these days."

Forest pulls his arm away from the back of Kirsten's chair. "With your battle-axe of a mouth, one might doubt that." He flicks a cigarette out of his pack.

Martha twists a matchbox in her hand, avoiding eye contact with both Forest and Kirsten.

I was too harsh again, thinks Kirsten, looking away. *When will I learn to rein in my temper?*

She almost never dates the same man more than twice. The first date is usually a success. The soldier is attracted to her Scandinavian looks: her blue eyes and fair skin. And probably also her straightforward demeanor. At least at first. But her manner inevitably ends up scaring them off. They rarely invite her out on a third date.

"If only they had a bit of humor, but they take themselves so damn seriously!"

Being around Forest feels different. Unlike other guys, he's not afraid of her temperament. He knows her, doesn't take her attitude for more than it is. If she crosses a line, he rolls his eyes and tells her bluntly to cut the crap.

"Drop it, Kirsten," he growls when she provokes him.

Kirsten blows cigarette smoke in his direction. If only she could meet a man she respected! The minions she meets at parties are too easy to manipulate. Her thoughts drift to the previous night, and a shiver tingles through her body, making her cross her legs.

"Beauty is fleeting," says Forest, holding her gaze as he stubs out his cigarette.

He's right, Kirsten thinks. *Time is not on my side. The stream of interested men will dwindle.*

"Are you saying I'm too difficult, my dear brother-in-law?"

Martha's head jerks up. She looks pleadingly at Kirsten.

"Your temperament is of a different character than Martha's," Forest replies, stirring the coffee he's already poured sugar into three times.

Kirsten gives her older sister a thin smile. She doesn't feel like arguing. She dips her apple strudel into her coffee and takes a bite that makes it impossible to reply. *No, my mind is not as gentle as Martha's. Still, I do dream of getting a man.* She sends the two of them her most apologetic eyes. "Maybe it'll work out. Just think about it! Wouldn't it be marvelous if we ended up going to America on the same bride ship?" Kirsten says.

She has until the fall. Then Martha sails off to New York, and from there to Texas with Forest. Before Forest, Kirsten knew little about Texas or San Antonio at all. Apparently, the state is something special, with golden sand-colored plains, warm breezes, and a rugged landscape.

"Palm trees along the sidewalks as tall as buildings, so you have to tilt your head back to see the leaves," Forest says when he talks about the San Antonio River that runs through the city.

Martha sits beside him, beaming. "Everyone has a Chevrolet or a Cadillac."

Kirsten pictures herself with sunglasses and a scarf around her hair, driving down a sandy Texas street in a shiny chrome cruiser.

Forest describes the cathedral, making it sound more magnificent than St. Peter's Church in Rome. "You're going to love it!" he nods at Martha. "As soon as we're settled, we'll bring your mother over."

He knows just what to say, thinks Kirsten as Martha lights up.

Forest talks about the dome-shaped streetlights and how there are never power outages like they are so used to in Europe. "On Houston Street, six people can pass each other on the sidewalk with no problem. The Pedersen family could walk arm in arm down the street," he laughs, while Kirsten cringes at the thought of linking arms with the rest of her family.

"There's outdoor dining all year round and at all hours," he says.

"Is it really open twenty-four hours a day?" asks Kirsten, widening her eyes. It's almost touching to see his reaction when she gives him the reply he so desperately wants.

He talks about a special Texan personality. "One fine day, the state of Texas will secede from the rest of the Union!" he declares, standing up.

When he talks about the dancing Texas dust that settles on eyebrows and between teeth, it sounds like part of the charm.

"What about cockroaches as big as your hand? Mosquitoes, bugs and snakes?" Kirsten interjects.

"You just have to shake out the rug before going to bed and hang mosquito nets around the windows. And we spray with DDT. It's very effective."

Kirsten isn't convinced, but for Martha's sake, she keeps quiet. Even though Texas is enormous, the state has fewer inhabitants than New York. Forest describes the gleaming coats of the horses, their manes in the wind, and the cowboys — who he calls "vaqueros" — loping across the plains with water jugs and lunchboxes in their saddles.

"No phone, no running water, and horses as transportation! I think I'll stay where I am," says Kirsten, elbowing Forest. After that description, she has no desire to live in a scorching-hot state with sweat dripping and insects buzzing. "I'd rather shop in the nearest town than spend my time in the countryside!"

She dabs lipstick on her chapped lips, "But if you can find me *'the one and only'* close to you guys, then I'll take him *and* Texas — cowboy hat, country music, blazing summers, and all," she says, winking at Forest.

OLYMPIA
KIRSTEN

At the office, the girls have typing races to compete over who is fastest on the typewriters. With her sixty words per minute, Kirsten is one of the fastest. The office is like a classroom: the women sit behind desks, performing the meticulous translation work, each assigned a folder with daily quotas to complete, translating letters from German to English.

Every morning, Kirsten goes to the shelf and fetches an Olympia. Then she finds an empty spot, places the typewriter case on the desk, and clicks open the lid. After work, she puts the typewriter back in its place on the shelf — hers, one of many.

⁂

THE BLACK RIBBON THAT SITS BETWEEN THE typebars and the paper moves up and down rhythmically, synchronized with the rapid movements of the typist's fingers. As Kirsten adjusts the machine's base, she inhales deeply, the scent of machine oil and ink filling her senses. The smooth transition of text from left to right on the paper is a pleasure, as is working with well-maintained tools.

With a steady hand, Kirsten lifts the metallic grid, focused on ensuring the line doesn't go crooked. She hesitates for a second before she lets the paper slide between her thumb and index finger over the cylinder. A smile graces her lips. As her fingers dance across the keyboard, she feels the weight of the spool, watches the fan of metal teeth moving back and forth, and listens to the sharp *clack, clack-clack, clack-clack-clack*. A sense of satisfaction fills her as she feels the resistance of her fingertip hitting a key, followed by the weightlessness before the metal tooth leaves its mark. Throughout the day, the triangular metal frame encompasses her world, displaying three letters at a time as the ribbon continuously unfurls from one side to the other. Abruptly, the drum reaches the paper's edge — a sharp ping signaling her to depress the typewriter's left-side handle fully and begin a new line.

Letters in poorly made envelopes lack the same collaborative spirit. These must be eased out of their envelopes without tearing the parchment-thin stationery to pieces. It requires a special touch. Following the established procedure, the girls are to arrange each document in a specific order: the letter first, then the translation, before filing the documents into the folder designated for the officer.

Thanks to the combined efforts of the women, previously unreadable German letters are skillfully translated into English for the American superior officer to understand. Thousands of letters from home and abroad pass through the girls' fingers, to the typewriter keys, before ending up on his polished mahogany desk.

Occasionally, he appears in the doorway and points at a

girl with his cigarette: "Follow me into my office. Bring the letters that were assigned to you today."

Most of the girls nervously wipe their palms on their skirts before following him.

❧

Kirsten is halfway through translating a run-of-the-mill letter. She's not giving it her full attention; it's one of many identical ones. Like most others, it is dreadfully dull. In this one, a daughter writes to her mother. In others, sons send encouraging signs of life to their parents. The vast majority of letters contain lists of everyday life and the lack of necessities. With a yawn and only half her mind on it, Kirsten continues reading Giesela's letter to her mother. The girl is experiencing bleeding gums and intense hunger.

> Dearest Mama,
> I miss hearing your voice... miss seeing your face...
> In this moment... I am hungry... You must not worry...
> Love you...

The experience is akin to peering over a stranger's shoulder, witnessing the intimate process of letter writing before the message is sealed and dispatched to their family. Initially, Kirsten was deeply affected, feeling a strong connection and empathy for the trials and tribulations faced by the Germans.

Even after work, she couldn't stop thinking about what the letters said. When she slept, she had nightmares about not being able to breathe. However, as time went on, the letters became monotonous, causing her empathy to diminish and eventually fade away.

Kirsten completes the translation. In the bottom right corner, she signs her initials: *K.M.P.* — Kirsten Marie Pedersen. There they sit, her initials, all alone. Without a title to announce her marital status, her availability on the marriage market is clearly signaled. *Will there ever be a 'Mrs.', followed by a man's military rank and surname?* she wonders.

She picks up the next letter from her stack, skims over the origin and destination, and begins another translation.

꽃

"OFF YOU GO!" SMILING, KIRSTEN ADDS ANOTHER completed letter to her folder. Before reaching for the next, she glances up at the army of women, watching their backs bounce rhythmically with the movements of their hands as they type. Their high heels, work suits, and manicured nails are a stark contrast to the grim task at hand, as the women methodically uncover the individuals responsible for Hitler's concentration camps, contributing vital pieces of a puzzle that provides daily help to the Allied forces. Kirsten lets her fingers glide over today's pile of letters. Every day she has the same thought: *Will today be the day I catch a Nazi?*

Few of the girls had a clear comprehension of the job's specifications and demands in the early stages. The women believed they'd struck gold with the translation work. Many hoped to find and marry a suitable American man while working on the military base.

The job is exciting, filled with fun colleagues and a constant stream of attractive men. The translations, however, are not for the timid. Horrific new discoveries about the Nazis' wartime actions are constantly being made. Children were buried alive. Concentration camp prisoners and mental institution patients were subjected to medical experimentation. Some experiments involved prolonged submersion in ice water, and the deliberate insertion of dirt and stones into open wounds to study infection. The Nazis showed no mercy to those they deemed 'subhuman' — Jews, Roma, homosexuals, and communists.

Kirsten feels a shiver and jagged jolts up her arms. She exhales, letting her worries drift away with the cigarette smoke.

When she's in a good translation rhythm, her hands fly effortlessly over the typewriter keys, clacking a steady beat. It's as if they're playing a sonata; each note, each comma, perfectly placed, flawlessly executed. Her favorite words to type, as her octopus-like fingers dance across the keyboard, are *time*, *woman*, and *hunger*.

While she works diligently at the typewriter, supporting the Allied cause, she also finds healing, although the emotional toll and difficult memories occasionally become overwhelming, making the work a constant, arduous struggle. A stiff drink and a smoke after work help.

Kirsten straightens her back, weighing the next letter in her palm.

꿍

AND THEN: THE REASON THEY'RE HERE. THE buzzing sensation, the heart's galloping rhythm when her eyes scan a letter, and the alarm bells ring. The vibrations, the familiar rush in her ears, the readiness in her fingertips.

Over time, Kirsten has practiced reading between the lines. Her awareness is finely tuned, allowing her to recognize and react to the signals. One telltale sign that awakens Kirsten's alertness is when the handwriting is deliberate and clearly not written in haste, as is often the case when the German girls send letters home between peeling potatoes and scrubbing floors.

The pressure of the pen against paper shows that the sender cared enough to take their time and write the message deliberately. When the language is precise, it stands out. When the writing is meant not to stand out, it raises her suspicion. Before her eyes, the ordinary content shifts and reveals its hidden codes, making her adrenaline pump.

In the right margin, she carefully uses a pencil to mark words and phrases that need extra attention, ensuring these aspects of the text receive the detailed examination they require. The mention of either "The Eternal Jew" — a piece of antisemitic propaganda — or any work by Adolf Wissel, a known Nazi propagandist, could serve as a coded message, suggesting a hidden meaning or agenda. This job requires more than just strong language skills. Understanding Hitler's propaganda machine is crucial. The coded messages within the Third Reich's art and cultural production necessitate a deeper analysis that goes beyond mere linguistic interpretation and a nuanced understanding of the historical and cultural context. Such letters go directly to the officer and not into the pile of translations collected after work.

It's that type of letter that Kirsten holds between her trembling fingers. She rises from her desk, adjusts her skirt and hair, and steadies her breath. The solid, imposing, always-closed wooden door leading to the officer's office serves as a constant reminder of the reason for her presence in this place.

☽

Kirsten hesitates at the door. Her breath is tight in her chest. *Damn these nerves!* she thinks. Then she knocks.

"Come in," a gruff voice calls from the other side.

A scent of cold spring wind and tobacco fills the room. And a faint scent of fish. A cool breeze drifts in through the open window. With each gust of wind, the long curtain snaps as it folds, then settles back into place. There, behind a large, highly polished mahogany desk, sits the officer.

He looks like any other Air Force soldier in his olive-green uniform. But Kirsten's trained eye sees the US insignia on both lapels: a golden star in the center of wavy stripes on the sleeves, the name tag above the right pocket, and his medals above the left. Subtle clues to his position.

Kirsten pauses mid-room. Unlike the typical meticulous nature of German organization, his desk displays chaos. Letters, newspapers, and folders are piled high across the surface. An ashtray is conveniently placed at the table's edge, yet he's sprinkled ash in a gray-dusted arc.

He looks up. "More Nazis for me, Ms. Pedersen?"

"Yes, sir."

"Nice work, Kirsten." He nods toward the tray of special-delivery letters. Then, he looks back down at his work.

Kirsten steps forward, taking her time as she places the letter in the tray.

His neck remains bent, just as it had been when she came in. But there's something about his breathing. He's distracted from his work. He can either maintain his focus on the stack of papers directly in front of him, or he can choose to look up, allowing his posture to relax and subtly signal his amenability to engaging in conversation with her. *Which do you choose, soldier?* Kirsten ponders, straightening her posture.

In a single fluid motion, the officer picks up his cigarette case and presents it to Kirsten, a slight smile playing on his lips. A wedding ring gleams on his finger.

This is too easy, Kirsten thinks. *What would I even talk to him about? I wouldn't mind accepting one of his Lucky Strikes — feeling the slight tremor in his hand as he shields the lighter's flame and I lean forward, arching my back, inhaling the familiar scent of his cigarette. The burning tobacco's crackle would cue me to straighten up and project a sense of openness. I'd make a coy wrist movement. Then, while we share the cigarette, our eyes would meet and I would look away in a cat-and-mouse game. A game I know all too well. But I'm not in the mood today. Why bother if it's just going to be a brief fling?* She eyes the ringed hand offering the cigarette case with a gesture of invitation. *Plus, I'd rather not have that reputation among the girls.*

She takes a step back. She can't stay here much longer if she wants to avoid gossip. If she gave in and he later boasted about his conquest to his soldier buddies over drinks, it could ruin her prospects on the marriage market. Just as a single feather possesses the potential to turn into five hens, a young woman's reputation can drastically affect her future marital prospects. There's a difference between what she can allow herself during work hours and what's accepted at parties. She shakes her head.

He leans back in his chair and gives her a scrutinizing look before tapping out a cigarette and balancing it between two fingers. "Ah, well. Another time."

Kirsten smiles faintly.

"Anything else, Ms. Pedersen?"

"That's all, sir." Kirsten turns to go. Heat rushes to her cheeks as she feels his gaze on her butt. Swaying her hips, she heads for the door, slips out, and closes it quietly behind her.

Jargon
Kirsten

As is their custom, the female office workers gather at one of the cafés on the base to discuss and process the day's work-related experiences. As always, men circle them like sharks in the water.

"Care for a drink, my dear?" A soldier hovers over the prettiest girl, who turns her body away in response. Her blonde hair cascades down, partially obscuring her face. The soldier, spurred on by her demeanor, continues his quest.

Kirsten observes the scene. The office girl is one of the quiet ones, long since engaged. "Leave the poor girl alone, soldier." Kirsten squeezes in between them and taps her cigarette, so the ash falls on his pants.

When he turns to look at Kirsten, there's fire in his eyes. He lets them wander up and down her body.

Stare all you want, Kirsten thinks, and grinds out her cigarette under her shoe. "She's already taken by a young man with a higher rank than you," she whispers, holding his gaze.

The soldier backs off, and the office girls avoid his eyes.

Some applaud Kirsten, while others shake their heads in disapproval.

"Phew, Kirsten. You've got guts!"

Kirsten shrugs, smiling coquettishly, flattered by their recognition. "His sort can just try me," she retorts, stiffening her spine.

I'm not entirely useless when the girls need help ditching an unwanted suitor, Kirsten thinks, lighting a new cigarette.

The women return to their conversation around the table. "…Auschwitz… gold teeth… those goddamn Germans…"

Kirsten watches their red lips move, listens as the conversation flits from topic to topic. The words they use, and their particular way of speaking, reflect the specialized language used by their profession. After workhours, the office closes with one of them announcing, "All set for a new sucker in the morning," before they head out, handbags swaying, switching off lights as they go, for a post-work drink and a smoke at a nearby bistro. A mixture of workplace adrenaline, the weight of their knowledge, and a yearning to escape the war's brutality creates a tension within their bodies that finds an outlet in verbal outbursts. That's what it feels like to the women who help bring Nazis to light.

Sharing excerpts from translations is a café tradition. One girl imitates a German letter:

> *Dear daughter, your cat lost its tail…*

The office girls burst into laughter.

"Well, we finally have a nickname for you," says the girl they call Miss Chalk. She got her own nickname when she shared the contents of a letter in which a farmer's wife suspected her neighbor of having something going on with the village schoolteacher. "We'll call you Jenny after the books about Jenny Linksy and all her feline friends."

Laughter and the clinking of glasses fill the air as the women toast to the name. Then the conversation falls somber. Out of nowhere, a girl's harsh voice declares, "They got what they deserve: rotten teeth, awful skin, and ragged clothes!"

Kirsten listens and laughs along. But is that really how she feels? *Not all the time*, she admits to herself. She shakes her head. She has a soft spot for some of the German girls. They never asked for the hand they were dealt. But that's the price women and children pay when thirst for power consumes men.

A sharp sting makes her look down. A glowing ember from her cigarette is making a tiny hole in her stockings. "Damn it!" Kirsten glares at the large run spreading across her thigh. Behind her eyelids, she can feel a persistent burn. Trivial matters derail her. If she can't maintain the integrity of her stockings, what else in the world can she control?

"Strong as steel, thin as a spider's web," says one girl, quoting the DuPont ad they all know by heart.

Kirsten lets out a sigh. "Add these to the mending pile."

The girls mustn't see that it bothers me, she thinks. "There's no use crying over spilled milk," was always her mother's advice. Kirsten taps the ash off her cigarette. But simmering anger boils beneath Kirsten's calm exterior. These stockings are fragile; a cigarette ember or fingernail could snag them. She glances at the other girls. *We all look the same*, Kirsten thinks. *Our perfectly manicured nails, painted lips, and styled hair hide what we're really carrying.*

A girl puts her hand on Kirsten's arm comfortingly and says, "There are plenty more where those came from."

Kirsten is grateful. She's right, it's just a pair of stockings.

Why does she react so strongly here at the café when she cares so little at Red Cross parties? Beer in hand, a cigarette dangling between her fingers, and a soldier's rough hand possessively on her thigh, she doesn't think twice about her stockings. With the music playing and her body reacting to a man's touch, the condition of her fragile stockings holds absolutely no significance for her. Oblivious to everything else, she focuses on the secret thing happening under the table, her legs subtly parting to allow his hands access. To the most audacious, she whispers a hushed warning, "Not past the cotton," as his fingers move up her thighs.

The sound of an office worker's boisterous laughter pulls Kirsten back to the café. She crosses her legs and moistens her lips. Patting the girl's hand, she thinks, *I will not let a pair of nylon stockings ruin my mood.*

"Look at that guy!" says a plump girl, tossing her head toward a soldier walking in their direction. The table giggles as he passes them, red up to the roots of his hair.

"Things aren't too bad," says Kirsten, stubbing out her cigarette.

Butterfly Wings
Kirsten

The air is charged with scattered voices and muted laughter of women. Their meticulously bobbed hair, painted lips, and polished shoes speak of careful preparation. This week's Red Cross party is a highlight. The fun will begin when the doors open.

Kirsten feels a familiar sense of anticipation. Has she remembered her invitation? Will the person she's hoping to see show up? What's the food like this week? How will she decide if she has multiple suitors?

Handbags click open and shut with hollow snaps. A complex mix of floral perfumes, musky colognes, and the faint scent of sweat fills her nostrils, revealing a spectrum of social standing and personal hygiene. Miss Dior from those who bathe regularly, and bad gums, cabbage, and fish from those who stink of poverty. The cloying odor of sweat and sourness assaults Kirsten's sense of smell.

"Ugh!" Lifting one arm, Kirsten brings her nose close to her armpit to check herself before sidestepping away from a woman who gives off a potent mix of mold and the stale air of an attic.

Later in the evening, nobody minds body odor.

❧

Kirsten finds herself in a land of freedom yet still bearing the scars of defeat. The American military base has everything she could want. Food unavailable to Germans and other Europeans is in high demand and easy to find.

A harsh, unpleasant noise grates on Kirsten's ears, filling her with irritation and a sense of unease. Someone's speaking German nearby. *Why are German girls allowed here?* she thinks. Why should they be permitted to steal a soldier right out from under her? How dare they? Their position should be at the back of the line, restraining from any ogling or suggestive looks.

She averts her attention away from the language that sounds like harsh commands. It's remarkably convenient how swiftly they've abandoned the ideology that once so blindingly shone from their Aryan eyes and outstretched arms. Kirsten feels like stomping her feet in anger. Prioritizing access to sausages, fresh fruit, and pudding has replaced their fanaticism.

The American military should have enforced its rule against personnel fraternizing with German women, she thinks.

Forest disagrees. "War can be won in many ways," he said when they discussed it. "If we fill the Germans' stomachs, they'll see us as more human than when we dropped bombs on their heads."

Survival, Kirsten thinks, *was a larger factor in trumping the German ideology.* Out loud, she replies, "Hunger makes you forget your principles."

※

THE DOORS SHOULD OPEN SOON. KIRSTEN WATCHES Martha. Her older sister is stoically calm, as usual. What's going on in her sister's mind? Is she thinking about Forest? Kirsten flattens her tongue. To capture the southern accent, his name is pronounced in a deliberate, slow, lingering manner, with an emphasis on long, soft vowels. "Forest Edgar Rhodes," she whispers. Does Martha pronounce his name that way when they are in bed together?

Forest and Martha are quite a pair. Like a ship's mast, Martha stands tall with an introspective gaze, her dimples a perfect reflection of her temperament. Present in the world, yet unapproachable. A stark contrast to Forest, whose senses are wide open and whose gaze hungrily scans the world.

When she's with them, Kirsten prefers to stay in the background. Among the long-legged shorebirds, she feels like a tiny, flitting sparrow. At five foot four, she seems to gather leftover glances meant for the tall couple.

※

NUMEROUS ARRANGEMENTS ARE MADE WELL IN advance of the parties. Food preparation, table setting, and the organization of music and entertainment are all necessary. The Red Cross sisters throw parties tirelessly for the local soldiers and eligible young women.

Still waiting outside, Kirsten hears her stomach growl. "I could eat a cow!" she says to Martha.

Just imagining the airy lemon cake, the burst of flavor from the fresh strawberries, and the irresistible sweetness of the caramelized bananas makes Kirsten's mouth water and her jaw muscles tense with anticipation. *Think of something else*, she tells herself.

And then there are all those rules about who can attend the Red Cross parties! Kirsten feels her palms grow clammy. A complete background and status check is conducted on all girls before they receive invitations. She tosses her hair. Because they work on the base, she and Martha are automatically invited. She's glad their parents weren't required to write letters of recommendation, like other women. *Martha would have passed that inspection with flying colors, but it might have been tight for me.*

There's more to the parties than just fun and games, though. Women who are lucky enough to find a partner and get married hope for happiness in America as they bid farewell to their homeland and family.

A Red Cross sister always gives out condoms at the entrance. Kirsten smiles at the memory of her reaction the first time they were thrust into her hand.

"Just pop them in your bag," Martha said, nodding.

Mortified, Kirsten rushed to the restroom and tossed them in the trash. It didn't matter at the first party; she was so awkward around men that she didn't need them.

Kirsten brushes the clasp on her handbag. It's become second nature to her now; she carries contraception in her bag without a second thought. Having transformed from a helpless caterpillar into a beautiful butterfly, she sends a tender thought to her former self. Like a chrysalis hanging from a branch, she was in stasis back in Denmark, almost devoid of life, waiting for the emergence of a new stage. When she arrived at the airbase, the chrysalis cracked, and her crumpled wings unfolded.

It is only after Martha and Forest have secured a seat that

Kirsten joins them, her hands trembling as she searches through her bag for cigarettes, eventually extracting one, tapping the case to dislodge it, and carefully positioning it between her lips before striking a match. Leaving the case on the table, she returns the matches to her bag. Each drag brings a moment of dizziness before the nicotine hits, as she holds the smoke in her lungs.

Forest leaves and returns from the bar moments later. He's always the first one to get the drinks.

"Thanks, Dusty," says Kirsten, taking a good swig of the foamy beer he places in front of her. He empties his glass in one gulp, still standing. It feels to Kirsten as if they're in on a secret together.

The beer's rough carbonation coats her throat and dulls her mind. Kirsten's routine is to survey the room and assess the atmosphere. A soldier will come along eventually.

This, however, only happens once the doors are open, and the women have selected food from the buffet. Fully aware that they must allow the women to indulge in the spread first, the soldiers understand that any attempts at courtship must wait.

A SCRAPING SOUND EMANATES FROM BEHIND THE door, like something heavy dragging across the floor. The doors swing open.

"Welcome!" A Red Cross nurse spreads her arms wide. Her Dilly uniform is tight across the bust. A crisp, chalk-white collar clearly displays a Red Cross emblem on the left breast and upper arm. *Volunteer American Red Cross worker* is written around the cross. "Girls, remember your manners and virtue! Let the festivities begin!"

Choo Choo
Kirsten

Kirsten's heart beats in time with the music. She's got dancing feet. A collective organism of bodies sways on the dance floor, its rhythmic pulse generating a palpable heat. Hands touch, skirts move, eyes meet. Will the evening be a fleeting flirtation, or will she meet *'the one and only'*?

She's familiar with the game. With a polite, "Allow me, miss," a soldier will offer his lighter. Then the familiar hollow click of the lid springing back at a flick of his thumb. A sweep across the textured wheel, the flame igniting soundlessly, mirrored in the lighter's polished brass. The distant clunk as he flips the lid shut. The ritual, comfortable and intuitive, will conclude with a meeting of eyes before the decision-making process. A "thank you" and a turned away face, or a smile and an upward gaze; either reaction precedes consideration of the next move.

WHO'S IT GOING TO BE TONIGHT? KIRSTEN LOOKS around the room. If she sits for a while, things happen on their own. In her mind, she runs through her best one-liners.

"Imagine you're a song. Which one are you and why?" To the more sensitive ones, she says, "Tell me something about yourself you don't normally share with others." When faced with a repeated question, she'll smoothly transition the conversation by mentioning a ubiquitous dance hit. For those who find her too assertive, she offers, "I have a softer side, too." Subsequently, the soldier always thinks he will be successful in making her open up emotionally to him.

Sometimes it's not that complicated. Just a familiar song snippet can be enough to create a bond and a shared energy between them as they sing along together.

A FEW MINUTES PASS BEFORE SHE NOTICES THE first gentleman caller of the evening from the corner of her eye. He saunters closer. Sparkling eyes, a straight back, khaki pants, full lips, and golden lashes. He radiates confidence. Kirsten slowly raises the cigarette to her lips then exhales smoke as she looks up.

"Howdy, ma'am. Swell party," he says, making a gesture toward the dance floor. "With those blue peepers of yours, you look like something out of a Scandinavian fairytale!" He extends his hand; looking questioningly at the empty chair.

Kirsten straightens and takes his hand. "Kirsten Marie." Ready for the game, she nods towards the chair.

From there, she falls into the routine.

"Are you cold?" Before she can answer, his arm is around her shoulder.

"Need a light?" His lighter awaits before she's even opened her cigarette case.

He keeps at it all night. Kirsten lets herself be seduced and lulled into a soft cocoon of compliments. She finds his one-liners over the top. Still, she can't help but bask in his attention. He is not *'the one and only'* though, even if he's doing his best.

Her choice hinges on subtle details. His jawline reveals an under-bite that leaves Kirsten with the impression of a simpleminded man. She stubs out the cigarette, crushing the embers. *What a shame.* The stub lies broken in the ashtray with a red kiss around its neck. For one night, however, he'll do. She fans her face, as though smoke has stung her eyes.

"What a fine hand." He grabs the tips of her fingers and mechanically runs his thumb back and forth over the back of her hand. Her skin soon becomes sore and irritated. Kirsten retracts her hand. *I hope he shows more imagination later tonight.*

It's easier said than done to find a quick-witted, humorous man. At least this one tries. He asks about her work, expresses his gratitude for her translations, and seems genuinely interested in her job. But then he says, "Who would've thought women could do the same work as men? In factories. In banks. Even in the oil and aviation industries!"

With great effort, Kirsten keeps her poised eyebrow from leaping onto her forehead. *Shut up, don't say anything*, she thinks, taking a long sip from her glass.

"Who would have thought?" he says again, amazed.

If only you knew! thinks Kirsten, nodding at him.

"Goodness!" he continues, holding up his glass in a gesture that resembles a salute.

Kirsten feels like letting slip a few words about how

women can be more than 'eye candy'. Instead, she lights a cigarette so her mouth doesn't run away from her.

"The women I know have made firepower!"

Kirsten removes a piece of tobacco from the tip of her tongue.

"Without you, we wouldn't have had the gunpowder and bullets to take down the Germans," he says, smiling. "My older sister works at an Oldsmobile factory. It's an American car brand."

Yes, duh, thinks Kirsten. She knows perfectly well what an Oldsmobile is. "Like a Buick?" she asks.

He nods. "They didn't produce cars during the war. Do you know, Miss Kirsten, what the car factory was converted into?"

"Your sister made ammunition, tanks, and military vehicles in Michigan."

He looks down at his beer. She almost feels sorry for taking his chance to lecture away from him, but she's utterly tired of the topic. She straightens her back. As she looks at his broad shoulders, straining the shirt across his angular frame, her gaze softens. The fabric bunches at the collarbone. Her eyes drift to his thighs, the outline of his muscles visible beneath his trousers. Their eyes meet in a long exchange. In one smooth motion, he slides his chair nearer to hers. A shiver runs down Kirsten's spine as their thighs touch. She finds herself captivated by the soldier's presence, his physicality, a blend of soft contours and stark edges.

Then the familiar notes of Duke Ellington's *Take the "A" Train* sound, and they jump up.

Choo choo…
You must take the "A" train,
Do, do, do-do, do-doo…

Désirée Ohrbeck

You must take the "A" train
To go to sugar hill
Up in Harlem...

Like people rushing to catch a train, men and women leap from their tables and line up. A special dance routine always accompanies the song. The soldiers lead the way and show the new girls how it's done.

Kirsten shakes her shoulders, bending her upper body forward and feeling the movement of her breasts against her firm bra. With a steady hold, her soldier leads her forward with his hand on the small of her back.

The best part of the song is the middle. The women stand shoulder to shoulder. The men form a line facing them, shifting their weight in time to the music. The women's movements require coordination of their whole bodies.

Kirsten moves her hips in rhythmic jerks and claps her hands, keeping her bare forearms away from her body. Every time she reveals her ankle and lower leg, twisting at the waist to form an S shape, her hands flutter and dance like a ballerina's. The spotlights reflect off her shiny nails, the color of deep red cherries — even though the lady in the shop said the color was called 'lollipop'.

After the dance, Kirsten and her soldier sit to catch their breath. Kirsten finds her cigarettes and lipstick in her bag. If it weren't for the alcohol, she'd feel silly about dancing. She lets the smoke seep out between her lips. There's a method to this madness. The dance highlights the women's physiques, and Kirsten has nothing to be ashamed of in that regard. She gives her soldier a long, lingering look. Regardless of how he performs later in bed, he's a brilliant dancer with a lovely scent.

The Body's Sigh
Kirsten

Kirsten awakens in an unfamiliar bed. Her mouth has a sour taste. The room reeks of intimate body odor. The man beside her is fast asleep. His scent drew her in last night. Fresh breath, a crisp shirt, and the manly notes of Old Spice. Later, the smell of his member evoked memories of the washcloth back home.

Men can be divided into two categories: one-night flings and potential suitors. Kirsten willingly surrenders to the former when the potential isn't there for the latter. Then she dials down the more serious version of herself and turns up the carefree one, flutters her eyelashes, dances closer, and lets her light shine brightly and provocatively.

The liberating feeling of being in Germany, far from the suffocating expectations of her parents' prescribed notions of proper feminine behavior washes over her with a sense of profound relief. Neither her father's fists nor her mother's dishcloth can reach her here.

To think that my freedom was found in Germany, Kirsten muses, letting a hand slide between her sleep-warm thighs.

She brings her fingers to her nose and inhales the soldier's scent.

Kirsten recalls a snippet from a Tove Ditlevsen poem, loves bathing in the author's melancholy. It is as if the poet's fine, raw poetry is written for her. After the Nazi occupation, they talked about Ditlevsen's poems in school. Talked about the innocence of childhood versus the brutality of war. Kirsten feels her muscles tighten at the memory. What the Danes had to endure during those years! What she and the rest of Copenhagen experienced! She'll never regain those years.

Kirsten turns her face toward the man beside her. The American GI-Joe was a talented dancer. And his teeth were perfect. He was charming; a gentleman. She smiles. While searching for her true prince, one might as well kiss a few frogs.

There was something irritating about his manner, though. This one explained the simplest things with a ramped-up pathos that grew in accordance with how much he drank. *As if women can't think for themselves!* No, he was a bit too fond of hearing his own voice.

"Duty over honor. We can think for ourselves, and we think quickly," he said about the American Air Force. He looked solemnly at her as if expecting applause. "When decisions have to be made in a split second between being bombed and bombing the enemy, we don't have time to smoke a cigarette and think about what to do."

Kirsten pulls the blanket up to her nose.

She'd done as he expected: batted her eyelashes and said in a sugary voice, "What if you pay the highest price?"

He enjoyed the attention, drawing out the moment as if pondering the question. "In the Air Force, we look out for each other. I would sacrifice myself for my brothers. They would do the same for me."

Even though he was too much, Kirsten was drawn to his talk of belonging, honor, and ideals. The unreserved surrender in it. He was so sure of his place in the world.

He stubbed out his cigarette, and some of the ash from the ashtray spilled onto the table. "Keep calm and stay Air Force strong," he said, slamming his empty beer mug on the table before pulling her onto the dance floor.

What a thought; belonging and being part of camaraderie and obligation. But God, how unbearable he was to listen to! Had there been potential for a deeper connection, she would have made more of an effort during the flirtation. Controlled her inner 'slut', as her father would say. And: "How you behave in the company of men!" her mother would chime in. Fortunately, Kirsten no longer needs to worry about them.

Following the dance, they continued their conversation at a table. Meeting her soldier's gaze, Kirsten stubbed out her cigarette and smiled. "I think we're in for a wonderful evening, soldier," she said.

And so, the game of body language and words continued:

"Do you have plans for tomorrow?" Later, on the dance floor, he pulled her close so she could feel his desire.

"Are you always so forward with strangers?" she asked and pulled away. Not because she was shy, but because it's what he expected.

"Are we strangers?" Again, he pulled her closer to his hardness.

Kirsten placed a hand around his neck, looked him in the eyes. "You're playing with fire," she said and brushed his cheek as she let her arm fall, wanting the evening to last a little longer.

On such occasions, Kirsten feels like a cat playing with a mouse. She flirts and then turns her face away, each time leaving the man in doubt over her intentions and drawing out the moment before inviting him to continue his courtship.

"Are you a princess from a fairy tale?" he whispered.

"Wish for anything you desire. I won't disappear in a pumpkin carriage."

Back and forth, like a dance, taking turns leading and never breaking contact.

The cigarettes are part of the game. At the table, Kirsten held his gaze as she leaned forward invitingly with an unlit cigarette. When he moved toward her with his lighter, she made sure her 'sweater puppies' appeared voluminous and took her time with the flame, inhaling his scent.

Lying next to her soldier, Kirsten feels desire rising again. Maybe she should wake him up? As if he has heard her thoughts, he sighs and farts beneath the blanket. Kirsten sighs. On second thought, she hadn't appreciated his kneading hands, which never really softened her body.

If it wasn't for his healthy teeth, he looked like he could be from Scandinavia. Kirsten looks at the blond curls on the back of his head. Didn't he mention something about his 'heritage'? She didn't really pay attention; doesn't understand the Americans' obsession with their origins. And by that point, he had rambled on for so long her ears needed a break.

Resolutely, she'd risen from their table. He looked somewhat taken aback when she grabbed his shirtsleeve. "You're coming with me, soldier," she said, and pulled him out to dance.

He stumbled after her like a puppy. *We might as well get started*, thought Kirsten. Experience has taught her that if a man can dance, there's a good chance their bodies will perform just as well in bed.

⁂

THEY BOTH UNDERSTOOD THE GAME'S INEVITABLE outcome. Later, he silently helped her into her coat, held the door open for her, and offered his arm as they stepped onto the street.

"I hope you will act like a gentleman," Kirsten slurred. Her tongue felt like a potato in her mouth.

"Of course," he smiled and pulled her closer so she could snuggle under his arm.

In the cold, she sobered up. "My landlady doesn't allow male visitors."

"And I don't want to share you with the guys in the barracks," he retorted.

I refuse to stand in an alley with my back against the wall while he finishes his business with me, she managed to think.

But he was determined: "I know a place."

Kirsten remembers the sound of her heels on the cobblestones, the floating sensation, and the taste of smoke and beer between them.

She'd hoped it would be a pleasant experience under the blanket. But the first time went too fast, like a champagne cork that pops before you're ready with your glass. The second time, he took his time, maintained eye contact, explored her body. Still, she didn't reach her climax.

Kirsten slips three fingers into herself. *I'm sure he did his best*, she thinks. At least he was kind and gentle. But when he'd fallen asleep and rolled away soon after, her body still screamed for satisfaction.

Sometimes her desire is spontaneous, and her body

takes over. Other times, she needs time before the climax comes in waves. Sweet words, kisses, and caresses aren't always enough. When her body is out of sync with the man's, desire turns to irritation. And since he couldn't satisfy her, she'd had to help herself along. Only then had she curled up against his back and fallen asleep.

❧

Love me, love me! Peep-peep, peep-peep!
The intense springtime chirping of mating birds draws Kirsten away from her thoughts. The high-pitched tweets repeat incessantly. In a few weeks, they'll have found their mates, built their nests, and be so busy tending to them that their early morning cries will fade and turn into a subdued trilling.

Behind her closed eyelids, Kirsten breathes in the bedroom's scent. She stretches silently, smiles, wiggles her toes out at the foot of the bed to play with the sunbeam. Those feet sure know how to move on the dance floor.

❧

The scent of men's semen varies. One smells of bleach, another of walnuts, and a third of almonds. Some men's semen smells like a freshly wrung-out dishcloth. And then there are those who smell like fish. If they want sex multiple times, their private part smells like a cleaning rag that needs to be boiled.

The first rays of morning sun touch her face; a familiar rough caress after a night of celebration. Above the blanket, dust motes dance in the sunbeam, reminding her of childhood winters and the glittering diamonds the sun's rays made on the snow.

Kirsten turns her face toward the man beside her. A smell of sweat and sourness hits her nose. Yesterday, the scented mix of Old Spice and his sweet, nutty scent was appealing. Kirsten sighs. To drown out the sensory impression, she rolls over and breathes in her own scent from the pillow.

Through the curtains, the strip of light has shifted its angle. Kirsten can't bear the thought of the awkward atmosphere and polite small talk if she is still here when he wakes up. Nor do the girls at the boarding house need to know she didn't sleep in her own bed last night.

She sniffs her hands. *I need to go home and wash before I can go anywhere*, she thinks. *Two more minutes, then I'll get up.*

A deep, sleeping sigh comes from the soldier. He lies stretched out on his back. There's no sense of alertness in his body's position. Not a wrinkle on his forehead, not a hint of a tremor in his muscles. Kirsten feels the urge to dig her nails into his eye sockets. Press against the softness. Feel the gelatinous resistance. Scratch his cheeks. Bite a chunk out of his ear. She'd love to see how he'd react if he woke from his Sleeping Beauty slumber to a furious Valkyrie.

Kirsten blinks, and the feeling is replaced by something softer. *He's a sweet guy*, she thinks, *lying there, looking innocent*. Where the room's darkness and a sunbeam meet on his neck, his bright face is divided from his shadowed body. She pictures the tip of her index finger tracing his jawline, mimicking the shadow in a long, gliding, decapitating motion.

☽

DANISH MEN — NOT LEAST HER OWN FAMILY members — could learn a thing or two from American soldiers when it comes to treating a woman with decency. In Denmark, her brothers and the guys she's met don't know how to behave toward their girls.

Kirsten's teeth grind against each other. She knows what they'd say if they knew where she slept last night. But it doesn't matter. They already think of her as nothing more than the dust they tread on. Kirsten snorts scornfully. The sunbeam from the window tickles her nose, warming her cheeks. She's safe now, but her body remembers. She touches her neck, tracing her spine, trying to erase the memory of her father's harsh grasp. Will she ever be able to relax? Will her body ever understand that those bad times are behind her? Will she always feel the wounds of her childhood as a physical pain, like an imprint?

Despite the dishcloth, she misses her mother; wishes she could share her thoughts and experiences with her. Kirsten sighs. She only has one mother. But her mother has seven children. How can you ever truly connect when you keep each other at arm's length, hiding your true feelings? In her letters, Kirsten includes censored excerpts of her life for her mother. As she writes them down, she almost convinces herself they are true.

Sighing once more, the man shifts onto his side. *Better get to it!* Kirsten thinks before rolling away and getting out of bed. Her soldier stirs in his sleep but continues to slumber. Then he grunts, and Kirsten freezes on the floor beside the bed. In a single, graceful movement, she gathers her skirt, blouse and nylon stockings from the chair with one hand, while bending down and picking up her shoes from the floor with her other. As she tiptoes to the door, she carefully places the stockings in her handbag. Then, pulling her skirt up over her hips, she buttons her blouse while sneaking out into the hallway.

She's looking forward to her workweek, but even more so to the weekend that follows.

Ingrid's Shame
Ingrid

Ingrid is in the living room, an overflowing mending basket at her feet. With the darning needle in her right hand, she stretches the sock with her left, exposing the hole.

"Now you know better than to ever trust men," her mother had said when Ingrid was still too sick to get out of bed, closing the window and yanking the curtains shut.

Any desire to step outside has drained out of Ingrid, along with the last of the blood and discharge from her visit to the quack doctor. *What's out there for me anyway but disappointments?* she thinks. It took months of wiping blood from her private parts before she was finally free of the clots.

Ingrid scratches her abdomen but abruptly stops her movement; the scar is still tender.

It's unbelievable to her that she went out every weekend, just as her friends do now. *I wouldn't dare*, she thinks. *The party can end all too quickly. Better to stay home and mend socks, even with a father who refuses to look at me.*

The Scandinavian War Bride

Is that really all that there is to youth? It's Friday night, and her old friends are out enjoying themselves. Ingrid patches the damaged area of the sock with needle and thread. All the things she used to enjoy mean nothing to her now. Emotions reach her through a padded layer, muffled, as if under a thick blanket. One feeling, however, is overwhelmingly sharp. The family shame weighs heavily — especially the disappointment of her father, who remains silent towards her.

The way she treated Erik after that terrible experience at the quack's haunts her, too. She felt so broken after lying on that table. A few days later, Erik visited her at home. He kept twisting his cap, saying very little. Finally, the silence became unbearable, and she asked him to leave.

"I have no one to share this with," she whispered, seeing his hurt expression.

The following day, he came back, and the same thing happened. More than anything, she craved the feeling of his arms around her, his closeness, and his comforting smell. But the sorrow consumed the love she'd barely had a moment to say goodbye to.

His clumsy caress on her cheek made her turn away. "You and my father. You're both just the same," she sobbed, feeling like the loneliest person in the world.

After a few days, Erik probably decided he'd had enough and stayed away.

Ingrid examines the sock in the light — not so much to inspect her work, but more to catch a glimpse of her father in his armchair. With meticulous care, he takes his pipe and gently fills the bowl.

He still won't look at me, Ingrid thinks and clears her throat. Her father pauses, his hand hovering over the tobacco. Just a fraction of a second, but enough for Ingrid to notice. Leaning forward, he carefully shields his pipe with his hands as he lights it. Before he leans back, he holds the unfolded newspaper up high, so he will not have to look at her.

Ingrid's hands flutter about before she settles them neatly in her lap. Tears stream down her face, an echo of the childhood pain of her mother's swiping dishrag.

Things weren't supposed to go this way, Ingrid longs to tell him, *I'm still your good girl.* She jabs the darning needle into her palm but feels no pain. *Can you even imagine how helpless I felt, not knowing what to do? How I feel now, afterward?* Imagine if he knew about the nausea, the dizziness, the exhaustion. How much disgust she felt at having to hide her condition as time passed. Would knowing all this change anything for him? Does he ever think about what she's had to give up? Friendships, schooling, her place as his favorite.

What followed the procedure was even more dreadful. Pain consumed her, coupled with the sensation of her body rejecting its own contents in a desperate attempt at expulsion. Everything happened at once, and the weight of her father's disapproval added to her burden. Visiting the apartment for a follow-up examination, she learned the truth about her body's reaction to the illegal abortion. Like a punishment she hadn't even considered.

"That's how it goes sometimes when you're not careful," the man said with a shrug.

Now she will never know the sensation of carrying her own child and giving birth. The cramps and bloody tissue served as a farewell to both the unborn child and her dreams of motherhood.

No one is there for us, Ingrid thinks. *For girls like me who get into trouble. For women like my mother, who give birth to one child after another, working themselves half to death to pay the rent and put food on the table while still managing the household. Is rejecting Erik really my way of getting back at Dad?*

Ingrid carefully weaves the needle in and out of the rows of stitches to mend the hole in the sock. *How much longer must I put up with his rejection? How much longer must I atone?* She clutches the sock, knowing she will regret her decision and its repercussions for the rest of her life.

My greatest wish was to get married and become a mother, she thinks. *How can I bear the weight of my actions? How do I continue forward?* Her thoughts emerge from the darkest corners, and she cannot stop them. *I should have kept the child. Erik and I would have found a solution.* She feels tears blurring her vision again.

"It was a boy," the man informed her afterward. A tiny, delicate boy, no bigger than a doll. The sobs sit in her throat like a soreness. Overwhelmed with despair, Ingrid stops darning. *I will never be able to carry a child, I've lost Erik, and there's no one here who will miss me.*

Shades of green and brown contrast against the gray sky outside the window. Ingrid picks up the sewing from her lap and runs her hand through the sock to finish her darning. Carefully, she ties off the ends, snips the threads, and announces, "There, Dad. Your sock is whole again."

Not a single word comes from the armchair.

Ingrid puts the sock onto the mending basket. Tiptoeing quietly out of the living room, she murmurs, "I'm going to bed."

I don't want to die, but how can I live like this? Ingrid thinks as she lies under the blanket. *What reason is there to keep going? They would all be better off without me. Ending my life would bring me peace.* She rolls onto her side and concentrates on breathing.

I can't bear the pain inside my soul. Maybe it would help if I did like Dad and numbed my emotions with the contents of a bottle? Would the turmoil inside me finally calm? Or would it just be a temporary reprieve before I sobered up and the anxiety returned? Ingrid sobs into her pillow. *How long must this fight within me continue? When will I come out on the other side, freed from the mire I'm stuck in?*

Isolating myself helps, she thinks. *I'm not worthy of being around anyone. And I don't have the energy for it either. But I cannot run away from the tormenting thoughts inside me.*

Ingrid folds her hands in prayer: "Dear God, please let everything be better tomorrow," she whispers.

"This can't go on." Martha kneels next to Ingrid's bed so their eyes are level.

Ingrid must have dozed off; she didn't see or hear her sister come into the room.

Martha has made the trip back from Germany for a weekend visit. "Let's get some color back onto your face." Martha furrows her brow, then declares: "I know exactly what you need." Ingrid looks questioningly at her and Martha continues: "A pen pal!"

"No, thanks," Ingrid whispers, folding her arms across her chest.

"Oh, come on!" Martha pulls a picture out from her purse. "Look at this guy. Isn't he good-looking? He's all alone down at his base in Germany, just waiting for you to write to him."

Ingrid shakes her head.

"Well, what about this one, then? He's got a nice smile, don't you think?"

Again, Ingrid shakes her head.

"Come on, Ingrid." Martha fetches another picture from her purse. "Give it a chance. If nothing else, just for distraction." She holds out the third photograph.

Warmth shines in the man's eyes, and his lips are curving into a smile. Ingrid almost smiles herself. *Charming*, she thinks, studying the knot of his tie, which sits slightly crooked. Everything else about him is perfectly straight, except for the cap, which sits just enough askew to make him appear both professional and boyish. His close-cropped military haircut, combined with his clean-shaven face, accentuates a strong yet refined jawline.

"What's his name?" she asks.

"Robin," answers Martha, "But everyone calls him Rob."

"Robin," Ingrid savors the word, "Just like a red-breasted American bird."

"If you say so," says Martha. "Does that mean you'll write to him?"

"They eat caterpillar larvae," Ingrid says, mostly to herself. Then, "Yes," she replies to her older sister.

"Great! Let's hope he can bring out the happy butterfly in you again," Martha smiles. "The address is on the back of the picture. Write to him soon, okay? A few words from a sweet girl like you make them so happy."

Ingrid sits with a piece of paper and a fountain pen. She'd find it funny to write about the irony of Robin being in the navy, given that he shares his name with the land-based bird. But that would be too strange, so instead she writes a neutral letter and introduces a side of herself she wishes was the whole truth. Erik, Tivoli, and everything that came after, she of course leaves out. She finds a picture of herself and places it with the letter before moistening the envelope and setting it ready for Hansen's morning round.

After a few weeks, a reply comes from Robin, who asks her to call him Rob. "That's what my family and friends do," he writes. Although Ingrid feels like neither family nor a friend, Rob's immediate kindness, like a warm sunbeam, softens her initial apprehension, lightening the dark gray shadows in her mind.

Once a week, Ingrid writes a letter, and once a week she receives one from her pen pal Rob in Germany. Ingrid likes to think about their letters crossing paths. Since mail takes so long, they write new letters before the previous ones are answered.

One week, Ingrid receives two letters, and a few weeks after that, three more.

"I think about you all the time," writes Rob. As the weeks pass, Ingrid must admit she feels the same way. The thought crosses her mind: *Could this correspondence develop into something more serious? Could this relationship be a fresh start, a world away from my past?*

Ingrid feels less desperate, less despairing, and less lonely with the arrival of each envelope. Still, each day, the sight of her father brings a fresh wave of guilt, shame, and humiliation. *Maybe I should do what Martha did,* she thinks. *Is it possible* to start afresh in America rather than ending everything here in Denmark?

Once the thought has taken root, it's hard to shake. Through her letters, Ingrid tries to determine if Rob takes their correspondence seriously, or if she's just a source of entertainment for him. The mere thought of him seeing her body if they became a couple gives her sweaty palms. She pushes aside the thought of his response.

Time will tell, she thinks. *Time will bring solutions.*

※

INGRID CAN'T EAT A SINGLE BITE, EVEN THOUGH she likes the stuffed cabbage her mother has prepared. Tonight is the night; she might as well just say it. Carefully placing her cutlery on her plate, she clears her throat. With a worried look, her mother stops chewing. Unfazed by Ingrid's interruption, her father continues his meal.

"My pen pal, Rob, has asked me to marry him," Ingrid says quietly.

Ingrid's mother's face goes white, as though all the blood has drained from it.

"I've accepted," continues Ingrid.

Her mother lets out a sob-like sigh.

"I'll go with Martha when she sails to America."

Ingrid's father finishes his beer. "He's in for a surprise when he finds out he's been tricked."

"Karl!" Ingrid's mother turns to Ingrid, exclaiming. "Does he know?"

"No," Ingrid whispers.

"But he will," Ingrid's father says, "once you're undressed." He shoves his chair back and rises to his feet. "Don't come crawling back when he doesn't want you."

Farewell
Karl

Hands in pockets, Karl walks toward the garden gate.

The girls have such contrasting personalities, he thinks. *Martha is the sensible one, level-headed and practical. Ingrid...* Karl snorts. He's not ready to think about her. *And Kirsten. Kirsten does as she pleases, that much he's learned. She is — and always will be — stubborn as a mule. Maybe Germany will tame her, somewhat.* The apple doesn't fall far from the tree, he must admit. But it's different with girls. They need to learn to be submissive and obey their father — and later, their husband.

Now the daughters are scattering to the winds. Martha is going to America, and Ingrid probably will too, if everything goes as planned. *And Kirsten? I wonder what will become of her,* he thinks.

Karl hears one of the Jeep doors slam shut. Forest calls out, "Willy is ready whenever you are."

Karl stops. *Who the hell gives their car a nickname?* He spits on the stone path.

The American walks around the car and places a flag in a holder. Red and white stripes, like the Danish flag, but with a blue corner and stars. With practiced ease, Forest inspects the vehicle's tires and canvas. The girls' suitcases are secured to the back of the Jeep.

Karl, digging in his pocket for his tobacco tin, thinks, *Not much room for the three of them inside that sardine can. All this commotion. Why the rush? It's all happening so quickly.* Edith nervously wrings her hands beside the car. *Why can't that woman show some dignity?* Karl packs his pipe for the third time. Gently at first, like a child's touch, then with the grace of a lady, and finally with the firm hand of a man, he presses the tobacco into the pipe bowl.

He watches his oldest daughter as he lights his pipe. Martha stands with her eyes downcast, cheeks flushed. Her face has an inner radiance. Her dimples are subtly visible. *America will treat her well*, Karl thinks, a satisfied grunt escaping his lips. *We did a good job with that one. We can be proud to send her off. The American is lucky with our Martha.*

Martha holds a bouquet. A quiet murmur passes between her and her mother, who nods in response, her shoulders slumped. Behind Martha, Ingrid steps forward, and the anger inside Karl boils over again. *How could she embarrass me like that? To be so utterly humiliated by one's own daughter!* Karl almost throws the pipe but changes his mind. *Breathe*, he reminds himself.

But Karl's rage still burns. The memory of weeks of her tiptoeing around him, visibly in pain, makes him want to yell. *Damn near unbearable to listen to! Naughty girls must pay the price for their actions. How often have I told the girls that they'd better not come home with a baby in their belly, out of wedlock? Ingrid, ever-submissive, was always at my feet, gentle and devoted to her household tasks. Of all my daughters, I never expected her to* disappoint me so much. Just when you think they're ready to leave the nest, they come crawling back with their problems! And what happens when Rob finds out she's been cut open and had a baby removed?

Karl reaches the garden gate. *It's out of my hands,* he thinks. *Whatever will be, will be.*

☽

SHOULD I OFFER FOREST MY BLESSING TO TAKE THE GIRLS WITH HIM? Karl burrows his hands in his pockets, tilting his head back, watching the clouds drift across the sky.

It dawns on him; there's no competition between them. The battle was lost long ago. Forest far outshines what Karl, and the rest of the family can offer. Something changes within Karl — from feeling like the patriarch, the man of the house, to feeling inadequate. He turns to face Forest. *Isn't that what we hope for our kids?* he thinks. *That they surpass us, do better in life than we did?*

Karl steps through the gate and pauses in front of Martha. "Well, goodbye then. Don't forget what your mother and I taught you." He lets his arms fall, gripping his pipe to occupy his hands.

"Yes, Dad," says Martha, giving him her quiet smile before turning toward the car.

Ingrid creeps in front of Karl. *Just like when she was a child,* he thinks. Karl spits a wad of tobacco to the side. She stands there, swaying slightly, her hands folded in front of her stomach, ready for whatever he might have to say with pleading eyes. "At least let me say a proper goodbye, Dad," she whispers.

Karl snorts, giving her the look he knows scares her. He feels like an old fool she's made a mockery of. Her meek voice irritates him. His thoughts careen wildly and far too quickly down paths he isn't even certain he wants to travel. *Be kind, Karl*, he can hear Edith thinking. He takes a step toward Ingrid. A mix of tenderness and frustration makes him clear his throat. *She's only sixteen, for God's sake.*

"It's almost time," he says, turning away.

Farewell
Martha

Turning in her seat, Martha looks at Ingrid, who is sleeping on her side, her knees slightly bent. *The fact that she can sleep on the uncomfortable Jeep seat shows just how exhausted she is.* Martha feels the urge to reach out and stroke her little sister's hair. One arm rest on Ingrid's rounded hips, the other cradles her head, ignoring the jarring engine noise and whistling wind that howls through the Jeep's pipes. *I just hope she likes her new boyfriend when she sees him*, thinks Martha. *Many girls end up with an American soldier that way, so hopefully it'll work out if the chemistry is there?*

Good thing they convinced her to go. Ingrid needs to get away from this place. Given everything, her relationship with Erik inevitably ended. After that, Ingrid became even quieter than usual, withdrawing into herself. The idea of a pen pal wasn't such a bad idea after all, Martha smiles to herself. Things moved quickly between the two after a few weeks — maybe a bit too quickly. But who can blame Ingrid for wanting to escape everything that reminds her of the time before and after the abortion?

Martha looks down at the Jeep's floor. The flowers are less vibrant than they were this morning when she and her mother picked them. Before they left, she wrapped wet newspapers around the stems and stuffed a soaked, tightly crumpled page into the bottom of the newspaper cone.

"Take care of yourself in America," her mother said, her hands folded behind her back and her body swaying in rhythm with her steps.

"We're going to be all right, Mom," Martha said, stooping to pick chamomile. "Can I dry these leaves and then brew tea with them?"

Nodding, her mother gathered cornflowers and chicory, binding them with a blade of grass. She placed the bouquet in Martha's hands, her fingers intertwining with her daughter's. "In memory of your blue-eyed Danish family and our country's history."

"I can make coffee myself if the American coffee is too weak for my liking." Martha attempted a light tone, but her voice cracked, forcing her to avert her gaze and regain her composure.

As they walked along the road outside the garden, Spot crisscrossed from side to side, his nose glued to the ground, completely oblivious to the fact that Martha would soon scratch him behind the ears for the very last time.

"I can't help you from so far away." Her mother wrung her hands in front of her stomach.

"Forest's mom is excited to have a daughter," Martha reassured her, patting her arm.

"You know what's best, my girl," came her mother's quiet reply.

WHISKEY
FOREST

Forest is not completely wasted, but he's not sober either. He sighs, feeling the burning sensation down his throat, as he takes a sip from his infinity bottle, breathing in through his mouth so he can taste the soft aroma without smelling the alcoholic fumes. The golden liquid between his thighs is warming up, yet the cool flask against his crotch feels pleasantly tingly. The bottle cap is in his pocket; it's just a matter of bringing the bottle to his lips.

He likes having it close at hand. When he wants a swig, he doesn't need to take his eyes off the road or ask Martha to pass it to him. Feeling her eyes on him from the adjacent seat, he is overcome by a sudden irritation. Damn, he hates her silent reproach.

Caressing the Jeep's slender steering wheel, Forest lets his fingers trace its smooth circumference. With his hands at ten and two, he leans forward, adjusting his posture for a more comfortable position.

Inside the car, the rhythmic snap of the American flag against the canvas is a constant, comforting sound. His flag, the most beautiful in the world. With every flick of the wind, it gives a sharp crack, reminiscent of a whip. To balance things out as they left Copenhagen, he put it on the girls' side before Martha and Ingrid said their goodbyes and got in the car.

"*Light my cigarette!*" he yells to Martha above the roar of the engine.

He loves the rugged look of the Jeep and its no-nonsense attitude, typical of a muscle vehicle. What you see is what you get. When he drives by, people stop, and traffic gives way. The five-pointed star takes up most of the grille. The fluttering American flag waves in its holder. 'USA' in white lettering is prominently displayed on either side of the grille. There's no denying it; here comes a representative of the victorious American forces!

Is he, like the Jeep, exactly what he claims to be? Always torn between the values he believes in — honor and duty on one side, longing and desire on the other. But just like the Jeep, respect is based on appearance. He must project the image that will make people want to give it to him.

Circumstances have led him here, sitting beside Martha, as her husband. She embodies everything his reason dictates he needs: stability, predictability, and unwavering loyalty. Still, he occasionally finds himself wishing for something different. Given a second chance, would he choose her again? With Martha, he can see exactly what their life together will be like. A simple life, a house, kids — everything a man could dream of. He should be happy with this woman and the life she offers. But he's not sure he's made the right choice.

Expectations! Forest clicks his tongue. Does life consist solely of fulfilling the expectations of others? His pop grew up in a different time with different ideals. Unlike Forest, he remained on the family farm in Texas. Forest is a veteran, a man who has seen the world. He looks over at Martha and flicks the lighter's flame. War's not all duty; it's about dreams and desires too. About choices.

Martha is my future, he thinks, as she places the cigarette between his lips. *But is she the right future for me?* With his hand on the wheel and the cigarette between his index and middle finger, he takes another swig. Martha is the epitome of strength and loyalty. Then why doesn't he feel a stronger love for her?

He sighs. *In Texas, I'll be the man I know I can be.* He glances back at Martha. The Jeep's split plastic windshield provides a shared view of the world as they gaze out at the same scenery. Behind them are the evergreen trees Denmark is known for. Ahead lies Germany with its shattered, war-torn landscape. Maybe he should paint their house in Texas OD, Olive Drab, the same color as his military Jeep? Would she like that? He might convince her, likening the idea to the Danish trees.

Martha removes her hands from her stomach, where they've been cradling their shared secret. His Danish in-laws don't know; he couldn't bear the guilt of taking their oldest daughter to America and depriving them of their first grandchild, so he convinced Martha to keep her pregnancy a secret. *Besides, you never know, so much can happen — who knows if it'll even come to anything?* With a flick of his wrist, he casually ejects the burning cigarette butt out of the car window. *Another swig,* he thinks, *then I'll save the rest.*

Martha finds the pack of Lucky Strikes, taps out a cigarette, puts it to her lips and lights it, shielding the flame from the Jeep's draft. As she straightens, he feels her gaze on his temple. He keeps his eyes directed forward, concentrating on the view through the windshield.

"Dusty, don't you think you should take a break?"

A tightness is building up in his thighs. "Can't a man have a drink?" He turns to her sharply, seeing her flinch. "Break!" He tilts the bottle and takes a long swig. "What I need a break from is a woman telling me what to do and what not to do!"

Stop Sign
Martha

Reaching toward Martha's face, Forest encircles her neck with his right hand. The firm pressure feels like a warning — similar to the way she would place her hand on Spot's neck to communicate to the dog that his behavior had reached its limit.

With a heavy sigh, Forest lifts the bottle to his lips. As the smell of his breath wafts towards Martha's nose, her stomach reacts with a violent lurch, preceding a wave of nausea that rises in her throat. As she swallows, she fixes her gaze on the indistinct shapes of the buildings, their outlines blurring.

Forest presses firmly on the accelerator and the vehicle surges forward with a sudden, jerky movement. The speed at which Munich's streets rush past makes it nearly impossible for Martha to differentiate between the various buildings that fly by. The auditory experience each time one block ends and another begins mirrors the sensation she experiences amidst a bustling crowd, when she covers and uncovers her ears in response to the levels of noise. She closes her eyes to the rising and falling roar.

"I need to rest," she murmurs softly, dropping her cigarettes beside the bouquet. The musty smell of wet newspaper and rich, dark earth, makes her open her eyes again and stare at the flowers on the floor.

꽃

SHE MUST HAVE DOZED OFF. IN HER DREAM, Martha was in an open field with wildflowers, feeling the undulating movements of the wind's touch in the tall grass.

The Jeep's acceleration is a jarring mix of hard jolts and softer bumps as it hits uneven patches on the road. Martha opens her eyes.

Through clenched teeth, Forest's voice is thick with anger: "I'm an American! We won the war! That damn German better yield to me!" His knuckles are white on the steering wheel.

Martha perceives it both instantly and slowly. She sees the stop sign; the orange light at the intersection. Through the window, further ahead, she sees the German truck and admires the curved shapes that arc over the front left wheel of the vehicle. She sees the headlight's beam: white light shooting forward into the darkness. And now she sees the cargo, filled with gray-white cobblestones.

Martha's mouth tastes metallic and sour. Her eyes meet the truck driver's across the blurry division of their respective car windows, and in that instant she sees his expression morph from one of puzzled uncertainty to one of utter horror. As if in slow motion, she watches him jerk backward in his seat, his arms rising to shield himself behind the wheel.

US ARMY HOSPITAL MUNICH

Ambulance
Forest

Forest groans. His head is pounding. As he draws air into his lungs, he feels a sharp pain in his ribs. A wave of nausea washes over him as the stench of urine and excrement reaches his nose; only then does he notice the dampness between his thighs. He loosens his grip on the steering wheel and turns his face to the right.

A jolt runs through his body. Martha and Ingrid's faces! Tulip petals of white skin around a glistening burgundy mass. A jagged bone protrudes from Martha's gaping back wound; a wine-red splatter marks the small hollow of her dimple.

His gaze jumps to Ingrid. Her ballooned fingers lie limp like a glove, a few threads connecting the flesh to the underlying bones of her hands.

Forest tumbles from the Jeep, staggering along the sidewalk before his legs give way beneath him.

He wakes to find Martha and Ingrid already extricated from the wrecked Jeep and receiving treatment in separate ambulances. Doors slam open and shut. Further away, a man is hosing down the road.

☽

"Go sit with your wife." The ambulance driver taps Forest on the shoulder. "Talk to her," he says, before exiting the cabin, leaving Forest with Martha.

The sound of the engine starting and the shrill pitch of the siren reaches Forest's ears before he feels the ambulance's acceleration. He sits for a while, unable to look at her. Then he rips the bandage off his forearm; it seems pointless to wear it.

"Sergeant, you were lucky," the doctor said as he treated Forest's minor injuries outside the ambulance. "Just some cracked ribs, minor cuts and abrasions." The doctor gave him a tube of ointment. "Apply this antiseptic cream and you'll feel much better soon."

Nodding, Forest recalled his air force training and the importance of preventing infection and tetanus.

"If it becomes tender, see a doctor," the man advised, shaking Forest's hand.

"Thanks, Doc," Forest replied.

He detests hospitals, particularly their sterile smell and overall atmosphere of illness.

"Rest for a few days," the doctor added, already turning to leave. Forest muttered in discontent. What was the point of him being in the barracks alone on sick leave? Gasoline fumes reached his nose from the ambulance's exhaust. He prefers to keep himself occupied, both physically and mentally. No able-bodied man should remain inactive. The mind cannot wander when there are orders to follow, and the body is busy executing them.

※

Forest doesn't know where to look.

"Talk to her," the ambulance driver had said.

What is he supposed to say? "I'm sorry," he whispers and places a hand on the white sheet. "I promise I will do better." He glances at Martha's face. Can she even hear him? "Do you remember...?" The words disappear in a sob.

Unable to face the consequences of his actions, Forest turns away. His inner eye conjures images of Martha: her hands folded over the barely visible baby bump; her dimples. He wants to remember her like that, not as he sees her now, still and lifeless on a stretcher.

Vegetative
Kirsten

Kirsten is completely disoriented. She can't find her way, neither on the streets nor in her thoughts. It's always been like that, but it's gotten worse since Ingrid and Martha's hospitalization. As Kirsten navigates the complex layout of the hospital, her sense of direction repeatedly fails her; just when she believes she's in one specific area, she finds herself opposite to where she thought she was.

The hospital comprises seven identical three-story buildings, all interconnected by a network of corridors. Grasping the logic took some time. Once, Kirsten unexpectedly found herself in the maternity ward amidst the cries of newborns, the groans of women in labor, and the click-clack of midwives' hurrying footsteps. Kirsten had no business being in that hallway full of commanding voices and furious screams, yet fascinated and terrified, she froze. Through an open door, a nurse appeared with a bundle in her arms, and Kirsten witnessed a man increase in height after receiving the swaddled infant.

The Scandinavian War Bride

SECLUDED IN A PARK AND HIDDEN BEHIND A WALL, the hospital is like a patient isolated from the outside world. Stepping out of the building, Kirsten feels the warm spring sun on her skin and breathes in the fresh, prickly air.

The seasons here are about a month ahead of Denmark. The sun feels warmer and more intense. In the hospital's kitchen garden, she can see how quickly onions, leeks, and carrots grow. Lowering her gaze to her white blouse, she shields her cigarette from the wind to prevent ash from falling. According to the latest fashion, her bust tapers to two points. *To become the person you dream of being, you must let go of your past self*, she thinks.

A woman in a lab coat walks past carrying a basin of laundry and Kirsten gives her a nod. The rhythmic thwack of a tennis ball echoes softly in the background. A microcosm of a community lies inside these walls, complete with laundry facilities, a kitchen, power generator, laboratories, staff housing, dining hall, swimming pool, and tennis courts.

Crunch-crunch. The sound echoes under her shoes as she jogs through the park. During the day, the gate is open wide to the world. She slows her pace, finally arriving at her destination: a bench on a patch of grass, surrounded by a boxwood hedge.

Facing the bench with her arms at her sides, Kirsten exhales and lowers her shoulders. Inhaling deeply through her nose, she holds the spring air in her lungs. *Here!* she thinks, tilting her head back, *I can breathe. Here I can turn my face toward the sun, feel the cool breeze, and walk on the grass with the chirping of birds and the buzzing of insects in my ears.*

Kirsten removes her shoes. Cold grass squishes between her toes as she walks on the trimmed lawn. At first it feels unpleasant, but then a tingling sensation spreads up her thighs. Holding her shoes by the ankle straps, she squints at the sun, enjoying the warm rays tickling her skin. As the tingling fades, she takes a seat on the bench.

The building up ahead has a fresh coat of paint. *There is much to say about the Germans, but one thing's for sure,* Kirsten thinks, *they are efficient!* Post-war renovations have revitalized most buildings, creating a bustling atmosphere. However, there's also something eerie about the meticulous orderliness. A shiver runs down Kirsten's body. A few kilometers from the hospital is Dachau, Germany's first concentration camp, infamous for its horrific experiments. Lethal injections and submersion in freezing water. Every detail was meticulously recorded in the protocols of the precise and methodical Nazi doctors. The US Army Hospital Munich was previously called Krankenhaus Schwabing. Word is that the hospital's physiotherapy department is at the cutting edge of hydrotherapy research, due to its experimental immersion programs.

A bird cries overhead, making Kirsten jump. A doctor in a white coat passes nearby. When their eyes meet, he briefly salutes her. She nods curtly. Did the doctors here take part in wartime experiments on concentration camp prisoners? What became of the people who died from their injuries before receiving medical attention? Were they taken away on those notorious white buses? Are those the same doctors who experimented on concentration camp prisoners now rushing around in their pristine white coats? Kirsten sighs. *If you ask them now, no German was ever a Nazi,* she thinks.

Kirsten furrows her brow. They *must* have known what was happening. They saw the smoke and smelled the stench of burned human flesh. Gazing across the park, she pictures a thick blanket of ash-like snow covering the gravel paths and flowerbeds, envisions children on swings with gray flakes softly dusting their faces, and sees laundry hanging on the clothesline, streaked with gray.

She has asked the staff several times. Kirsten glares at the back of a doctor's neck as he walks between two buildings. She can't help herself. How can they move among each other silently? She refuses to pretend nothing happened. But instead of answering, they stare at her, implying she is in the wrong.

"We don't talk about the war," they say.

How convenient! Just because a conversation falls silent doesn't mean there's nothing to talk about. They want to forget but Kirsten needs answers. With all their construction work, it's as if they can't erase the evidence of the past quickly enough.

She flips open her metal case and takes out a cigarette. Even the expansive lawn in the park has been mown so finely that not a single trace of the previous shell holes remains visible. The flowerbeds are so perfectly trimmed, they look as if someone used tiny nail scissors. She lights her cigarette and takes a deep puff.

"Ahhhhhh." Nothing beats the first drag. Leaning back, she stares at the ancient trees with their gnarled surfaces, shaped by centuries. She loves tracing the rough bark with her fingertips. How can the outermost dead tissue of a tree make her feel so alive? Despite all they've witnessed, they remain majestic. Time has left its mark in the deep grooves, curled edges, and knotted contours. If she stands by a trunk long enough, faces emerge from the cracks in the bark. Mostly, it's Forest's face she sees in the lines as she caresses the firm, rough bark.

With a furrowed brow, the doctor speaks in German: "Vegetative." Each day, he adds a new word to Kirsten's medical vocabulary; words that push Martha further away from life.

In his hand, he holds a thin flashlight. Shining the light in her eyes, he uses his other hand to lift her eyelid and says, "No quality of life."

Kirsten nods.

"What's he saying, Kirsten?" The tendons on her mother's hands stand out, white against her liver-spotted knuckles as she clenches her fists. Her gray-blue eyes flicker between the German doctor and Kirsten, trying to decipher from Kirsten's expression what he means. Deep lines are permanently etched around her mouth. Kirsten wishes she didn't have to be the translating pendulum between her mother and the doctor.

"He's talking about her condition, Mom."

"Yes?" Does her voice convey hope or despair?

"Martha won't regain her mobility. Or ever be able to speak." Kirsten starts to reach out for her mother but instead bolts toward the window. "The doctor doesn't expect any improvement," she says with her back to the room.

Kirsten hears her mother sigh, the way she does when she bows her head.

☽

Who feels the deepest sorrow? In the cruel hierarchy of the heart, parents who have lost a child are always the winners. Is a parent's grief over losing a child more intense than a sister's sorrow over losing a sibling?

Kirsten mourns the sister who was always there, who taught her to tie her shoelaces, let her crawl into bed with her, stroked her hair when she couldn't sleep. The one Kirsten will never chat to again, never share a cigarette with. Kirsten mourns the sister Martha was — the sister who is now fading away.

She turns away from the window. The doctor said more, but that's enough for now. Now is not the right time to translate the words "vegetative" and "medical treatment" to her. There are limits to how much a mother can bear to hear.

Kirsten walks over to Ingrid's bed. Her bluish-purple balloon-like hands rest on top of the blanket. The contours of Ingrid's body only fill half the oversized cot, making her look like a child lost in a giant's bed.

Behind her, Kirsten hears footsteps. A second later, her father steps into the room and comes to stand beside Ingrid's bedside.

"At least, I don't have to listen to her playing that awful caterwauling on the fiddle." He fills his pipe, pressing down the tobacco. "I wonder what I can get for that thing."

A wave of anger washes over Kirsten, fueling an overwhelming urge to swipe and scratch at his face, flailing wildly, before finally wrapping her legs around him and bringing him to his knees.

Instead, she feels her vision blur as tears streak her face. Turning away, she hears her father snorting behind her. Gurgling with rage, she storms out of the hospital room, nearly knocking Forest over in her haste. She can't bear to see her helpless sisters, her apathetic mother, and her despicable father. Least of all can she bear the bitter taste of her own cowardice.

꥟

In the daily rhythm of the hospital, one day blends into the next. Getting up from her seat, Kirsten walks to the window. Waiting makes her both lazy and insane. *Why can't they decide if they want to live?* Mortified, she looks over at her sisters. *Who thinks like that?* What a despicable person she must be!

Ingrid looks as if she's sleeping, her straw-like hair spread out over the starched pillow. Though pale, her cheeks have a faint rosy hue. Martha's face is smooth and waxy, devoid of expression. Her dimples are gone. Her ever-worried forehead crease is a groove against her light skin. There's something about her body that suggests she's no longer present. Her complexion is yellowish, her cheeks sunken.

Their blankets, pulled tight and snug, seem to both shelter them from the cold and shield the family from the sight of their actual condition. Kirsten looks away. Those helpless figures swathed in white bedding are not her sisters.

"I'm going out."

Reluctance
Forest

Forest would like to linger a little while longer in the park. It's never easy to walk through the hospital's front doors. Leaning against a tree, he lights another cigarette.

Up there, in the sterile hospital room, Martha, pale and still, is no longer his vibrant Daisy. He takes a deep drag from the cigarette. At their wedding, he promised, "In sickness and in health, for better or for worse, until death do us part." So why does he dread visiting hours, but longs for walks with Kirsten? City strolls with her make him forget, almost completely, that he's a married man.

Finishing his cigarette, he lights a fresh one using the still-burning end of the previous one. The crackle of the tobacco, followed by a slight dizziness, dampens his guilty conscience.

He was happy with Martha, of course. They had fun in the beginning. He thought it was all in good fun, that is, until she made it clear what she expected from him in exchange. He watches the cigarette's glow eat its way through the tobacco. And so, he proposed to her as a way of achieving his real objective, if he were to be completely truthful about his intentions. A man has his physical needs, after all. Forest stares at the cigarette.

Things did not go as planned, and as his deployment came to a close, he contemplated the option of abandoning Martha in Europe. He could go back to Texas and allow the memories of her to fade. He wouldn't be the first soldier to do this. It would be easy. Back home, he had the chance to begin anew, keeping his two lives separated.

He sighs. Alcohol and girls' giggles are a dangerous cocktail. How can a man resist the flirtation and swaying hips?

But while he was still weighing his options, Martha got pregnant, and soon after, plans were made for Ingrid to join them in Munich. The trap closed, catching him. Women always bring trouble.

Forest flicks his cigarette onto the lawn. "No littering," he mutters and pockets the butt. He looks up at the hospital building. Kirsten is in there. He knows he shouldn't think of her. He should be thinking of Martha. Calm and gentle Martha. This is not how he wants to be. He wants to be decent and honorable. Martha is loyal, faithful, and devoted. But Kirsten makes him feel alive. Her directness helps him open when they talk.

Martha's presence made him feel proud; more like the man he wanted to be. He thought, or perhaps believed, he wanted a family, a house, and children with her. That's what he's always wanted. What she confirmed he wanted. The safe choice. But his focus has shifted. He's no longer sure of his priorities, his life choices. Is it a betrayal of Martha that he now feels like a stranger compared to the man she married?

Kirsten makes him uncertain in a way that makes him feel young. Her spirit is untamed and wild, like the mustangs that freely roam the vast and open plains of Texas. Initially, he gave little thought to their conversations. But as time passed, something in him softened. With Kirsten, there's no pretense. After all the whispering voices and accusatory glances in the hospital, Kirsten's company is refreshing.

Desire and reluctance go hand in hand when he's on the hospital grounds. The desire to be in Kirsten's company, her fine figure beside his. The contrast between her delicate features and her direct language is striking. A smile crosses Forest's lips. The private nature of the innermost thoughts they share can only be understood by the two of them: the accident, the hospital, and their relationships with their parents.

Reluctance, though, is also ever-present, causing Forest to grimace. Day by day, Martha has withered and shrunk before his eyes, losing color and form. But it's not just her physical shell that brings him discomfort. As soon as he steps into the room, the weight of her parents' silent judgment settles on him, their eyes burning into the back of his neck. As if his own shame and guilt weren't enough! Forest spits. There must be a way he can pay his emotional debt to them and still move on with his life.

He looks up at the hospital building and takes a deep breath. *Act like a gentleman now*, a voice in his head says, before he bounds up the steps.

WAITING
EDITH

A mix of spring air and disinfectant fills the hospital room. Between her daughters' beds, a fresh bouquet sits on the table. The sun's rays, streaming through the window, amplify the whiteness of the starched sheets, making them blend with the high-ceilinged room. Wrapped tightly in their sheets, the girls resemble mummified pupae.

As always, Edith and Kirsten sit in their chairs at the foot of the beds, keeping watch. Several times, Edith has tiptoed over to check her daughters' breathing gently, just as she did when they were small. Every now and then, a nurse comes to turn them. *That's how life is too*, Edith thinks. *We're placed in the world, pushed here and there, and can only wait and see what life brings us.*

Edith fixes her gaze on Martha's mattress. Not a single wrinkle in the chalk-white bedding. *How do they keep the sheets so white?* She wonders. Shame washes over her. What would the staff think if they knew what she was thinking?

The Scandinavian War Bride

In the morning, the sun shining through the window marks the beginning of the rounds. When the movement of the sun's shadow across the floor reaches approximately half a chair's width, the nurse arrives to adjust the bed linens. Without the windows, the difference between night and day would be nearly imperceptible.

Edith takes her eyes off the girls. The stark contrast between her current surroundings and her ordinary life is as striking as the unexpected journey that brought her here. Hurried footsteps, approaching and receding, add to the unsettling atmosphere, heavy with chemical smells and the overwhelming palette of metal and white. Click-clacking heels, muted beeping, a light blinking orange-red, coded messages across the facility, and seconds later, the galloping sound of wooden clogs rushing to a room where a life may change forever.

The hallways are always lit; illness doesn't care about regular working hours. Edith is one of many women in a long line of mothers, daughters, and sisters. But for her, the world seems to hold its breath. This will never feel routine. Edith clutches her handkerchief. Martha's precise stitching is visible in the corner.

She looks up. Did Ingrid make a sound? Waiting is a strange paradox — present yet distant, filled with imagined noises and heightened senses, and utterly draining. The ventilator's rhythmic hum blends with other sounds, creating a constant beep and buzz. Waiting by the bedside of a loved one in the hospital is a distinctly unique experience compared to waiting in everyday life.

As a youth, you long for love, and marriage. Then comes the uncertainty while you wait for the child growing in your womb. When the little ones arrive, one waits for them to be potty trained, learn to walk, eat on their own, dress themselves, and go to school. When you can't bear the thought of one more childbirth, you wait anxiously each month for your period. You wait for the end-of-work whistle, wait with dinner ready, wait for the children to grow up and leave the nest. And yet, time flies, even if it feels like an eternity. In the end, you find yourself alone with only the ticking of the clock for company, longing for someone to need you.

Harsh, guttural 'rei' and 'sch' sounds — the sounds of German conversation — jar Edith back to the hospital room. With a jerk of her head, she turns towards the window, her lips pursing into a thin, displeased line.

"Germany!"

This Germanic country with its imperial dreams! First came the Great War, followed by the worthless currency of the 1930s. Then came the ugly years of the Second World War. When it was all over, she felt such relief. Edith looks at Martha's yellowish face. But then the American soldier came and turned her eldest daughter's head.

"America!"

Edith winces. Her back aches. *What's wrong with Denmark? Doesn't family matter at all? How can Martha be so casual about moving halfway across the world? And with a man who is so much like Karl it's unsettling!* She shrugs. Once youth are determined, nothing can stop them.

No, Edith thinks, *it's all been too much to get used to. Martha in Germany. Forest and his mannerisms. His drinking. And now the accident. Traveling all the way here, when she has never been outside Denmark's borders!*

Edith crosses her arms. Forest returned to his military base practically unscathed. *How much do we actually know about him and his family history?* her thoughts continue. *We should have asked more questions. Why did we let him sweep us off our feet? If only Martha had married a Danish man. Life is easier when you accept where you come from.*

☽

A GURGLING SOUND COMES FROM ONE OF THE tubes. Throughout the day, a nurse visits Martha and Ingrid, taking their vital signs and disposing of waste. Except for the quiet sucking and gurgling of the machines, the room is still.

Today, a nurse has turned the girls' faces toward each other. *Like the twins in the dresser drawer*, Edith thinks, wringing her hands. Losing your little ones before they've properly grasped life feels like a personal attack. But this is worse. Like a taunting whisper, suggesting all her hard work has been for naught. Diaper changes, overflowing washbasins, mountains of peeled potatoes, and the extra shifts at the cigar factory. Back then, the deaths of her babies left her heart consumed with blackness. Ever since then, she's lived in fear.

☽

THE DOCTOR COMES INTO THE ROOM, GIVES A BRIEF nod in Edith's direction, and walks over to Martha and Ingrid's beds. It's time for his round. Edith straightens in her chair. Kirsten stands beside the doctor as he reviews the charts and examines the girls. German, English, and Latin tumble from his lips. Watching the doctor and Kirsten, Edith tries to decipher what's going on through their body language. The doctor protectively covers Ingrid's hair with his hand as he speaks. Things are looking up for her, it seems. Turning, he shines his torch into Martha's eyes.

"She may not wake up again," he says.

May, Edith thinks. There is the potential for two contrasting outcomes within the meaning of the word. *May*. Maybe she *will* wake up again.

"For God's sake, don't treat me like a fool!" Edith straightens her fingers, the blood rushing to her knuckles. The flames of grief burn in her heart. "How am I supposed to go on?" she whispers, her mouth filling with mucus and salt.

☽

IF HER CHILDREN ARE NO LONGER IN THIS WORLD, will she then forget their childhoods? Will the joy of her daughter, born after three sons, be erased by the fear she felt for Martha's life?

Edith smiles, remembering Martha's unsteady first steps and Ingrid's scraped knees from crawling. Will she forget Martha's proud, gap-toothed smile? Martha's early crooked attempts at cross-stitch, Ingrid toddling along behind Kirsten, and Martha's triumph when she finally managed to peel an apple in one long strip?

With time, all wounds heal. Edith gazes out the window. That's what people told her when she lost her baby twins. Now she finds herself in a similar situation. How can the seasons change and life go on while her world crumbles to dust? Those who have been wounded in war are easily identified by their missing limbs, but those who are grieving are indistinguishable from anyone else moving through the city streets.

"Doctors aren't always right, are they?" she says to Kirsten.

"Mom."

Edith raises her hands and Kirsten falls silent.

The curtains flutter. Soil and freshly cut grass perfume the gentle breeze drifting through the open window. Edith bows her head. Sometimes tears come unexpectedly, like a warm, soft wave. *May the girls soon find peace. May Kirsten step into the life she stands on the threshold of.* Rising, Edith stands between her daughters, gently touching their cheeks.

"That's enough now."

※

IT'S THE MIDDLE OF THE NIGHT. SHE NOTICES THE hospital's smells and sounds most intensely when she first wakes up. The steady rhythm of the IV pumps blends with the sucking sound of the respirator. Edith sits, letting her eyes adjust to the darkness. Absence. A sense of alarm washes over her. Then the hair on her arms stands on end.

Prinzregenten Theater
Kirsten

One foot in front of the other, *Kirsten thinks. Her vision is blurred as she wobbles along the path. Although a strange detachment has settled over her, a heavy weight still presses on her chest. Only here in the hospital park can she let her mask fall.*

Martha is gone. Despite the simplicity of the words, her heart stubbornly refuses to accept their meaning, no matter how many times she forces her brain to comprehend them.

Once the doctor pronounced Martha dead and the nurse disconnected her from the medical equipment, Kirsten left the hospital room quickly. Having had weeks to prepare and say her goodbyes, she has committed each detail of Martha's face to memory, from the largest features down to the smallest, most insignificant beauty marks.

Kirsten waited in the hallway as the nursing staff prepared Martha's body. When she was called in, the window was open and a candle had been lit by the bedside. On the mattress, with ample room to spare, lay her older sister, covered with a white sheet. The cloth revealed the contours of her slender body, every part clearly defined. The shroud was draped at the edges, as if the angels had already taken her. Her head lay slightly raised on the pillow; her hair styled in a way she never would have chosen herself. The comb lines were clearly visible in her bangs, standing out against her pale skin.

You remember the strangest things when your world falls apart. Like Martha's slender, gray-white fingers folded around the bouquet's green stems. Kirsten shudders at the memory. But it was the Bible under her chin — not the gray-blue lips, not the waxen cheeks or glassy stare — that kept drawing Kirsten's eyes back. Like a bookend, the holy book was meant to keep her older sister's mouth closed. Yet it hung open in a grimace, as if Martha was shocked at what was happening; that life was leaving her before it had truly begun.

For a brief moment, Kirsten stood at the bed, looking at her sister one last time as relief washed over her body. "Now you're finally at peace." Kirsten let her gaze caress Martha's cheek before turning and leaving the room.

In the park, Kirsten's senses return, and her legs give way. She falls to the grass. Curling up, with her arms bent over her head, she sobs into the soil until exhaustion numbs her body.

⁌

KIRSTEN TAKES A SIP OF THE SODA FOREST BOUGHT her. The spring sunshine is warm and bright with a refreshing coolness. She observes him over the bottle. A boldness has developed between them; an understanding that they share a bond of fate that no one else understands. As a result, they are seeking each other's companionship more frequently.

"We only get one life," Kirsten sighs.

Forest gazes at her. "Facing the present means living it." He looks away, embarrassed.

Kirsten nods. *But I feel guilty,* she thinks. *I feel bad about meeting secretly like this. I feel guilty for having feelings for the man who killed my sister.*

Out loud, she says, "Just smiling makes me feel guilty." Kirsten picks at her cuticle, then looks up at Forest. "Maybe our feelings for each other are a way for the grief to exist without us falling apart?"

Like a jolt, a new thought hits Kirsten. It's not right of her to feel these emotions so close to Martha's death. Kirsten crosses her arms. Did she feel this way from the moment she first saw him? Does grief work in such a way that it opens emotions at the other end of the spectrum? Overwhelmed by her internal turmoil, Kirsten fans her face with her hand.

Forest nods in agreement. "Both of us will always carry her in our hearts."

Change and loss, Kirsten thinks, *closely connected. How does one deal with loss and the changes it brings? Who will I become now?*

Kirsten buries her head in her hands. "If we continue, I'll have to face my family's anger and disapproval."

"Maybe that's the thing that connects us," Forest sighs.

Kirsten looks at him questioningly.

"You've always been a bit of a thorn in their side." Forest blows a gray puff of smoke upward.

Kirsten follows it and thinks about how her mind and heart must accommodate the choices she's facing. "With you, I'm never sure of anything." Leaning over the table, she locks eyes with Forest. "How can I be more than just Martha's replacement?"

A penny for your thoughts, Kirsten thinks as she studies Forest's expression.

"Who says I want the same thing again?"

Kirsten hasn't considered that Forest might not want to be with the same woman again. *Maybe I don't have to live up to her.*

KIRSTEN IS BACK ON HER FAVORITE BENCH IN THE hospital park. Forest should arrive shortly. It's become a habit for them to go out to get food. Their foraging trips are a welcome break. With his large strides next to her smaller steps, she finds herself believing that if she follows his lead, everything will work out.

The hospital has its own mess hall with Opa and Oma in the kitchen, but they rarely buy food there. Kirsten fantasizes about them being a couple. For an hour, she creates her own reality.

In the beginning, her walks with Forest were awkward, punctuated by long silences and clumsy attempts at conversation. Both knew the reason Martha lay in the hospital; that Forest was to blame. But slowly their conversations changed and they created a space where they could be together. As a sense of ease grew between them, mentions of Martha became less frequent.

Soon, Kirsten looked forward to their walks, which were no longer just about getting out. She missed Forest during the day, and often thought of things to tell him. She's noticed his glances when he thinks she's not looking. Should she feel guilty? Maybe. But in this country, neither his, nor hers, morals and expectations are different.

Then, one day, he invites her to the Prinzregenten Theater. Aware it will intrigue her, he mentions, "It's Jacques Offenbach's *Tales of Hoffmann*, a Jewish composer's work."

Knowing she is behaving improperly, Kirsten keeps it from her parents.

As they wait outside the theater, the anticipation for the show is palpable. A sign hangs on the wall:

> THE THEATER'S TASKS ARE TO ENTERTAIN, INSPIRE, AND EDUCATE THE MASSES.
>
> BERTOLT BRECHT

"That sounds a bit too socialist for my liking," Forest frowns. "Nah, give me entertainment!" he says, throwing his arms wide.

Good thing Dad can't hear him, Kirsten thinks. *He believes art should depict real people, especially working people like him.*

"Maybe you can have both — entertainment and something to think about?" she says, trying to bridge the two men's differing perspectives.

Forest narrows his eyes. "Don't trouble your pretty little head with that, Kiki."

Kirsten's stomach tightens and all her boldness drains

away. "Yes, what do I know about anything?" Watching him visibly relax, Kirsten continues: "Can you believe it! We're going to see a performance that was censored during the war!"

Forest looks like someone whose worldview is falling into place.

The theater doors open. All around them, American servicemen wait, each with a girl on his arm. Fürstenfeldbruck Air Base personnel have been given free tickets by the theater. German civilians also queue in the spring showers. Initially, Kirsten is touched by the show of support. As she contemplates the situation, however, a surge of anger begins to build within her. *Now they show up? For a theater performance! Solidarity should cost more than a spring cold. True heroism is shown when it can cost you your skin*, she thinks, before heading into the theater.

っ

SHE CAN'T CONCENTRATE ON THE OPERA, FEELING like an adult with a little girl's mind. She glances at Forest, who seems relaxed. In the auditorium, he settles into a plush red chair and rests his arm on the back of hers. Stiff as a plank, Kirsten misses the performance, her mind focused on the arm.

Eventually, emboldened by the darkness, she leans back in her chair. Sitting side-by-side, they remain in that position until Forest slowly shifts his arm to put it around Kirsten's shoulder. Without looking at each other, they sit like that through the first act. During the intermission, Forest takes her hand, and she lets him.

Courting Disaster
Kirsten

Grief feels different from how Kirsten imagined. Besides a constant headache, she feels a physical emptiness. As if her heart is missing a piece, making it hard for her body to function. Seated on the bench, which she now regards as her own, she raises her eyes to the hospital's main building as she lights a cigarette. A ladybug lands on her skirt while a stray gust of wind ruffles her hair, making her want to scream and cry. Instead, she bites her lip. *Get a grip! Don't dwell on your sorrow*, she thinks. But what role does she have now? What will the future bring? Who will define it?

Ingrid's fate is still up in the air. According to the doctor, she will either wake from her coma and slowly recover or pass away quietly. Kirsten obstructs the ladybug's path with her hand, creating a barrier that compels the insect to crawl onto her outstretched index finger. "Fly up to the Lord and ask for a miracle," she whispers.

Did Ingrid feel Martha's absence when the undertaker

came to take her away? Does she hear them when they talk to her? Does Ingrid feel a void now that she's alone?

When Kirsten looks up at the sky, the ladybug is nowhere to be seen. *Ingrid is still here among us,* she thinks. *Thank God.* Seeing her lifeless sister in the hospital, her expression vacant and personality gone, feels like watching someone lose their entire history. Thankfully, the bruises around Ingrid's eyes and mouth have faded, but Kirsten is still terrified by her erratic, shallow breathing.

"Life offers hope," Kirsten murmurs, smoothing her skirt.

THINKING ABOUT INGRID'S ABORTION MAKES Kirsten tense up. Overnight, her little sister transformed into a woman. Afterwards a quiet, gray mood hung over the house like a misty fall morning. Ingrid fell apart, in shock at what her body had been subjected to.

Kirsten crosses her arms. Maybe it was also the shock of putting her life in the hands of someone who came so close to taking it away from her.

The bucket of blood by the bed and the sobs Ingrid tried to hold back are forever etched in Kirsten's memory. Her face was the same color as it is now in the hospital. Then, as now, her body appeared gaunt and empty. And just like then, she left as one person and came home another.

After the abortion, Ingrid staggered under the reaction from their father. Disbelief and contempt were etched on his face. She fell from grace, losing her place as his favorite. Accustomed to her father's affectionate grumbling, his behavior had been a shock, too. His icy silence emanated from behind his newspaper in the armchair by the stove.

Whenever Ingrid walked past, his knuckles turned white as he held the paper up to his face.

How Kirsten recognized his behavior! Seeing Ingrid, not herself, in the line of fire, and being unable to help, was painful. But to tell Ingrid that everything would work out would have been a lie, and her little sister would have known it.

Kirsten lets out a sigh. The scent of blood marked the end of the life growing inside Ingrid, as well as the end of her life as she knew it. "Dear God," Kirsten whispers. "Hasn't my sister suffered enough?"

☽

KIRSTEN SHIFTS HER GAZE AWAY FROM THE hospital and looks around the park. Ahead of her, a young girl pushes a stroller along a path. Gravel crunches under the wheels. Some new mothers have no one waiting after they give birth. Pushing a hospital-issued stroller, they walk alone. Other mothers disappear and leave their babies in the care of the nurses. They risk being turned away at home if they show up with a newborn. Times are hard, and not everyone can cope with another mouth to feed. Kirsten nods as the stroller passes by her. How quickly she has learned that all women have their reasons for doing what they do.

And then there are babies born with Slavic features. In such instances, the girls nearly always vanish. No one wants to marry someone who has been with a Russian, even if it was against her will.

☽

After Kirsten became more familiar with the hospital's layout, she returned to the maternity ward several times, sneaking up to look through the peephole of the room with the new mothers. Sometimes eight of them lie side-by-side. The sheer number of people in one room makes Kirsten question how anyone can recover after childbirth. Perhaps that's why breastfeeding, changing times, and mealtimes follow a strict schedule.

In another room, twenty infants are nestled in tiny, crib-like beds. It's a mystery to Kirsten how the nurses can keep track of which baby belongs to which mother. A single child's cry is enough to start a chorus of wailing. Side by side, they scream their little lungs out. But the nurses only come when the schedule says it's time for feeding. Then they take a bundle in each arm and bring the babies to their mothers. It is said that the pediatric and maternity wards are operating according to the latest standards, which seems to prioritize efficiency over individualized care, treating newborns like an assembly line. Kirsten's mother had a very different approach to motherhood. Whenever the little one cried, she pulled up her blouse and breastfed her baby. The nurses here are highly skilled and knowledgeable, but witnessing a baby so distressed overshadows Kirsten's understanding of the procedures.

She sighs. Ingrid's life would have taken a different turn had she not had an abortion. Continuing the pregnancy would have had significant costs, however. Would Erik have stayed? Kirsten shakes her head. Ingrid would have had to walk around with a growing belly, faced with contempt, and been forced to drop out of school.

Kirsten grinds out her cigarette, heading back to the hospital and the familiar, endless wait.

Martha's death hasn't changed Kirsten's daily life at the hospital, even though it's only Ingrid who remains in a coma now.

Rising to her feet, Kirsten announces in a clear voice, "Ingrid, I'm going for a walk."

Kirsten crosses the hospital's quiet park with hurried steps. On the other side of the wall, the world comes rushing toward her. She wants to cover her ears. Since Martha's death, she hasn't been able to taste or smell, but now she is hit by an explosion of sounds and scents. Gasoline, soil, and the cool touch of the spring breeze compete for her attention. People hurry to and from work, buy bread, toss a cheerful comment her way. Kirsten wishes the world would stand still to give her mind time to process the loss she hasn't yet accepted.

"Kirsten, wait!" someone calls from behind.

She turns to see Forest running towards her. He reaches her and a silent moment follows. Then Forest pulls her into his arms.

"I'm so sorry. For both of us," he whispers into her neck.

The icy thorn within Kirsten thaws and she accepts the embrace. They stand like that, in the middle of the sidewalk, as cars, bicycles, and pedestrians continue around them. She closes her eyes. The sounds fade, leaving only a clear tone ringing in Kirsten's ears.

When she opens her eyes, the city noise comes flooding back. Motionless, she inhales the mixture of tobacco and sweat emanating from Forest's jacket. *You!* she thinks, looking at him. *You were at the wheel. The car accident, the hospital, Martha's death — it was your fault!*

Fighting back tears, she lowers her eyes to the asphalt,

staggers away from Forest, cannot bear being so close to him. How could she surrender to the comfort of his arms? His actions stifle her, despite the attraction she feels. Moving away, she hears her heels scraping against the street, her feet like lead weights.

A firm grip on her shoulder jolts Kirsten back to reality; the blare of a truck horn, loud and close, vibrates through her.

"Kirsten!" Forest lunges forward and pulls her away from the road, his arms tight around her, using his body as a shield.

Did she walk toward the road fully aware of what could happen, or are her senses so shattered that she doesn't know what she's doing? Kirsten doesn't know the answer, but with her heart in her throat, she follows Forest, who leads her to the nearest café.

He seats her at a table and returns shortly after with two cups of coffee. "Kiki, that's not the answer," he says, taking her cheeks in his hands.

"Why her and not me? She had everything." Kirsten angrily wipes her eyes.

"If anyone is to blame, it's me." Forest stares into his coffee cup.

Kirsten lights a cigarette and watches the smoke curl away as she exhales. "I am blaming you," she says. "Every time I look at you." She sees his wounded expression. "But I also feel something else," she continues softly, holding his gaze.

Forest's eyes change expression. As he reaches his hand across the table, she places hers over his.

"Making you the villain won't bring her back," whispers Kirsten.

They sit like that for a while, watching each other. She can feel Forest's thumb moving under her palm with a gentle, caressing touch. Withdrawing her hand, she brings the coffee cup to her lips.

Silently, they sip their coffee and smoke. *Apparently, grief, love, and guilt also go hand in hand,* thinks Kirsten.

"We're both courting disaster," she says, stubbing out her cigarette. Forest looks at her questioningly. "I always do the wrong thing; disappoint those I love. And you will always be the one who drove Martha to her death."

Forest bows his head. "But we are so much more than that," he says, seeking her eyes.

A softening feeling washes over her again. *This constant emotional push and pull between contempt and love, how do I deal with it?* she thinks. "Imagine," she says aloud, her voice barely a whisper, "if we understood our experiences in the moment we lived them, and not afterward."

Forest nods. "I'd do a lot of things differently, if I could."

She stares directly at him, an image of him drinking in the Jeep flashing into her thoughts. She reaches across the table and brushes his hand: "How do we do this? Us?"

Leaning back, Forest drains his cup. "I'm not sure, Kiki."

What should I do? thinks Kirsten. *I should stay away from him, but I can't. There's more to my attraction than just chemistry. He understands my thoughts, knows me, and can see beyond what others can't. I don't have to measure my words with him or be afraid of scaring him away.*

They leave the café and walk silently side by side. Kirsten feels the presence of his body like a pulling force. What will happen if they let this develop into something deeper?

Hasn't my mother been through enough? Am I destined to always be the one who causes her pain? she thinks. *What if things don't work out between Forest and me? Then I've burned my bridges and have no one to turn to for support. I wish I knew how to navigate this.*

"Forest, what are we doing?" Kirsten whirls around to see Forest freeze, as though she'd struck him.

"Kiki…"

"No! This isn't right! You're my sister's husband!"

"Maybe that's exactly why it makes so much more sense." Forest lowers his face. "We're both grieving the same person. Maybe we can both make it right together." He lifts his eyes to hers. "We have so much to offer one another."

Moving closer to Forest, Kirsten places her hand on his upper arm. "But how do I know you'll stay away from the bottle? How do I know I'm not just a replacement for Martha?" *Say something that convinces my heart*, she thinks, letting Forest find the words.

"I give you my word, Kiki." He stares intently at her. "If there is regret," he asks, "isn't there also room for forgiveness?"

Funeral
Edith

The pastor holds Edith's hands in his. Feeling her body sway, Edith tightens her grip to maintain her balance. The red bricks of Sundby Church remind her of Martha's lips when she was a child and came inside with bright eyes and rosy cheeks from the crisp air. Edith lowers her eyes, unable to bear the clear, bright rays of the spring sun. Behind her lies the cemetery.

"There is no greater sorrow than having to bury your child," says the pastor, squeezing Edith's hands.

How do you know, Pastor? Have you personally experienced that? Edith could ask, but of course, she doesn't. Instead, she keeps her face bowed as snot runs in a long strand. Grief is ugly. There is nothing beautiful about the body's expulsions when the mind is in turmoil.

Inside the church, she walks to the front pews and sits down in the seat closest to the casket. Behind her, she hears shuffling footsteps as the church fills. The sound of soles on tiles, scattered throat-clearing, and noses being blown fills the air.

Edith glances at the casket. Parents should never have to experience losing a child. If she had the strength, she could reach out and feel the polished wood of the coffin beneath her fingertips. No sermon can make sense of a mother having to say goodbye to a life she brought into the world.

What reason do I have to continue to live? Edith thinks. *I am falling apart. My heart is shattered.* A scream threatens to rip from her throat; a desperate plea for the comfort of an embrace. No! If anyone were to try to comfort her, she would ask them to leave her alone. She wants to keep her grief close, wrapped up inside of her. Her muscles tense. Her heart pounds in her chest. She looks at her hands. Her knuckles protrude sharply. How can they look like human hands when they feel like bear paws, waiting for the opportunity to deliver a swipe?

As she sits in the pew, she feels herself leaving her physical body, floating up and out through the rose-tinted window. The vibrant green spring grass, fragrant with the sweet scent of new life, entices her to lie down on its soft, bright carpet.

꽃

Edith recoils as the organ's pipes swell polyphonically. Funerals have always brought her a sense of peace. She would find solace sitting at the back of the nave, away from the mourners; placing her bouquet so far from the casket that her heart was safe from heartbreak. Through the ritual of hymns, bible verses, and the pastor's careful guidance, a space was created for the bereaved to adjust to life without the deceased. A space where peace and tradition joined hands and made the unbearable bearable.

That's not how Edith is feeling today. A life summed up

in a few sentences does not do justice to the layers of grief. What does the priest know about Martha? His words could apply to anyone. Edith looks around. The congregation stands, sits, and sings. She remains seated; cannot muster the strength to move a muscle; is not even able to find the right page in the hymnal. His muffled sermon is lost on her. Her throat tightens, a lump forming as she forces herself to open the hymnal, the notes catching in her chest.

> *The dear God and creator of the smallest worm is near: He feeds...*
> *But the children of men He loves most of all...*
> *God breathes on the eye when it weeps...*
> *...even a child...*
> *His cradle stood on earth without a path...*
> *...so dear...*
> *...carries the child up to God...*
> *...earth, but the children played...*
> *...took the little ones in his arms...*
> *One morning we will see you in paradise.*

In planning the funeral service, the pastor asked her what hymns she would like to be played. The only one that came to mind was the lullaby she'd hum to her children when they were small. *Nature, the rays of the morning sun, children embraced in paradise. Why didn't he take me instead of Martha?* Edith thinks.

She winces, feels the pew beneath her thighs. Why do church pews have to be so uncomfortable? Narrow and varnished, forcing everyone to sit up straight. Lacking the strength to tense her back, she lets go and allows her body to do as it pleases.

"Compose yourself, woman!" Karl hisses.

As he pulls Edith upward by one of her shoulder pads,

she feels warm breath and tiny droplets, like rain, in her left ear. The stitches in the cloth break, making a clicking noise.

Give her this last honor, maintain dignity! She can tell what he's thinking just by looking at him. Edith tries to make her eyes say sorry. Karl sighs deeply, his body shuttering. She knows the rhythm of his breathing, the subtle shift of his weight, the tremor in his hands. In her mind, she tells herself to compose her face and simply do what he wants. Straightening her spine, Edith folds her hands in her lap.

The coffin's presence beside her is palpable. *Martha is inside*, Edith thinks. Maybe she will lift the lid and tell them all this was one big mistake. Edith shakes her head. *My smart and beautiful daughter.* In her coffin, she awaits her descent into the earth. Transform into soil. Once the worms are done and she's reduced to dust... *Stop!* Her brain screams, while her heart bleeds.

The priest raises both hands, looking at Edith: "Jor hæsd sgi di ta åsd sgo tan sdol flæsg." Edith squeezes her eyes shut, then opens them again, and sees the pastor reading from his bible: "Væm sægs pragtisg drægge sirgus fabræg æfder."

Swallowing, she turns her ear toward his voice in an attempt to make sense of the words, then gives up and instead lowers her gaze to the floor. Out of the corner of her eye, she sees the bouquets and wreaths in the center aisle. She wants to tap Karl on the arm and say, "Look, Karl! There's our wreath. It's a good wreath, we did well." But no, that would anger him.

She'd requested blue flowers and a single white lily. The same color as Martha's eyes, and the ocean she never got to cross. The florist poised her fountain pen above the order form impatiently, tapping a fingernail on the counter with a steady thump. "Do you want a silk ribbon? How wide do you want it to be? What color? What message would you like?"

What words do you inscribe on the ribbon for your daughter's grave? The silk ribbon Edith chose to go around the wreath is white. *Pedersen*, it says in swirling, golden letters, each character intertwined. Nothing more. Forest's heart-shaped wreath made of red roses is nestled behind their bouquet. The inscription reads: *In Loving Memory*.

Edith feels her scalp itch. That's too little too late! Is Martha already just a 'memory' to him? Does he not feel the sharp shards of loss? She let him take her eldest daughter, trusting that he would give her a good life. How can it be fair that he gets to continue living after this?

"Dear God," Edith whispers, "Hold him accountable for his actions."

The floral arrangements are displayed in a long row, their size graduating from largest nearest the casket, to smallest at the far end. Like a funnel, they narrow towards the nave's base. *My little girl was baptized and confirmed here*, Edith thinks. Both symbols of a journey, of life's movement. Who could have foreseen that journey would end before it had truly begun?

The damp scent of the floral arrangements brings Edith back to the nave. The size of the bouquets is like a hierarchy, demonstrating the relationship to the deceased. Each individual flower, its petals bursting with life, was cut at precisely the moment it was either in a tight bud or just starting to unfurl its bloom. By tomorrow, the vibrant energy the flowers currently possess will have faded and wilted. When the first rain falls on the grave, they will yellow, taking on a uniform brownish hue, until they become part of the earth they've been laid upon, and no one will be able to distinguish roses from lilies.

Man to Man
Edith

After the funeral, they rejoin Ingrid at the hospital in Germany. Edith stands beside Karl and opens the window. Birds chirp in the park below. Is Ingrid aware of any of it in her state of unconsciousness?

"You should talk to her," the doctor said. So, Edith does. She tells her youngest daughter what she and Karl had for lunch, what she saw on the way here this morning, that Ingrid needs to hurry and recover. That's become routine, too — the quiet, one-sided conversations with her lifeless daughter.

Edith turns from the window. Young people in hospital beds look dead. She glances at the foot of the bed, where there are too many chairs now that Martha is gone. She pushes two chairs against the wall. What will family get-togethers be like in the future? Sunday lunches, Christmas, Easter? What is she without her daughters?

Sitting on one of the chairs by the wall, Edith thinks back to the first time she met Forest. As if the chair senses her thoughts, it creaks when she shifts her weight wearily.

Edith tries in vain to shake off the uncomfortable memories. He sat at her lunch table, scarfing down his food while she watched him and Martha. A radiant glow seemed to emanate from her daughter. She drank in every word Forest spoke. His eyes sparkled with life as he confidently held hers, his animated gestures and stories drawing the attention of everyone at the table. It was hard not to be captivated by this strange American man, Edith admits to herself.

He began by selecting a slice of rye bread, to which he generously applied margarine before finally topping with several halved boiled eggs, resulting in a high-piled open-faced sandwich. He finished it by applying a remoulade sauce. Did he understand the immense effort and preparation that had gone into crafting each of the delicacies on the lunch table? And did he realize just how much she had scrimped and saved to afford such a lavish feast? Edith, still struggling with English sentences, rose and approached Forest. Reaching across the table, she scraped the remoulade onto his plate, then spread mayonnaise, salt, and pepper on his egg sandwich.

It was difficult to get a proper read on him. He stood out from Danish men like a long-legged exotic bird; an intriguing stranger rather than a threatening one. Maybe she should have seen then that he was too different. Considering how he behaved during just one meal, how would things be for Martha in America?

Martha will never get to experience that. Edith furrows her brow. And neither will Ingrid. She doubts Rob will stay engaged to her, given her disfigured face. If Ingrid ever wakes up, that is. Edith's body twitches. What do you do when rage consumes you, but you are completely helpless to do anything?

"There, there, my girl. Everything will be all right," she says, her gaze caressing Ingrid's cheek.

Laughter floats in through the open window, accompanied by the sound of gravel crunching outside. Is this all there is to life? Gradually, the things that once gave your life meaning disappear, leaving you empty and contemplating death. Edith clenches her hands around her handkerchief.

And now this! Kirsten and Forest! She'd suspected something wasn't right, but attributed it to her overactive imagination. And then they came and asked for a word with her and Karl. Edith feels her jaw tighten. *I can't lose Kirsten to that man!* she thinks, pursing her lips as if she has a sour taste in her mouth. *How dare he?* The thought makes her want to spit. Instead, she buries her hands in the handkerchief. How dare he take her last daughter? Doesn't he have any shame? And what about Kirsten? A scornful snort escapes Edith's nose. Kirsten has always made decisions with no regard for the ramifications or consideration for others. How can she be so different from her cautious Martha and submissive Ingrid? *What is that girl thinking? It's one thing to follow your nose and go to Germany to work, God help her. It's quite another to throw herself into Forest's arms. After all he's done to the family! Ugh,* thinks Edith. *I've endured much, but this is unbearable. How does Kirsten even tolerate being around him?*

Rising, Edith fetches a chair from the wall and positions it next to Ingrid's bed. Taking her daughter's hand, she stares at her scarred face and damaged fingers. *Maybe she's better off staying asleep,* she thinks. *What man would want her? And then with that scar from the quack doctor!* Edith bites her lip. Shouldn't a mother be overjoyed her daughter survived both an abortion and a car accident?

Edith summons her courage; the words have to be just right. "I only have the one left."

She can tell from Karl's breathing that he's heard her. He turns away from the window.

"He'll listen to you," she continues.

"It's sick." Karl's voice is barely audible.

Is Kirsten trying to punish me? thinks Edith. *If only her nature were gentler, like my other two girls'.* Edith wipes her eyes. Martha's fine stitches are visible on the corner of the handkerchief sticking out of her clenched fist. "It's because of him that I'm suffering."

Karl sighs.

"You can mend a vase, but the cracks will remain," Edith whispers.

Karl grunts.

He's not dismissive, thinks Edith. *The idea must feel like it originated with him.* "Do you remember how your mother tried to keep us apart?"

Karl nods.

"In her mind, you were going to marry the girl from the neighboring farm."

"Vera," Karl sighs, "But you put an end to that."

"We've lived a good life." She waits. "Your parents intended for you to inherit the farm."

"My brother also had mouths to feed."

"We all did." Edith purses her lips. It's not meant to be an argument. "The farm would have been yours if you'd picked Vera."

"Could've, should've, would've," grumbles Karl. They sit in silence. Then: "I'll speak with him."

FAREWELL

Donut Dolly
Kirsten

Forest runs ahead in his dark blue uniform jacket. Kirsten tries her best to keep pace, holding tightly to his hand. Out of the corner of her eye, she sees the sunlight reflecting off the silver planes of the base. Zigzagging between trucks, people and Jeeps, she hears the sound of tools behind her. Forest's back seems to radiate with military pride and a palpable sense of anticipation for what is coming. *I'm running from the shadows of war toward the future*, thinks Kirsten.

"You'll love it!" he shouts over his shoulder as he continues on. Right, left, around a barrack. Kirsten loses her bearings before he finally stops.

"Club mobile!" he exclaims, his eyes shining as he spreads his arms wide. Kirsten sees a shed on wheels. "Like *The Ugly Duckling*: once it was a GMC truck, now it's a donut stand." He beams, leading her to a table at the back of the truck.

A woman in a Red Cross uniform and a smile in her voice welcomes them. "Howdy, soldier."

"The usual, Dolly. And the same for my guest."

Two cups of coffee and round, golden-brown donuts dipped in sugar are placed in front of them. Dark, greasy stains spread across the napkin.

"Follow my lead." Leaning over the table, Forest grabs the donut like he would a burger. It disappears in two bites.

Kirsten emulates him. Her brain explodes in a soft sugar dream, filling her mouth with water. Her first impulse is to lick her lips — the cake has left behind a layer of sugar.

"Aaaahhhhhhh." Forest leans back. "It tastes just like home!"

※

THE NEXT DAY, KIRSTEN IS BACK AT THE DONUT truck.

"I recognize you from yesterday."

Kirsten takes the woman's outstretched hand. "Kirsten."

"Donut Dolly."

Kirsten raises an eyebrow.

"That's what we do," the woman laughs. "That's what they call us Red Cross volunteers who make donuts for the boys." A smile graces her lips. "It boosts morale. The soldiers forget everything else for the time it takes to drink a cup of coffee and eat a donut."

Kirsten looks at the selection in the booth. "I'll take cigarettes, bubblegum, and the newspaper." She slips the cigarettes into her purse and tucks the newspaper under her arm.

"How about coffee?"

Kirsten's first impulse is to say no, but then she changes her mind. *I need to be more open, let go of some of that Scandinavian reserve,* she thinks.

"Play some music, Patty," Dolly calls up to the cabin. A

crackling speaker fills the cabin with Billie Holiday's soft, nasal tones. Strength, fear, and fragility are woven together in her rhythm and tone.

> *It's cost me a lot,*
> *But there's one thing that I've got,*
> *It's my man,*
> *It's my man.*

From her purse, Kirsten retrieves her cigarettes and offers one to Dolly. "Tell me about America," she says, settling in more comfortably.

Dolly narrows her eyes at Kirsten. "Are you from Germany?"

"What? No, for heaven's sake! I'm from Scandinavia!" Kirsten looks at Dolly indignantly. "I'm from Denmark."

Warmth returns to the Red Cross girl's light brown eyes. "That makes me feel better," she says, winking. "I have complicated feelings about Germans."

"No kidding! You and I both." Kirsten rolls her eyes.

"America." Dolly sighs and taps her cigarette ash into the coffee cup on the table. "Mountains, oceans, lakes, and stunning natural beauty — we have it all." She's somewhere that brings a softness to her eyes. "We don't have the buildings and culture like you do in Europe, but you won't find a more beautiful place on God's green earth."

"Where are you from?"

"Boston, it's on the east coast." Kirsten nods and Dolly asks: "Where are you headed?"

"San Antonio, Texas."

Dolly whistles. "Did he prepare you? Has he told you about the south?"

"He's said it's beautiful. And hot."

"He hasn't said too much then."

Putting aside her questions, Kirsten stubs out her cigarette. "How did a girl from Boston end up here?"

Dolly runs a hand over her uniform. "One of the girls back home was going. It sounded exciting and exotic." She straightens in her chair. "It was really hard to get the job. Only one out of seven applicants gets to go. You'd think I was going on a secret mission. To be considered, you need a bachelor's degree, good recommendations, and then must go through an extensive course in Washington DC." A smile plays at the corner of her mouth. "I mean, we make donuts, right?"

"Good heavens!" Kirsten blinks. "And you have to be good-looking." She forms an hourglass shape with her hands, gesturing towards Dolly. "What were the requirements?"

"Applicants have to be at least twenty-five years old and pass a medical check. I don't know if it was to see if we were healthy enough to run from the enemy if we got caught in our little tin shacks on the battlefield." She laughs hoarsely. "It's not just our boys who live dangerously. I could've been blown up as many times as I've made donuts. But at least I have it in writing that I have an 'outstanding character'."

"You worked at the frying pans while bullets flew overhead." Kirsten struggles to make sense of her mental image.

"We're expected to represent America. Be 'eye candy' for the boys." Dolly uses her fingers to make quotation marks in the air. "Make them feel comfortable. Oh, and amidst the fray, make donut batter, of course."

"What were you taught in Washington DC?" Kirsten leans forward.

"All sorts of topics, so we could engage in conversation that would make it easier to listen to the boys. History, politics, how the ARC works, and about the American military," Dolly says, waving smoke away from her eyes.

"ARC?"

"The American Red Cross," Dolly smiles in explanation. "But all that with the uniforms was a bit much." She fiddles with a button on her jacket.

"What about the uniforms?"

"Ten whole pages in a manual dedicated to how you should — and shouldn't — wear your uniform. What kind of make-up and nail polish we're allowed to wear, rules about jewelry, and all that jazz." Feigning a book in her lap, she runs a finger down an imaginary page, then flips it and repeats the action. Kirsten chuckles. "Although there are thousands of us, every single uniform is tailored to fit each individual girl." Dolly caresses the outfit once more. "Getting measured for it makes you feel special."

"I must say! You're certainly qualified to stand over a fryer!" Kirsten smiles apologetically as she realizes how her remark might come across.

"It's a chance to go on an adventure." Dolly gives Kirsten a wounded look. "See a bit of the world before we settle down with a husband and kids."

"With your personality, you must have someone waiting for you?" Kirsten licks the sugar off her fingers and can smell the sour tobacco.

Dolly turns her face away. "I did." She blinks, and the softness returns as she looks back at Kirsten. "I was young when I left. I'll come home an old soul." She flicks a piece of ash off the table. "Will history remember us, I wonder?"

"You're as much a war veteran as those who bear arms." Quickly patting her hand, Kirsten stands.

Dolly finishes her coffee. "We fight with smiles and games, not with gunpowder and bullets."

Wedding Day
Kirsten

Sitting on the edge of the bed, Kirsten bends over the laundry basket, tossing blouses, underwear, and skirts aside as she searches the hamper for a pair of wearable nylons. Finding a pair, she slips her hand inside and holds them up to the light. There's a run at the heel. With a fingertip, Kirsten prods the stocking, stretching it to watch the run grow. "These have a run, too. Just what I needed!"

"We got to be there in five minutes." Forest is leaning against the wall. Kirsten hears the click of his lighter and the crackling sound of tobacco as he inhales. "Can't you just use a pair of Martha's?"

Kirsten stiffens. "On our wedding day!" She clears her throat to lessen the shrillness of her voice.

"They're just stockings."

"Absolutely not!"

KIRSTEN FIDDLES NERVOUSLY WITH THE PINK button on her jacket. The ceremony is complete. Two of Forest's soldier buddies and a girl they'd met on the way to the military chaplain witnessed the wedding. Now Kirsten finds herself at one of the cafés on base.

Everything happened so quickly. She looks around the room. European women marry Allied soldiers daily in a swift, assembly-line process. To ensure everything was finalized before Forest's deployment, Kirsten and Forest's application was fast-tracked.

We're scapegoats; it's us against the world, Kirsten thinks. Turning to Forest, her emotions ease. Her fingers trace the line of his jaw. *I never fit into the family, and he carries the heavy burden of guilt.* Gently, she slides her hand under his. *I'll follow him, come what may. Even if the war bride ship sinks, at least I've achieved something. I can't bear to explain things to anyone. Nothing changes anything. To survive, I've chosen self-exile from my family and accepted the necessity of letting go.*

FOREST WAS RIGHT THERE, AVAILABLE. NO, IT wasn't just that — it was much more. Kirsten loves the feeling of weightlessness she gets when his body wraps around hers. Finds comfort in his unquestioning acceptance of her. With Forest, she doesn't have to feel ashamed. He knows where she comes from.

She never imagined that grief would be the foundation of her romantic choices, but that's how life turned out. *And really,* she thinks, *love and grief aren't so different after all. Each is a life-altering circumstance.*

Or maybe the girl from the office was right: "Kirsten,

you're still in shock. Take a moment to grieve. For your mind to think clearly."

Kirsten snorts. *I don't have time to "take a moment" when my body and mind are starting to function normally again. Martha is gone but my life is just beginning, despite my nerves. I will not risk opportunities arising and disappearing while I "take a moment".*

Still, Kirsten feels the grief as a constant presence. Her thoughts are sticky, sliding apart. Everything feels muffled, as if a thick blanket separates her from the sights and sounds. Her emotional barometer is either overly sensitive or reacts with indifference. Instructions don't stick in her memory. At times, she has trouble retrieving words that are on the tip of her tongue.

Since the accident, she experiences the world with a heightened, unfiltered sensitivity. The wind feels like a strike to the face, the sun's rays sting like needles. Kirsten feels her eyelashes getting wet. In her mind, she envisions herself as a fly, desperate to escape through the window, to find refuge from the cacophony and unsettling presence of strangers.

☽

NEXT TO HER, FOREST IS BEING LOUD. KIRSTEN glances at him. He smiles, and she feels a surge of warmth flood through her body. Holding a glass in his right hand and delicately balancing a cigarette in his left, he makes a series of expressive gestures. *Like a conductor,* Kirsten thinks, as flakes from his cigarette fall on the table. She places a hand on his neck, lets her fingertips glide over his crisp military haircut.

Forest looks at her with a glazed expression and finishes his drink before getting up. "Do you want another one, Kiki?" he asks over his shoulder, already headed for the bar.

With a shake of her head, Kirsten's eyes follow him as he approaches the bartender. Has the car accident changed him at all?

At twenty-one, the same age Kirsten is now, Martha arrived home in a whirlwind of infatuation, her clothes carrying the lingering scent of chewing gum and American tobacco. She and her unborn child now lie together in the cemetery. Has Kirsten's life been eclipsed by Martha's? Suddenly, she is overcome by an urge to scream across the café table. She blinks and blows cigarette smoke upwards to intensify the stinging sensation in her eyes.

Did I take something that doesn't belong to me? Kirsten shakes her head. *If Martha's ghost always has a seat at the table, things will be too difficult to bear.* Kirsten exhales and follows the trail of cigarette smoke with her eyes. *Will Martha always lie between us?*

"Martha," she whispers, "Forgive me."

※

RICH AND DARK AS AMBER. KIRSTEN WATCHES AS Forest sets the beers on the table. The strong, dark lager that Forest prefers is called Dunkel by the Germans; its flavor is intense and the alcohol packs a punch. Kirsten wishes Forest would drink Radler like her: beer mixed with lemonade.

He slams his hand on the table, making her jump with a squeal. Her fingers tingling from the shock, she looks at him. *It's clear to anyone that he is drunk*, she thinks, her eyes dropping to the tabletop.

Everyone knows his wife was killed in a car accident. They also know Forest was behind the wheel that day, and that he'd been drinking. Kirsten wants to hide, but if she moves any further into the corner she'll blend into the wallpaper. She watches the ash from his cigarette, which he has let burn for too long.

"I could eat you up, skin and all," he mumbles in her ear, his voice slurring, while his hands force her legs apart under the table.

Kirsten squirms. "Dusty, stop." She tenses her thigh muscles. Is it even her he wants? Unfazed, he casually removes his hand and continues his conversation with his friend.

If only he would build a space for us where both intimacy and physical touch existed, take my hand in his, Kirsten thinks. *See what I need, reach for me.* Still, it's as if she can't resist him. As one thought leads to another, a pleasant warmth begins to blossom and spread throughout her body. She feels the chair's edge against her groin, the throbbing sensation intensifying. Lazily, she brings the cigarette to her lips, enjoying the feeling, and reaches for Forest's hand. When he looks back at her, his eyes are unfocused. Kirsten doesn't care; she has her own buzz.

"A picture of the bride and groom!" shouts the girl Kirsten still hasn't figured out who is. Apparently, one of Forest's wedding witnesses brought her along. The girl holds a polaroid camera and clings to one of the soldiers' arms. Kirsten stubs out her cigarette. With trembling hands, she grabs a piece of bubblegum from her purse.

What if her wings fail to carry her in America? What if the hope and fight for a better future amount to nothing? Forest is drunk. That's why she got him to promise. Was it naïve to think the accident had deterred him?

As he kneeled and proposed a few weeks before, she revealed, "My biggest fear is marrying an alcoholic and being isolated in America."

Placing a hand on his chest, he replied, "I give you my word, Kiki."

Kirsten smiles bitterly. *He's dancing on Martha's grave, a cigarette dangling from his lips, a glass sloshing in his hand, the wedding ring a mocking glint on his finger,* she thinks.

Forest turns to her, squeezes her shoulder, and a warmth washes over her. She shoves aside her gloomy thoughts. *We all fail,* she thinks. *Isn't there room for forgiveness if there's remorse?*

Kirsten envisions an American house with a car in the driveway. In her mind, she's preparing his lunch and sharing a quick kiss as he leaves for work. She pictures herself waving goodbye, wearing a headscarf and striped apron.

Time will mend things. My family will eventually forgive me. And if not? She reaches for Forest's hand, which is still on her shoulder, *I'll be so far away, I'll need to rely on my new family.*

A SHATTERING EXPLOSION OF GLASS ABRUPTLY silences the table's conversation. Feeling glass on her ankles, Kirsten instinctively runs her fingers over her instep. A puzzled Forest shifts his gaze from his hand to the floor.

"Take it easy, Forest." Kirsten's hand rests on his arm, and she feels the tension in his muscles under his uniform.

As he yanks his arm away from her, the back of his hand strikes her cheek, his knuckles leaving imprints that feel like they've carved holes beneath her eye. Covering the humiliation with her palm, her mind blanks momentarily before she regains her composure. *Alcohol makes movements rougher than intended,* she thinks.

"They need time to process their wartime experiences," the Red Cross nurses explained at the briefings.

They must know what they're talking about, and if that's what helps, she will gladly wash clothes, iron shirts, and cook his meals. Retrieving a cigarette from her case, she leans toward Forest and gently strokes his cheek with her thumb. "We're okay, honey," she whispers.

He flicks open his lighter. His thumb rotates the flint mechanism's wheel, causing a spark to ignite and a flame to spring forth. When he shields it, Kirsten leans into his hands, lingering within their dome. She inhales and slowly straightens up, holding eye contact. *With him, I will feel alive, experience the world sharply*, she thinks.

Finding her powder in her purse, she dabs her warm cheek. The war has shown her the unpredictability of the future. Ingrid taught her to follow her passions but to stay safe. Martha taught her to live each day as if it were her last.

She looks at the wedding ring on her finger. As Forest takes her glass and brings it to his lips, the cigarette between his fingers traces a glowing arc in the air.

*

Before Kirsten has a chance to plaster on her practiced smile, the girl jumps up and presses the camera's shutter. "Kirsten, what do you say in Danish to make people smile in pictures?"

"Appelsiiiiiiiin," Kirsten replies, pulling up the corners of her mouth.

Confused, the girl kneels to get a better view, then yells, "Say applesiiiiiiiin!"

Kirsten rolls her eyes as the flash lights up. A few seconds later, the girl places the warm, curved photo to dry on the table. Slowly, the image emerges. Kirsten watches herself surface as if from a fog. *Life is not static, as it is in a photograph.*

It is constantly interrupted, and a new reality arises, she thinks, and removes a piece of tobacco from the tip of her tongue, flicking it to the floor.

In a quick motion, the girl reaches across the table, takes the photo, and tears it — first lengthwise, then crosswise. Kirsten looks at the square pieces. She and Forest look into the camera from their respective frayed squares: he with his toothpaste smile and she with her skyward eyes. The other two scraps show Kirsten's half-full glass in one and Forest's empty glass in the other.

"Let's try this the American way." The girl puts a hand on her hip and looks sternly at them. Her nails shine red. "Say cheese!"

Kirsten parts her lips slightly. That must pass for a smile. A click from the camera. Her gaze falls on the ashtray, containing her two bright-red butts and Forest's four flattened ones. To Kirsten, they resemble ships sailing a sea of ash. A stack of torn Polaroid photos sits beside the ashtray. The girl is unhappy with her face in one photo and her posture in another. *Doesn't she understand that perfection doesn't exist?* Kirsten shoots a sharp glance in her direction and stubs out her cigarette in the ashtray. *It's my wedding day*, she thinks, shoving the torn photos off the edge of the table. Turning to Forest, she whispers, "Can we leave now?" Why doesn't he understand that she needs to be alone with him?

"My wife would like to say thank you for tonight." Forest stands up, a little unsteady on his feet. He offers her his arm, brings two fingers to his temple in a salute and says, "Wish a newlywed man good luck!"

A few feet from the café, he presses her against a barrack wall. With his head against her chest, she feels the warmth from his throat. A mix of perfume and alcohol envelops her face. She pushes him away.

"Kiki, it's our wedding night!"

Not against a wall with the mix of alcohol and sour tobacco in my face, she thinks.

"Don't be so prissy," he slurs, pressing his groin harder against her hipbones. His hand is on the wall beside her cheek. Kirsten tenses, her mouth opening as a thousand thoughts flood her mind. Her throat tightens. As apathy washes over her, a to-do list forms in her mind: she needs to sort the documents required for the immigration authorities, retrieve her garments from the cleaners, and clean her boarding room. Then she turns her face upward, unbuttons her stockings, and pulls down her panties. He forces her head back and she feels a sharp crackle at the back of her skull. A few thrusts, and he is done. She fixes her clothes, feeling a warmth running down her inner thighs.

☽

Lying in her boarding house bed, Kirsten traces her face with her fingertips. One of her cheeks is warm. A dull ache pains her lower body. The world feels off-kilter, out of its orbit. In the dim light from the window, she gazes at her hands. They look the same as usual.

MEDICAL CHECK-UP
KIRSTEN

Dust particles dance in the sunbeams slicing through the windows before settling at the feet of the women gathered at the military medical unit. A nervous mood settles over them, the feeling of anticipation is palpable.

After hearing other war brides' stories, Martha had been terrified of her medical examination. Afterwards, she stayed silent when the topic came up and never shared her own experience.

Kirsten lets out a sigh. *Now it's my turn,* she thinks. Officially, the checkups are meant to check for lice, fleas, and venereal diseases, but everyone knows that there's more to it than that.

"Onward! Let's just get this over with." Kirsten talks as much to her shaky legs as to the other women.

The war brides huddle together in a tight group by the theater door, where the examinations take place. Like a school of fish, they move as one until they have to go inside.

"Don't be so shy, ladies." An officer is waiting inside the

room. His eyes sweep over the women. "Take off your clothes!" he commands.

No one follows his order.

"No one is asking you to leave Germany. This was your choice." His hands are clasped behind his back.

The women exchange nervous glances, turn toward the benches and methodically undress.

"Shoes under the bench," his voice booms.

A few women keep their underwear on.

"All your clothes! Keep everything together so you can find it afterward."

Kirsten unhooks her bra and places her panties on top of the pile of clothes. She looks around. Counts: fifty women. Soldiers line the back wall, their eyes fixed ahead, caps pulled low.

"Line up!" The officer calls out names from a list. "Hannah Berger?" He looks up. No one responds. "Sarah Müller?" Still no reply. "Do you want to join your husbands? Your children's fathers?" It is clear from the tone of the officer's voice this is not a game he wants to play.

The women are stirring. A prickly, tingling sensation crawls across Kirsten's scalp as her nerves twitch. *We need to get this over with quickly,* she thinks. "I don't know about you, but I've had enough of the Italian and German prisoners' chatter on the base!" Aware of the impatience in her own voice, Kirsten glances around. "Do you want to stay in your overcrowded barracks?" She makes a sweeping gesture with her arm. "Do you want to go to America?"

Scattered murmurs.

"In this place, the doctor is God. Play the game!"

Several women nod.

"Give them what they want." Kirsten straightens up, pulling her shoulders back. "Let them think they have the upper hand," she whispers, sending a look toward the back wall. "Pretend they're not here."

⁂

EVEN UNCLOTHED WOMEN ARE EXPECTED TO adhere to strict military rules in this place. In one long column, with their hands folded in front of their groins, they stand at the ready to follow orders.

"Think of Roy or George, or whatever your chosen one is called." With a toss of her head, Kirsten gestures at the uniforms. "Don't cower!" Mentally, she dons her armor, so only her body is present. "This is just another hurdle."

"Go to the back wall and face it." The officer points. A nervous murmur spreads. Kirsten thinks of the swirling dust particles.

"He can't possibly mean that we have to face those men, completely exposed," a woman whispers, her voice barely audible.

The officer walks around to the front of the podium to illustrate where he wants them to line up. "Wait here." He stands facing the men by the wall, his hands neatly folded behind his back. A woman sobs. The officer walks back toward the podium in the center of the room, ascends the two steps, and addresses the women, "When your name is called, come up here and face the doctor."

⁂

A MIX OF SPEARMINT, TOBACCO, OLD SPICE, AND fermented fish hangs in the air around the men, standing with legs spread, staring off into space with their hands clasped in front of them. *I know what they're trying to hide,*

Kirsten thinks, glancing at their hands. The uniformed men shift their weight from one foot to the other.

One woman has a scarf wrapped around her body. "No scarves, hairpins, or jewelry!" the officer barks.

A shiver runs through Kirsten. Then she finds the familiar white spot in the back of her mind, focuses on that, and lets her consciousness leave the room. One day a funeral, the next a medical exam, tomorrow something else.

From his pocket, the doctor pulls out a crumpled handkerchief and blows his nose. The sound brings Kirsten back to reality. "Old, ugly man!" she whispers. *And those disgusting brutes along the wall!* she thinks. *It doesn't matter how many stars and medals they have! Dogs will be dogs! Medical check, my ass! It's a lie!* She takes a deep breath. "Follow me!" she says and strides past the uniforms without giving them a glance, followed by a trail of scurrying women. She stops at the last man and stands facing him. She counts to five before turning. Out of the corner of her eye she notices the doctor looking at her with a raised eyebrow and skewed smile.

"Quiet!" the officer growls.

Kirsten's gaze darts around. No one has said a word. She shudders, thinking of hyenas' barks, guttural growls, and musk.

꩜

THE WOMEN LINE UP BEHIND THE STEPS BY THE podium. The doctor waits with his flashlight. A woman wipes her face, smearing away snot and tears. Her other arm resembles a sash; wrapped around her at an angle, it covers one breast and her genitals. Another woman sniffles as she adjusts a child on her hip. The little one's arms are wrapped around her neck, legs dangling, partially hiding the light triangle in front and the dark crevice behind.

A silence settles, broken only by scattered whimpers. Everyone waits for the doctor to call their name. *Soon we'll be on the scaffold,* Kirsten thinks. *Three, four, seven. Inhale for three seconds, hold your breath for four, then exhale slowly over seven.*

"Ingrid Arendt?" A girl slowly walks up to the podium. "State your name and age!" The doctor's voice is low and hoarse.

"Ingrid Arendt, sixteen," the girl whispers.

The doctor checks off the list on his lap. "Bend over!" Wide-eyed, she looks at him pleadingly. The doctor raises an eyebrow. This will be on his terms. "Move your hair!" With a slender hand, she gathers her long blonde hair at the nape of her neck, revealing her upper body. Her skin is pale, almost translucent. The fine down on her arms and legs is like a delicate spiderweb.

Kirsten's gaze runs over the podium, searching in vain for an escape. She re-dons her armor and looks at the girl. A few years ago, the Germans would have adored her Aryan looks, if it wasn't for her nose. Noticing the angle the doctor is taking to inspect the girl's body, Kirsten shudders. He shines his light slowly through her hair, gently grazing her scalp. If anyone asks, he's checking for lice.

"Straighten up!"

She does so, the tension leaving her shoulders as she folds her hands in her lap.

"Spread your legs!"

Her expression changes from terror to a blank stare. *She's a quick study,* Kirsten thinks, before the doctor waves her off.

"Accepted!"

The mood shifts instantaneously, as if someone has snapped their fingers. A brief sense of relief washes over them and the women breathe again. The girl stumbles off the podium and darts toward the benches.

But unease spreads among the women once more as the doctor trails a finger down his list. A body breaks free. Bare feet on cement is the only sound in the room. Kirsten watches the girl throw a coat over her shoulders before grabbing clothes and shoes from the bench and running toward the door. A metallic clang as the door closes and the girl disappears. A second later, the room is completely silent, as if the scene had never taken place.

"One woman's misfortune is another's good luck." The officer points encouragingly toward the door. "Because of The War Bride Act, there is now a vacancy for one more fortunate Victory Bride."

The doctor interrupts. "Sarah Mertens?" A broad-hipped woman, visibly pregnant, steps onto the podium and walks with heavy steps toward the doctor. "State your name and age!"

Enunciating each syllable, the woman pronounces her name with emphasis. Her feet are firmly planted on the podium. Blue veins spread across her chest like streaks. Her thighs and stomach are covered with stretchmarks; skin straining to accommodate the life it holds. The woman stands with her hands on her hips, ready to face whatever may come.

"Stand on your tiptoes! Lift your arms above your head." Sighing, she obeys. "Slowly turn around three times." The doctor's voice is raspy. He crosses one leg over the other. The woman hesitates, as if about to speak, then thinks better of it. Clicking and popping sounds fill the room as her feet respond to the weight of her body. "If it creaks, it works!" the doctor scoffs. Laughter echoes from the back wall. Remaining on tiptoe, the woman raises her arms, thrusting out her rounded belly and highlighting her waist.

The cat-and-mouse game slowly dawns on Kirsten. *Are we really powerless against them?* she thinks. *Does our capacity to provoke that sort of look grant us power over them?* She looks at her trembling hands.

"Kirsten Marie Rhodes!" The doctor's voice reaches her as if through a blanket. His fleshy finger hovers over the list. Kirsten takes a step forward, placing her hands behind her back, on top of her buttocks. Surprise registers on the doctor's face as he looks at her.

Don't show fear, she chants in her head. She turns her gaze neutral. *Don't provoke, don't tease, don't appear indifferent.*

"State your name and age!"

"Mrs Sgt Forest Edgar Rhodes," Kirsten says in a clear voice, "Born Kirsten Marie Pedersen."

The doctor checks her name off his list. "Make a cross. Spread your legs!" he commands. Kirsten looks at him questioningly. "Hands above your head and spread your legs," he sighs, as if he is utterly bored.

Your trembling voice betrays you, you beast! Kirsten thinks, clenching her teeth. She stretches her arms overhead, tilting her head back. Then she spreads her legs. The doctor leans forward with his flashlight. Warmth spreads between Kirsten's thighs. A sweet, metallic smell reaches her nose. The doctor jerks the flashlight back, just as Kirsten feels blood trickle down her inner thigh.

"Leave the podium! Accepted. Next!"

Copenhagen Central Station
Kirsten

After a night spent in the sleeper car, Kirsten's senses are abruptly awakened. The shrill sound of a whistle numbs her mind as she watches the locomotive doors open. Copenhagen Central Station awaits her on the other side. The dampness of morning mist, a metallic smell of coal, and the stench of unwashed bodies fill the air.

Pushing her hair up under her scarf, Kirsten carefully steps off the train, avoiding the dizzying gap between the carriage and the platform. People push their way up the stairs to street level. Kirsten flows with the crowd, dodging commuters rushing to and from the platform. As if seeing with fresh eyes, she notices the weathered pavement, stained coats, and dust from the coal depot clouding the puddles on the jagged concrete.

This is her final visit to her childhood home before moving to America. Kirsten smooths her dress. Back in Germany, buying it had seemed like a good idea. Admiring the dress in the shop, Kirsten knew it would make her stand out in Denmark. The latest fashion is all full skirts and wide belts, while practical, military-style skirts remain a common sight on Danish women. *It's almost too much,* a voice muttered in the back of her mind as she turned and twisted in front of the mirror in the fitting room. Still, she couldn't resist.

Kirsten observes the Copenhageners. People here act like they don't care she's married to an American. She can see it in their eyes: *Don't think you're better than us.* The intoxicating feeling from the dress shop is gone. A woman shoves her in the back as she walks past and Kirsten's anger flares. *So damn petty! At least now it's clear to everyone that I never belonged.*

A newspaper seller's hoarse cry reaches her as she exits the station: "Danish Social Liberal Party: bring the brigade home from Germany."

Who do the Danes think will keep the Germans in check? Kirsten thinks. *The Americans? Why does Europe always expect the Americans to save them! When will the Danes take responsibility for anything?*

She lets her shoulders drop and inhales slowly. She needs to stay calm today. Kirsten glances in the boy's direction. He wipes snot from his nose and adjusts his sixpence. Perhaps she should read the newspaper to see what the Danish Social Liberals have to say. Stopping, she turns back to the newspaper stand, pays, and folds the paper to fit in her purse. Kirsten smiles as a woman walks past holding a little girl's hand and steering a stroller. *I wonder what the world would look like if women were in power?*

Weaving through a crowd by a hot dog stand, she makes her way to the city hall square to catch the tram. The train station is behind her; her family home is two miles away. Her travel bag weighs almost nothing; she's only brought the bare necessities. When she thinks about what the next twenty-four hours might bring, a feeling of dread washes over her. It's drizzling, and Kirsten struggles to open her umbrella, unable to feel the button through her gloves. *Buying them was foolish*, she muses, but they complemented her coat perfectly. Ripping off the gloves, Kirsten tosses them into her purse before continuing on toward the square.

☽

Two things Kirsten will be happy to leave behind are the rain and the indifferent looks people shoot each other. As the tram arrives, passengers tense up, shoulders stiffening in anticipation of the rush to board.

Tram number five clatters noisily down Rådhusstræde, its bell ringing at cyclists who weave between the tracks, seemingly oblivious to their disregard for traffic rules. When the tram stops, Kirsten hops onboard and buys her ticket. Out of habit, she takes a seat on the side facing the road.

Like a beetle with dark gold-framed windows like eyes and a green undercarriage, the tram eats its way through the city streets while Kirsten rests in its belly. She lets her hand glide over the travel bag, hoping she'll have the seat to herself all the way to her destination. The prospect of meaningless conversation with a stranger on her last journey home is unbearable.

"Never again," she whispers at the window. *After the war, that's the sentiment. We all hope for a better future*, Kirsten thinks. *One free from history's atrocities, but who knows how Europe will develop? Will the coming years bring stability and peace, or will a new madman plunge Europe into chaos and horror on his wild ride? Maybe the Russians will come roaring back. The red superpower has been meddling in elections and installing puppet governments in Eastern Europe.* Fear washes over Kirsten.

What if they attack Denmark? Could the recent defection of Olympic athletes to the West be a warning sign? *Hopefully my goodbyes go better than those negotiations. Sure, I'm not defecting,* she thinks, trying to dampen her dramatic thoughts, *but I am seeking a new life under foreign skies.*

Her father isn't a communist; he's a Social Democrat through and through. It's not just his ruddy nose from years of drinking that's earned him his nickname 'Red'. Although Kirsten likes the idea of community supporting the weakest, the Americans see communism as enemy number one, so she supposes she must too, now that she's become an American wife.

A flock of pigeons takes off with a flapping of wings. A moment later, gray and white feathers flutter past the tram's side window. Kirsten tries to hold her attention, wanting to imprint every building, every childhood memory — from games of hopscotch to teenage bike rides. Her brain, however, refuses to cooperate; the images slide over her retinas and disappear.

The tram whines and jerks, announcing its presence. Leaning her head against the cool windowpane, she seeks a moment of peace to escape her emotional turmoil. The tram steadily crawls from H. C. Andersen's Boulevard onto Amager Boulevard turning a corner and continuing along Amagerbrogade. A glimpse of the Church of Our Savior appears between buildings, then the tram screeches to a momentary halt and turns left onto Holmbladsgade. On this street, residents and buildings lean wearily against each other. Rows of dilapidated two-story houses stretch as far as the eye can see on both sides of the cobblestone road. Windows hang loosely and moss-laden roof tiles arch upwards like tired, old shoes.

This desolate edge of Copenhagen is populated by clusters of greasy caps and vacant stares. 'Aksel Jacobsen' is written on a handcart. *The poor greengrocer probably can't afford a proper shop*, Kirsten thinks. There are many like him. In the cold months, they retreat into the backyards and warm themselves by tile stoves when their fingers grow too stiff to pick out potatoes for customers. Peter used to earn 25 øre when he was a boy removing potato sprouts for a shopkeeper. He never saw that money, though; either their mother took it, or their father did. She used it to buy food, he to buy brandy.

Further down, Kirsten recognizes the cheese shop. Water runs down the window, so you can only see the cheeses once you're inside the shop. *Does it still smell the same in there? Sour and sharp?* Her brain remembers the nausea in her throat. She swallows. As a child, while waiting in the shop with her mother, she distracted herself by studying the peeling paint at the window's base. Glass-clear drops, like tiny pearls, clung to the windowpane before joining forces with other droplets, racing each other down the glass in a sparkling stream to form a puddle on the stone floor. Meanwhile, her mother haggled over the price and made a deal for cheese rinds.

The city where she took her first steps as a child has changed. *Or perhaps I have changed*, Kirsten thinks. *Is it because my childhood world seems small after being away, or is it the uncertainty of whether I'll ever walk these familiar paths again?* Turning to follow the golden facade letters at the intersection of Holmbladsgade and Østrigsgade, Kirsten experiences a sense of alienation and displacement. A feeling of being a stranger in her own city. In her childhood, whenever she saw visitors from the provinces staring out of the tram window she would deliberately avoid their eyes. Now she's the one staring. She blushes as she notices a few people raise their eyebrows at her.

A sign advertising dresses and a glimpse of the window display catch her eye. For a moment, she feels a surge of anticipation. *But heavens, how disappointing!* The outfit on the mannequin clearly shows that French fashion hasn't arrived in Copenhagen yet.

Gosh, when she thinks about how they dressed during the occupation! Their mother had to be creative, transforming potato sacks into clothes in an endless cycle of sewing and resewing. The hand-me-downs went from Martha to Kirsten and finally to little Ingrid. When the fabric wore out, their mother repurposed old curtains into skirts and blouses; adding from one piece, taking from another, making everything stretch. The family never got their hands on one of those coveted parachutes. All that cotton and silk could have clothed the whole lot of them, and they wouldn't have had to smell like half-rotten vegetables, scratching themselves like a pack of flea-infested dogs.

Kirsten feels a pang of guilt. *You ungrateful wretch*, she scolds herself. *Mom did what she could, even if the clothes weren't beautiful, or had pockets or collars like the ones in the ladies' clothing stores.* Kirsten flicks a speck of dust off her dress. Fashion is more stylish now. Voluminous skirts, nipped in at the waist, and gently curved shoulders. Fashion is an open, upward-looking face, seeking to break away from its rigid, inward-looking predecessor. *Each time I wrap myself in French-inspired clothes*, Kirsten muses, *the transformation of the war reveals its brighter side, I shed my childhood and spit on the Germans' legacy. I want to whirl out into the world, spread my arms, ready for embrace, for farewell and arrival and shout: Here I come — are you ready?*

THE TRAM PASSES BY THE NEIGHBORHOOD SCHOOL. Even now, Kirsten can recall racing back from the bakery carrying the bag of Danish pastries Martha had sent her for.

"Get us two Napoleon hats," her sister said, and Kirsten had darted off.

She smiles at her reflection in the tram window.

But when Kirsten returned, she stumbled into a whole new world. In a courtyard, hidden from the street, her older sister was kissing a boy. The urge to tattle itched all over.

The tram jerks, braking suddenly to avoid a crossing cyclist.

Kirsten, however, saw an advantage in remaining silent. At the courtyard gate, unnoticed by Martha, she discreetly turned back around. On the street, she paced back and forth, trying to figure out her next move. Finally, she sat on the curb and fiddled with the top edge of the bakery bag for a moment, before resolutely tearing it open and eating both pastries. Napoleon hats don't make much of a statement. The modest pastry bears no resemblance to a mad emperor's hat — looking more like draped fabric clinging to a soft bosom. But she still remembers the feeling of confusion mixed with a sweet sense of power.

"You ate both?!" Martha nudged Kirsten with her shoe, gesturing toward the empty bakery bag.

With her back to the courtyard gate, Kirsten sat licking her fingers. "Yes, and I'll do it again next time, too." As she turned to her sister, she watched her face cycle through a series of expressions; first irritation, then surprise, and finally, a look of fear.

"I'll come with you when Mom asks you to look after me," Kirsten said.

Martha nodded.

"When we reach the school, I'll go to the bakery for two Napoleon pastries, which I'll eat far enough away that I can't see what you're up to."

Martha's lips were paper-thin. "You'll stay away? And you'll keep quiet?"

"So long as you hold up your end of the bargain."

They shook hands. In the end, it was a pretty good deal. However, some things never change. Martha remained flawless in their parents' eyes. It's bearable now, knowing her sister had a few dents in her character.

"I'll never reveal what I know," Kirsten whispers to the window. Especially not now. After the accident, Martha is even more exalted, surrounded by the aura bestowed upon those who pass away too soon.

Their pastry deal remains a fun memory, though. At least, it's become so over time. During the weeks Martha saw the boy, Kirsten devoured many Napoleon hats on that curb. She smiles to herself. How she misses Danish pastries! The thought makes her mouth water. *Maybe I should get off and make a quick trip to get a bag of some sweet baked goods? No, I must stay focused*, she thinks. *I have more important things to attend to today.*

As the tram passes the hardware store, she remembers Knud, her older brother, who loved to press his face against the window. Who will she share memories with in America? No one there will understand where she comes from. They will not understand the distinct taste of Danish pastries, Danish holiday traditions, or the atmosphere of Copenhagen.

As the tram approaches the hospital stop, Kirsten prepares to alight.

"They added a stop last year. If you're going further, you might as well stay seated." The driver lets his gaze linger a bit too long on her clothes. "The route was changed back in '47."

"I haven't been around here much lately." Kirsten nods toward her travel bag.

"Our last stop is now Famosavej," the conductor announces.

"This must be my lucky day!" Kirsten says, a high-pitched happy lilt in her voice.

He gestures broadly with his hand. "Much has changed."

Is he for or against urban development? Is she? Kirsten decides she doesn't care. It no longer has anything to do with her. "There aren't many farms and fields left from when I was a child."

The driver grumbles and turns a corner. Then he stops the tram with a jolt and opens the doors.

"Thanks for the ride!" Kirsten shouts before hopping off.

Feeling something smooth and wet in her palm, Kirsten looks down. "Spot!" she exclaims, "Where did you come from?" Touched, she feels a lump form in her throat when the dog nudged its soft snout against her hand. *Now it begins*, she thinks. *But not in the way I'd expected.*

Kirsten scratches the dog's ear. "Are you glad to see your Aunt Kirsten?" Spot was Martha's dog. At the hospital, they talked about him all the time, hoping for a reaction from the hospital bed.

"When Martha went to Germany, he waited every day at the tram stop," her mother said a bit too loudly during one of those long vigils in uncomfortable chairs.

Kirsten seized the opportunity: "If only someone missed me like that," she said, hoping her mother would say something. But the conversation fell apart, landing like sharp little pieces of glass on the floor.

Kirsten pats Spot. "You might have been Martha's dog, but you seem to like me just as well." *Maybe coming home won't be so bad after all?* she thinks, and heads in the direction of her parent's house.

On her way, she makes a few steps, picking up groceries for dinner at the greengrocer and the butcher, while Spot waits outside. She walks intuitively through her childhood streets, turning right and then left. She straightens her back. *This is my neighborhood; I know how to carry myself here, know what to say, how to act.* She follows the staggered pattern of the square pavement tiles. "Almost there, Spot," she murmurs, carefully avoiding the cracks. Where the tiles finish, the road becomes a muddy mess. Tree branches overhang the road, their reflections shimmering in the puddles alongside the hedges.

⁂

HER PARENTS' STREET CAN'T DECIDE IF IT WANTS to be in the countryside or part of the city. A wheelbarrow leans against a wall. In the distance, toward Copenhagen, the new high-rises are visible. Time rushes forward while clinging to the past, marking its territory with remnants so the future won't forget where it came from.

And then she finds herself in front of her childhood home. The house is rather unassuming. Still, Kirsten needs a moment. She turns, picks up a stick, and throws it. Spot sprints off and proudly brings it back to her with his head held high. Kirsten throws it once more. And then again.

"Now I better get to it," she says and walks down the tiled path toward the house. The yellow bricks are covered in brown splotches. *Why are there no clean, bright colors in this country?* she thinks, letting her gaze wander upward. Descriptions of how her father and older brothers dug out the foundations spring from her memory. Earth, concrete, bricks, and countless wheelbarrows — these words were as much a part of her early vocabulary as the ones learned in school.

"It's a good thing the boys are so good with their hands," her father had commented from his armchair. At the time, they were still learning their trades and worked evenings to build the house. Finally, it stood there, functional, bright and spacious.

Martha baked a pound cake the day the yellow bricks were laid. "The house is like a giant yellow cake," she said, placing the biggest slice onto her father's plate. Mortar stained his skin a rough, gray color, and blisters dotted his calloused fingers.

Kirsten looks at the front door. Knud had made a few suggestions, including a peephole he persuaded their father to install. His dream was to become an architect, but of course that was never going to happen.

Kirsten looks through the peephole and meets her father's eyes. When she still lived at home, he would stand there like a captain on his ship, waiting to make sure she was home on time. She blinks, and sees only her own image looking back at her in the glass reflection.

Kirsten turns and throws the stick one last time with all her might, watching the dog leap over the ditch and disappear into a hedge. She whistles and Spot returns with the stick, his tongue lolling out. "I don't want you inside with those muddy paws." With a shake and a pleading look at her, the dog slinks down the front steps and curls up on the garden tiles, nose tucked between his paws.

The key is in its usual place. When Kirsten unlocks the

door, Spot raises an eyebrow, then looks away. A shudder runs through her as she hangs her coat on the hook. Her dad's shoes are in the hallway. In the living room, his pipe sits on the armrest of his chair. She looks around but the house is an empty husk. Why was she so scared? Nothing to fear but ghosts from her childhood.

❂

A SHRILL WHISTLE PIERCES THE AIR AS THE KETTLE on the stove comes to a boil. Lost in her thoughts, Kirsten is startled by the sound.

The moment she stepped through the front door, the smell of childhood enveloped her. Kirsten pours the boiling water into the zinc basin and scoops out a handful of brown soap. Her methodical, repetitive movements provide a temporary reprieve from the uncomfortable tightness in her chest, allowing her to focus on the task at hand. The rhythmic movements of her scrubbing create a sense of order that helps her manage her inner chaos.

As she plunges her fingers into the soft, yielding blob of soap, the water's heat scalds her arm. The floor cloth, stiff from having been left on the basin's edge, is shaped like a plate. Kirsten drops it into the scalding water. As the cloth makes contact with the water, a crackling and fizzing sound emits from the bucket. A splash of vinegar added into the soap mixture makes her nose sting. Grabbing the bucket and floor scrubber, she heads into the living room.

A fine layer of dust and dirty fingerprints cover the woodwork, furniture and door handles. "Monkey grease," her mother calls it. She is back at Ingrid's bedside at the hospital in Germany and in her absence, no one, it seems, has bothered to take over the cleaning duties.

Kneeling, Kirsten wipes the baseboards, wondering when the water has become dirtier than the surfaces she's cleaning. As the cloth glides up and down, she weighs the pros and cons, finally deciding to change the water once it reaches room temperature.

"Water, soap, vinegar, cloth, wring, scrub," she hums, feeling the calm settle upon her. She glances at the armchair. *Come what may.*

After a while, Kirsten allows herself a break. She lights a cigarette, holds the smoke in her lungs, and surveys her work. She's tired, but there's more work to be done. Retrieving a knife from the kitchen, she returns to the living room and kneels back down on the floor. Cleaning the floorboards requires a special method to lift the deeply embedded filth out of the grooves. Before long, a gray mound of grime lies beside her — the Pedersen family's accumulated dirt, ground down and compressed between the floorboards over the years. Scooping it up in her hand, she goes to the kitchen and throws it in the trash.

After cleaning the outhouse, she stops in front of her father's armchair. It sits beside the fireplace like a throne. "It's just an armchair," she whispers, perching on the very edge of the seat. Once her heart settles, she leans back against the backrest. If her father could see her now!

The tobacco pipe sits on the armrest, carrying the smells of her childhood. Carefully, Kirsten runs her index finger over the pipe's bowl. The wood is soft and oily. *Isn't it true that Native Americans in America smoke peace pipes?* She picks it up and lets the bowl rest in her palm, before closing her fingers around the wood. A shiver runs through her body as she brings the mouthpiece to her nose. A scent of wood and sour tobacco fills the air. She lets the mouthpiece slide between her teeth, finding a notch that feels natural to bite down on. A memory flashes before her eyes: her dad's lips smacking and sucking at the pipe. Kirsten rips it from her mouth. *That peace pipe didn't work out so well for the Native Americans, did it?*

⁂

KIRSTEN WIPES HER SWEATY NECK WITH THE towel draped over her shoulder. Her eyes dart around the kitchen. Pickled red cabbage simmers on the stove and the roast still needs a few more minutes in the oven. She measures out flour, finds fat, salt, and a dollop of jam to round off the gravy. Even though it's just going to be Kirsten, her father and Peter, she's boiled enough potatoes for an entire army.

Any moment now, he'll be here. *Breathe*, she reminds herself and whisks the gravy in tight circles, breaking down the stubborn lumps. There can't be a single flaw in her cooking. *I will make sure he has enough roast to burst.* She sprinkles sugar in the pan for her caramelized potatoes. Is her penance of washing, scrubbing, and cooking enough to change anything? She's willing to try, and what better way than through her father's stomach?

⁂

THE TABLE IS SET, ADORNED WITH A TABLECLOTH and candles. Gleaming in a bowl, the caramelized potatoes lie golden and the roast is sliced neatly on a platter while the gravy forms a skin in its saucer.

The distance to her father's heart feels as far as the end of the table. Kirsten watches his jaw clench with each bite. Peter eats quickly and passes dishes between Kirsten and their father. Clearing her throat, she feels an urge to raise her glass in a toast. She takes a sip as if it were wine.

"Milk!" Her dad snarls. "Who the hell drinks milk with roast?"

Kirsten flinches when he slams his glass on the table. She lowers her gaze. "You know why we're having milk, Dad." Kirsten's mind races, silently pleading, *"Please, don't let me voice your alcohol problem."*

He drains his glass and wipes his mouth with the back of his hand. "All right then, Mrs. Forest Rhodes," he sneers, "Was there really not a single man in all of Denmark good enough for you?"

"It's not like that." Kirsten bites her cheek.

"You'll never measure up to her."

Kirsten looks up into his narrowed eyes.

"You're never gonna!" he shouts, with a clatter of cutlery. "You've always had a big head, thinking you're better than everyone else."

Her brother finishes his drink with a toss of his head. "Thanks for dinner, Kirsten," he mumbles, pushing back his chair. Kirsten hears him swallow. "I've gotta run."

Kirsten gets up. "I may never see you again, Peter." As she moves in to hug him, he sidesteps deftly. In a few more strides, he's out in the hallway. He grabs his coat, opens the front door, and is gone. Kirsten returns to the table and sits down.

"First you were set on school, then you decided you

wanted to work in Germany." Her father's eyes gleam. "And now this!"

Kirsten swallows. Nothing has turned out as she had hoped. Rather, it has all turned out the way she'd feared. She considers whether it is safe to get up and leave the table. When her father is in this mood, timing is everything. Taking his time, he scoops potatoes onto his plate. His left arm rests on the table. His thumbnail gleams white from his grip on the edge.

"Even in that outfit," he lets his eyes run over her clothes, "you're nothing but a back-alley cat."

Teardrops hit her plate. Kirsten doesn't dare wipe her eyes or blow her nose. *He's right,* she thinks. *What kind of person am I? Less than four months after my pregnant sister dies in a car accident, I marry her husband.* Grateful for having let the dog back in after finishing dinner, she feels a gentle nudge from Spot's snout under the table; the warm fur of the dog's head in her lap. *I must leave,* she thinks. *How else will I break the pattern?* Kirsten looks up. "He swore he'd quit drinking."

"He misses having a woman around!" her father sneers.

Damn it, I won't be the scapegoat for their anger! Martha is gone! Why would I pass up a fresh start far from all that Scandinavian gray, cold, and pettiness? Kirsten gathers meat, potato, and gravy onto her fork before stuffing her mouth. Her teeth mash the food into a mushy consistency. *Stay silent, don't speak,* she repeats to herself as she chews.

"And now that woman is me!" The words tumble from her lips, despite the roast. Surprised, Kirsten instinctively brings her hand to her mouth, then quickly straightens her posture as she regains her composure. She did it. She found the courage. She's an adult woman; a married woman. *I am leaving for America. I no longer live under his roof.* Then fear sets in. She feels a tightening in her throat. Her hands shake violently when she tries to lift her glass to her lips. As she sets it back on the table, milk spills onto the tablecloth. Standing, she places her cutlery on her plate.

"Sit down!" His words are clipped and tense, each syllable emphasized.

Spot gives a low growl of warning. A heavy feeling settles in the air around them. Kirsten is intimately familiar with the nuances of her father's voice. A simmering rage — a dark, controlled fury — threatens to explode. She imagines herself as a fragile bottle in the vast ocean, about to be shattered. Overwhelmed, she feels her face splitting with tears, her shoulders slumping inwards.

The harsh screech of wood on wood fills the air as he shoves the chair back. It clatters onto the floor. Spot, hackles raised, teeth bared, blocks his path, positioning himself in front of her chair. Her father delivers a powerful kick to the dog's ribs. A shiver runs down Kirsten's spine as the dog yelps, fleeing into the kitchen with a whimper. In two steps, her father reaches her. Kirsten leans over the table. *Protect your face*, she thinks, pressing her forehead against her forearms.

"No!" A blow to her upper back makes her neck crack. "Shame!" With each strike of his hand, Kirsten's chest jars against the edge of the table. He groans from the effort, gasping for breath, and then the blows continue, like a hammer pounding against the back of her head, the shattering force spreading through her forehead and jaw.

Kirsten waits for numbness to replace the crushing pain.

"Unhinged..." The edge of his hand comes down on her head with the force of an axe. "Tramp!"

Finally, a combination of indifference and exhaustion engulfs her. Kirsten welcomes her sack-like body. A muffled muttering reaches her:

"Spoiled... Immoral...Your sister... Forest... Whisky!"

Kirsten drifts away, knowing only that if she stays, she will break.

"Cheap whore..."

The blows gradually find a slower rhythm.

"Have you lost your mind?"

No, dad. I've found it, Kirsten thinks, before darkness embraces her.

From Copenhagen to Bremerhaven
Kirsten

Most of the journey from Copenhagen Central Station to Germany has passed in silence, broken only by the occasional whoosh and clatter of passing trains. With every station the diesel train chugs through, Kirsten puts distance between herself and her father. Her shoulders and back remind her of their farewell every time the train jerks.

As the train boards the ferry, Kirsten touches her throat. She can't stand the dark, claustrophobic tunnel with its unsettling metallic clunks and sloshing. *If disaster strikes and we disappear through the foaming surface, hopefully it will be quick,* she thinks.

They make it off the ferry and into Germany. Kirsten and a quiet engineer have a compartment to themselves. As the train rocks rhythmically, a sense of calm washes over Kirsten and the hours pass.

"Hamburg, that's me," says the engineer as the train comes to a stop. "I wish you all the best in America." He buttons his coat, touches two fingers to his hat with a shy smile, and is gone.

Our lives briefly intersected, Kirsten thinks. *Perhaps one day he'll sit in a rocking chair remembering his train journey from Copenhagen to Hamburg, and the Danish woman he shared a compartment with. Perhaps I will, too,* Kirsten muses. *And in the intervening years, what sort of lives will each of us have led? What new experiences will have shaped us?*

The train lets out a hiss of air, its doors slamming shut. A mix of movement and quiet anticipation fills the train.

"May I keep you company, signorina?"

Kirsten looks up. "Definitely."

With a smile lighting up his features, the man proceeds into her compartment, adorned in a kimono of shimmering silk. As he moves closer, Kirsten notices his cologne — a scent that conjures images of olive-toned skin and a taut, muscular stomach. She leans forward and rests her face on her hand. He has a commanding presence that is both alluring and off-putting. The cigarette pack he retrieves from his pocket is labeled *Murad*. He offers her the pack with an inviting gesture. Kirsten shakes her head. "I have my own."

He lets out a sigh. "Mine are Turkish. You don't know what you're missing out on." He inhales deeply, holding her gaze, and spreads his arms wide. As he exhales the smoke, Kirsten is enveloped in a soft scent of burned sunshine and dry wood.

"I'll take my chances," she shrugs. The warmth and presence she initially felt around him vanish with the disdainful look he shoots at her American cigarettes.

Undeterred, he launches into long tirades about this and that in a mixture of Italian and French. As his swaggering, inflated manner begins to wear on her, Kirsten glances at her watch. He doesn't appear to require an actively participating audience, however — or even a show of interest in what he's saying. With minimal effort, Kirsten sprinkles in a few *ouis* and *nons*; just enough to avoid seeming impolite.

When they finally arrive at his destination, he executes a dance-like walk toward the compartment door, leaving Kirsten to sink back into her seat, utterly exhausted.

KIRSTEN MUST NOT SLEEP; SHE MUST KEEP WATCH until her eyes burn. A terrifying stream of images glides by as she stares out of the framed compartment window. A sudden lurch as the train switches tracks forces her eyes away, offering a brief reprieve. The train settles onto the new track with a groan.

Inch by inch, the train chugs its way through the rubble-strewn streets of Bremen. Her gaze drops to her hands, folded in her lap. But despite her best efforts, her eyes are drawn back to the war-torn urban landscape. Unforgettable images sear her retinas. Kirsten sniffles. The smells of the train meld together: dusty seats, where thousands of buttocks have left the springs slack; notes of the engineer's hair cream; and a trace of the Italian's cigarettes.

Neatly arranged along the roadside to allow for the safe passage of traffic, piles of rubble create mountain-like formations. Kirsten lets out a long sigh. *Will this place ever be livable again?* The train passes stray dogs and children rummaging through garbage. Rising dust clouds sweep across the landscape, reminding Kirsten of a jigsaw puzzle not yet assembled. Reading about the bombings in the newspaper is one thing; seeing the war machinery firsthand is quite another.

Here, the Allies dropped twelve thousand tons of bombs on German aircraft factories and oil installations. As bombers flew overhead, concentration camp prisoners clung to the hope of liberation. Perhaps some of them prayed that one of the bombs would fall on their barracks, ending a life that felt like death.

Yet again, the train comes to a halt, forcing passengers to endure another security screening. The endless procedures of the German authorities are nothing more than a charade. Even if they were to find something that didn't align with their protocols, they have no real power to do anything about it. No one can take Kirsten by the arm and lead her off the train and away from her destination. Because she is married to an American, even errors on her visa stamps would not impede her travel plans. Still, the controllers play their role, and the passengers act their submissive part. Kirsten smiles, hoping they find something in her papers to reprimand. How it would please her to tell a German conductor a truth or two; to watch the air seep out of his uniformed body as his face bends over her papers.

ONCE AGAIN, THE TRAIN SLOWS DOWN. AS IT MOVES between sections of track, Kirsten feels the rhythmic *clack-whoosh, clack-clack-whoosh* shift to a smoother ride before another shift back into the *clack-whoosh, clack-clack-whoosh* pattern once more. The movement is both sleep-inducing and a reminder for her to stay alert. The journey has been a smooth transition from a pre-war world of village landscapes to a post-war urban one.

In the city, the buildings stand so close together they almost touch. The sun illuminates the empty, windowless shells from behind. Hard, white flashes hit the train's carriage window through the gaping holes in the ruins as the train moves from the shadow to the light. Remnants of life are revealed, layer upon layer, a testament to lives lived by necessity. A mosaic of gray shades, where light transforms into darkness, and destruction into beauty. The silence is like the aftermath of a raging storm. Even here, there is hope. Kirsten bows her head. *Does the same apply to people? Can the right circumstances make us shine?*

It's time. Kirsten pulls her travel bag from the overhead net and places her purse onto her lap. Amidst the shrill of the whistle, the hailing of messages over a loudspeaker, and the coming and going of noisy passengers, she finds it difficult to focus. She must be prepared and stay composed, so her thoughts are not drowned out. In her head, she goes through the next phases of her journey:

First, I must find my bus stop, and make sure I'm waiting on the right side of the road. How I wish I had the sense of direction others seem to be blessed with. I'll probably end up going in the same direction I just came from. Kirsten pats her purse. *But I can barely navigate to the bakery and home without getting lost, so it's pretty impressive that I made it all the way here.*

From the train she drifts with a small crowd, half guessing and half hoping they are going the same place as her, until she ends up at the right place, finds the bus — the right one — and takes her seat. The engine roars as the driver signals and pulls out, calling over his shoulder, "Off to the Dependent Hotel!"

BEHIND HER EYELIDS, KIRSTEN ONCE AGAIN GOES through the next stage of her journey. American forces have seized a hotel where the European war brides will be housed until the next leg of their journey. The Dependent Hotel is one of the city's only intact buildings. Here, Kirsten will wait until all the logistical details have been completed and it is her turn to leave on the boat to America.

There is a burning sensation behind her eyelids. The fatigue draws her attention to the worn springs in the bus seat. Abandoning her attempts to sleep, Kirsten opens her eyes. Although she is aware it is just an optical illusion, her perception is distorted, causing the buildings to appear as if they are gently flowing past the bus window.

THE BREMERHAVEN TRIP SHOULD ONLY TAKE A couple of hours, but nothing in Germany runs on time anymore. First, it took forever to get out of the train station. Passengers arrive continually; women with weary, searching eyes; some burdened with screaming children. *They should have been better prepared, instead of making the rest of the world wait,* Kirsten thinks. Then the bureaucrats had to meticulously check and cross-reference each document before allowing the women to board the bus. When they finally pulled out of the parking area, they had to stop several times due to wreckage on the road.

MY KINGDOM FOR A BATH, KIRSTEN THINKS, TO WASH MY HAIR *and stick the damp corner of a towel in my ear canal.* Her poor ears have been chafed sore listening to the wheezing and groaning of trains and ferries. *I'll be glad to take off my nylons and put on fresh, clean clothes.* Slipping off her shoes, Kirsten wiggles her toes. A blister is developing on her right foot near the reinforced seam. She forces her foot back into the shoe, wincing as her toes squeeze together. *Maybe I can save the stockings with a dab of nail polish before wringing them out in the hotel sink. I need to remember to apply potato starch to my feet in case the smell bothers my roommates. Hopefully, I'm sharing a room with respectable women. I can't handle drama, especially if I have to share with a German.* Kirsten lets her fingertips run along her hairline. It's damp under the scarf and her hair is plastered to her scalp like a helmet. *Good thing I have my curlers in my suitcase,* she muses. *I'm so exhausted that I don't care about their poking and pricking tonight.*

She looks out the bus window. It's hard to imagine the city was once famed for its cobblestone streets, beautiful street lighting, and grand buildings. After the bombing, only the main shopping street and the area the Allies have taken over have access to basic necessities. Like stubborn ivy, metal wire snakes out of a pile of rubble. Scrawny barefoot children, their faces streaked with grime, scavenge for anything of value. Kirsten lights a cigarette and watches the smoke curl against the bus ceiling, the outline of the city fading into the background.

"You look like someone who's been on the road for a long time!"

Kirsten is about to retort sharply but then recognizes the flat accent in the woman's English pronunciation. "The same could be said about you!" she replies in Danish.

With a raspy laugh, the woman drops into the seat next to Kirsten. "It's beginning to feel real now." She offers Kirsten a hand, speckled with freckles. "Henny."

Kirsten notices her clean, manicured nails. Henny's blue eyes sparkle with life. "Kirsten."

"So, what's your soldier's name, Kirsten?"

"Forest. Air Force Sergeant Forest Edgar Rhodes."

"Ooh, fancy. Mine's just a regular GI. A scoundrel who doesn't treat me right. But what can I do? He's my man." Henny shrugs, then continues. "I'm from Parmagade on Amager. Born Pedersen."

"I'm from the Amager neighborhood, too!" *Does she know me?* Kirsten wonders. "My parents live on Røde Mellemvej. Our family name is also Pedersen!"

"Strange we've never run into each other." Henny leans back in her seat, sighing contentedly.

For the next hour, their conversation flows effortlessly, like a dance, as if they've always known each other. *This is how it should always be when meeting new people,* Kirsten thinks, *straightforward.* She glances at Henny's freckled profile. *She looks a bit like Ingrid before the accident,* she thinks, and closes her eyes for a second.

"I could eat a cow," Kirsten says, as her stomach growls loudly.

Henny laughs. "You're funny. I hope we get to be roommates. If I have to share a room with a German girl, it'll be over my dead body!" Henny rolls her eyes. She pauses and then turns sharply, "First they kill our young men and then they take the ones who are left!"

Kirsten rolls her eyes but thinks, *Wouldn't I do the same in their situation? Desperate times call for desperate measures. Isn't that what I've done myself?*

For the rest of the drive, Kirsten is too busy chatting with Henny to look out the window. A feeling resembling infatuation surges within her, like champagne served in a tall glass — a rising column of fizzy bubbles that burst on the tongue.

"Goodness, how refreshing it is to talk to a sensible person!" Kirsten sighs, feeling an urge to caress Henny's cheek. Instead, she lets her hand brush Henny's on the way to the clasp of her purse. "It feels like I've met my twin when I talk to you."

Henny nods. "We're going to have a great time. I can feel it all the way down to my big toe."

The conversation continues, but inside Kirsten's head, the insecurity begins to hiss. *Just wait,* the voice whispers, *She'll get to know you, and then she'll be sick of you in no time.* Kirsten waves her hand irritably and tries to focus on what Henny is saying about going to Hawaii. *She seems genuine,* Kirsten thinks, giving her new friend's arm a gentle squeeze.

"Perhaps you'll learn to hula dance." Kirsten raises her arms and lets her wrists dance in circles, hands moving like playful fish and hips swaying in her seat.

"Ha! Maybe you should go to Hawaii instead of me? Then I'll take your Forest."

"Promise me you'll take hula lessons."

"I'll write when I need advice on making a grass skirt." Henny laughs, then seems to retreat into herself.

Kirsten observes the corner of her mouth. Where did that cheerful girl go? "Should I be worried about you?" Kirsten asks, placing a hand on Henny's shoulder.

Henny's eyes are shiny. "What have I gotten myself into?"

"What other options do we have? What if we want to do something more with our lives?" Kirsten says, thinking not only of Henny.

"He just needs to keep his job, and I'll take care of the kids and the house." Henny talks about what she thinks it will be like to keep house. She says she hopes Carlo won't gamble all the money away. She lists a bunch of names they might name their kids. Although Henny is just as much a chatterbox as the kimono-clad man on the train, she's much funnier, enticing Kirsten to join the conversation.

Could it be because we're from the same country and share a similar culture? Kirsten thinks. *Or is it because, as women, we share an uncertain future? We both find ourselves standing at a threshold; saying goodbye to what we know, about to step into a new life we don't yet understand. But what lies ahead?* Kirsten considers the other women in the bus. They all have dreams and imaginations, too. But do any of them know what awaits? The road ahead is both alluring and daunting. Hope is one thing they all share — otherwise no one would leap without a lifebuoy, risking everything. Back home in Denmark, they don't understand. Either they find it heartless to leave, or they condemn the women for taking the opportunity. Or maybe they envy them for having the courage?

Leaning back, Kirsten offers her cigarette pack to Henny, who pulls a bar of chocolate out of her purse in return. The rumble of the bus's diesel engine almost distracts Kirsten from her exhaustion. *The notion that nothing can arise from nothing is incorrect. That formula only works in a classroom. If you look around like I have on this journey, you will see that from nothing comes a whole new country. Abracadabra, Marshall Plan.*

〜

As the driver decreases speed, approaches the curb, and finally turns off the engine, the vehicle emits a long, drawn-out groan before the doors open with a thud. Before them stands the Dependent Hotel.

Colonel Christensen
Kirsten

Someone flings a glass through the air. Tensions are high during meals in the communal dining room. Some shriek, others scream. It's always the same. Kirsten narrows her eyes. There's a high-pitched, grating shriek, like metal forks twisting in her ears.

She looks around as she and Henny wait in the doorway. The seating arrangements seem to reflect an unspoken agreement among the brides to segregate themselves. The Dutch and French women sit at separate tables, and the German brides sit far from the others.

"You're going to live in a ramshackle cabin in the middle of the prairie!" A woman nearby chats with her neighbor, "Forget lipstick, lollipops, and apple pies! It's going to be hard labor and spreading your legs!"

"You think it'll be any different for you? That you're going to live in a mansion with your lover?" the neighbor retorts.

Kirsten glances at Henny. "What's with the big grin?"

"This is a hoot! All these girls and their gossip. The only thing missing here is music and men!"

She's not shy, Kirsten thinks, exaggerating her wide-eyed reaction by bringing a hand to her mouth. "You're incorrigible!" Kirsten surveys the room for a place to sit.

"Allow me, ma'am. Your coat?" A waiter leads them to an empty table and pulls out a chair for Kirsten.

"You're an angel!" she smiles at him gratefully.

"Your attire is always impeccable, madam." His eyes travel down her body before he takes her coat and drapes it over his arm.

"A little ingenuity goes a long way," Kirsten says, her cheeks flushing.

Henny clears her throat. "We'd like the daily special. With plenty of gravy, please." As they sit, she eyes the German women. "Acting all high and mighty!"

"Henny, let's just eat."

"They're ruining my appetite."

A man approaches their table, his gaze shifting curiously between Kirsten and Henny. "Are you the two Danish girls staying in the hotel?" His Danish pronunciation is slow, lacks the characteristic guttural sounds, and uses soft American 'R' and 'L' sounds instead.

Kirsten studies him. He speaks Danish well, except for the preposition error. "That must be us. Who taught you to speak such lovely Danish?"

"Colonel Christensen, at your service." He bows his chin to his chest. Then, looking up, he continues, "I'm the commanding officer here at the hotel."

His eyes dart from Kirsten to Henny. He spreads his arms. "You brighten up the place with your Scandinavian looks. Come to me if there's the slightest trouble with the other guests." With a nod towards the Germans' table he adds, "We Scandinavians must stick together. My mother is Danish. I love the language. So please, speak Danish." He smiles.

Drawing a blank on Danish words, Kirsten stammers, "Potatoes... pork..."

Henny bursts out laughing.

Does he understand the words' meaning, or just their sound? Kirsten thinks. Her brain stutters and finally switches to Danish. She winks at Henny and says, "I love you..."

Christensen beams at the declaration. "My mother always tells me that."

Glancing at the colonel, she begins speaking rapidly, pronouncing the name of the Danish dessert that's impossible for foreigners to articulate correctly because of its lingual sounds and elusive vowel pronunciations: "Red berry pudding with cream." Next, she gives the title of the national anthem: *"There is a Lovely Country."*

"God, song, cigarettes, marriage," Henny chimes in.

"Oh, those Danish sounds — I miss them so much!" He bows. "Ladies, it was a pleasure meeting you." He shakes each of their hands. "And remember: you don't have to put up with anything here."

A clatter erupts from the German table as they fling their cutlery onto their plates. With a loud crash, a carafe of water topples to the floor, followed by more shrieks from the women.

"I admire the Scandinavians more than anyone else," the colonel grumbles, shooting a resentful look at the Germans, "That's something no one can take away from me!" With a final salute, he turns on his heel.

"Red porridge with cream, fair skin, and blue eyes. That will serve us well in America," says Kirsten, checking her watch.

The Scandinavian War Bride

Once a week between eight and nine o'clock, a palpable tension hangs in the air as everyone anxiously awaits the reading of the next passenger departure list. As the names are read aloud, the room fills with an expectant silence so thick you could hear a pin drop. Not hearing her name called always frustrates Kirsten. Another meeting looms, and the air crackles with anticipation.

"I hope we're on the same ship," Henny says.

"Of course we will be. We have to stay together for the last leg of our journey." Kirsten squeezes her arm.

Above the mahogany paneling, a succession of framed portraits of elderly men adorn the wall. There's little difference between eating here and at home with the old Prime Minister Stauning and her father looking down on her. She mixes mashed potato into the gravy and spoons it into her mouth.

Music flows from the speakers, weaving around clusters of women and children. A calm has settled over the room, and the scattered conversations are subdued. Lost in thought, Kirsten taps her cigarette, enjoying the relaxation of a post-meal smoke.

"Hurry up, Kirsten! They'll be announcing soon." Henny empties her glass and wipes her mouth. "Wouldn't it be amazing if they called our names tonight?"

Before following Henny, Kirsten traces the edge of the gravy boat with her index finger, then promptly sticks it in her mouth.

Bremerhaven Port of Embarkation I
Kirsten

As she passes through the hotel's foyer, Kirsten grabs an apple, gives it a quick rub on her skirt, and puts it in her purse.

Outside, there's rain in the air. Kirsten glances at the dark gray sky. She smooths the edge of her scarf, checking the knot under her chin.

Henny takes her arm. "I'll lead the way!"

Kirsten gives her a grateful wink. "All will be fine, then."

"Let's begin at the harbor, so we can get a sense of what we're getting ourselves into."

᠌

A FLURRY OF ACTIVITY FILLS THE DOCKS. WITH ITS giraffe-like neck, a crane lifts a full cargo net onto the ship. In the faint sunlight, a corner of a suitcase glints as it swings from its balloon-like cradle. A whole life is contained there; two suitcases per adult. Red Cross nurses and uniformed American soldiers are easily identifiable everywhere — on hand to assist and direct women and children amidst the organized confusion of departure.

Kirsten tilts her head back. "All this commotion is making my palms clammy!"

Henny pulls her away to a quieter space. A breeze caresses Kirsten's sweaty forehead. She takes the cigarette Henny offers her. "Now we know what to expect."

From a distance, Kirsten takes it all in. Passengers are divided into three columns, slowly snaking forward. One line is for German women, with and without children; another for non-German women with children; and a third for non-German women traveling alone. All of them wear identification tags around their necks. A sudden gust of wind blows a tag into a woman's face.

Kirsten puts a hand to her own neck. "It's unbelievable that such delicate threads determine our destinies."

Everyone has their birth and marriage certificates ready. Those with children have their hands full. Some children cry, while others stare blankly. A mother absentmindedly strokes the hair of a whimpering child, her eyes gazing off into an endless distance. At regular intervals, the Red Cross sisters and soldiers bark orders.

"I've seen enough." Walking around the building, Kirsten heads toward the moored ship. The crew must have stretched a canvas cover over the gangway to protect against wind and weather. Or to shield from curious eyes. "It's like a giant stomach, swallowing passengers as they go through the tunnel," she says.

At the dock's edge, Kirsten peers down into the gap between the ship and the gangplank. Several meters below, gray, white-capped waves churn the water. An icy wind blows. Henny seizes Kirsten's arm and yanks her back from the edge.

"Thanks, Henny. I felt a terrifying sense that I was about to fall into the abyss."

Henny nods and gives her a wry smile. Then she points toward a building with a sign that says *Bremerhaven Port of Embarkation*. "First, we have to get our documents processed and approved." Kirsten's eyes follow Henny's finger. "After that, we'll go through the back entrance for sorting." Henny glances over at the clusters of people huddled against the sea breeze.

It looks like the monstrous gangway is the only way to embark, but then Kirsten notices another gangway at the second-floor level. She points to a woman ascending the stairs alone. "That must be the one for us." Kirsten reads the name of the ship, "USS General Harry Taylor." She turns to Henny. "Can you believe it! That could be our ship!" A buzz runs through her body. "Or will be, when it's our turn."

A slender woman in a tight skirt catches her eye as she delicately places her heels on the metal stairs, stepping lightly to avoid scratching them. How does it feel to take that first step onto the ramp? Does the woman even give it a second thought?

"Kirsten, get out of the way!" Kirsten's reverie is broken by Henny's sharp voice, and she quickly steps aside.

A woman with a bag slung over one arm carefully parks her stroller next to the others already lined up. In one swift movement, she removes her baby from the stroller, enveloping the infant in a blanket before stepping without hesitation or a backward glance into American territory. In the blink of an eye, she disappears from Kirsten's view.

A photographer waits to take a picture of the next woman, who is struggling to lift her crying child out of a stroller. Kirsten watches the scene, considering the photographer's viewpoint. She'd never pose for a picture like that. The resulting image will be terrible, showing a nervous mother holding her crying child. In her peripheral vision, Kirsten sees the stroller swaying gently in the wind. Behind her, a huge American flag hangs from the side of the ship.

Down at the dock, family and friends are waving goodbye, singing hometown songs and waving scarves. They're wearing their best clothes — felt hats and long coats. Kirsten has a lump in her throat. *When it's my turn, there will be no one to say goodbye,* she thinks. She turns to Henny. "Let's get out of here."

Dogs
Kirsten

Endless indistinguishable days spill into each other at the hotel, and Kirsten fills them with invented errands to make the silence behave. Spending hours on hair and make-up is no longer sufficient. The weight of waiting for her old life to end and a new one to begin makes her restless.

Today, Kirsten and Henny visit the former Adolf Hitler Platz, which has been renamed Theodor-Heuss-Platz after the war. Kirsten tries to visualize the square before the war. Even after the devastation, the platz is imposing. The height of the buildings, the vast tiled centerpiece, and the vacant window frames are striking. The combined effect makes it easy to picture the square when it was one of the city's most important gathering points.

"Imagine them," Kirsten says, gesturing, "the Nazi party members, their voices filling the square with poison."

Henny shifts her feet nervously on the cobblestones.

"Relax, Henny. I'm not looking for trouble, but I'm curious what the average German thinks." Gently nudging

Henny's arm, Kirsten's eyes scan the people crossing the square, her mind forming a vision of the buildings draped with swastika flags. "Do you see it, Henny? Soldiers with armbands, outstretched arms, and a roaring crowd?" Kirsten can almost hear the roar of their bloodlust demanding release. "Just a few years ago, the dream of the Third Reich, of Germany's global domination, was still alive."

"It's creepy here with all these ghosts, Kirsten. Let's find a place to wander around instead."

The image of a cityscape made of yellow stars fills her mind's eye. "Those poor souls," Kirsten whispers, pulling a handkerchief from her purse to blow her nose. The square is quiet now, the wind swirling dust through the rubble. "Let's get out of here," she says, taking Henny by the arm.

A little away from the square, they find a sidewalk café constructed from debris with patched-up chairs and remnants of columns serving as tables. Kirsten shudders. "Sitting here with my coffee and vanilla-topped apple strudel is out of the question."

Henny nods. "Let's go get something to eat, then find somewhere we can sit for a bit and take a smoke break."

They walk down a block lined with closely packed stalls. "Over here, miss!" a woman shouts to attract their attention. "Chocolate? Coffee? Something to drink?" Each stall competes for customers. The sun smiles down in glimpses as it peeks through heavy, dark gray clouds.

"Hello, ladies. What would you like? We have good homemade beer. Weissbier, Helles, or maybe Dunkles?" says an older man, trying to lure them closer.

Continuing, they pass stalls stacked high with vegetables. "Those are almost as filthy as the German girls in our hotel." Henny gestures toward the salvaged wooden counter where artichokes, Brussels sprouts, and mushrooms lay piled.

"Now you're being crude, Henny." Kirsten tries to conceal her smile behind her hand. It's easy to succumb to the anti-German sentiment fostered by the war.

The aroma of grilled meat wafts toward her: a woman is selling pork knuckle and sauerkraut. A bratwurst sizzles in a pan. The scent of freshly baked bread, crisp and nutty, tempts those walking by. The smell triggers memories for Kirsten. She can almost feel the sausage skin popping and her teeth sinking into the soft, fatty meat. The intensity of the aroma is so powerful that she stops and takes a long, deep breath.

"Do you like sausages?" Henny's eyes sparkle mischievously.

"That depends on what kind," Kirsten retorts, winking at her friend.

Farther down the row of stalls, a pot of soup steams. Kirsten buys a cup and a loaf of bread from the woman. "Hallelujah for supply and demand aligning. They must pay their bills, and I want to make the most of my money."

Henny buys a piece of sausage, and together they stroll down the street looking for a peaceful spot.

Beyond the war-damaged buildings is a park. "Look," Kirsten says, pointing towards the skeletal buildings surrounding the greenery. "They're just like the Germans!"

Henny looks questioningly at her. The ruins of columns stand scattered here and there, their forms bent and broken, yet somehow still striving to maintain a sense of the grandeur of a past era.

"Look at them! Their remnants of pride and prosperity in shambles. They'll be all right," Kirsten nods, "Just like the rest of us, they'll have to gather what remains of their lives and begin again."

They enter the park, which has recovered faster than the rest of the city. Nearby, a group of American soldiers are playing gin rummy. Kirsten and Henny avoid making eye contact. Still, the soldiers whistle at them.

"Hey guys, we're just here to eat our lunch."

"Okay, sweetheart. Let us know if we can do anything for you," a soldier yells.

"Dogs! Always on the hunt."

The most outgoing of the group lets two fingers touch his cap in a gesture of greeting and licks his lips. His friends roar with laughter.

Kirsten looks up at the sky. "Let's hurry and get something in our stomachs." With their backs to the men, they quickly finish their lunch.

SCHOOL FOR WIVES
KIRSTEN

Tonight's Red Cross Club lecture is titled: *How to Be a Good Wife*. Henny and Kirsten sit together with the other war brides, listening.

"Try to be patient with your husband," the Red Cross nurse suggests. "They don't understand what you've been through here in Europe." She arches an eyebrow. "In America, the women won't look kindly on you. They feel they've made sacrifices."

"What sacrifices? They've had meat, butter, and leather shoes!" The outburst comes from one of the older war brides.

The sister gives her a stern look. "They've waved goodbye to their sons and brothers. Fought for your freedom. They've taken over the men's work so the wheels could keep turning in America, produced military supplies, and put food on the table for their children."

Kirsten looks down.

"You shouldn't expect sympathy from everyone; some will react with coldness or indifference."

"We're used to that," Henny whispers to Kirsten.

The sister continues: "Some soldiers are angry because you've taken their place in line and are coming to America before them. You must have answers ready if you're confronted."

"It was about time the rules were changed," whispers Kirsten, "Were wives supposed to stay behind with a child in their arms and another on the way, waiting for their turn?"

"And now let us proceed to a completely different topic." The sister slowly surveys the audience, her gaze lingering until every person in the room is looking directly at her. "The United States faces a housing crisis. Many of you will be living with your in-laws," she explains, eliciting a sigh from the room.

Henny offers Kirsten some chocolate from her purse.

"I hope my mother-in-law bakes pies and makes fried chicken," Kirsten says before stuffing her mouth with chocolate.

Henny's not usually this quiet.

"Chin up, Henny." Kirsten winks reassuringly at her friend and places a hand on her arm. "If things go south with that rascal of yours, you come and stay with me in Texas."

—

After the lecture, the sister's words echo in Kirsten's head: "You must learn to cook American food! You must know how to sew! Understand the value of the American dollar and how far it can stretch!"

We're always expected to jump through hoops for the men, she thinks.

After rattling off all the information, the sister talked about homesickness and the longing they might feel to share their experiences with others. "Perhaps you'll meet fellow war brides from your country, possibly even your own town."

Kirsten's ears perked up at that. Imagine how lovely it would be for her to find a Danish friend in Texas!

Lastly, the nurse discussed American fashion. "Browse the hair salon magazines to help you tailor clothes that match your new culture."

Kirsten glanced down at her own body. She only half-heartedly listened to the rest of the lecture while picturing herself at an American salon, imagining the feel of the rollers in her hair as time slowed to a gentle pause while seeing herself browsing through a glossy magazine, its images whispering promises of a brighter future.

The Bathroom
Kirsten

Kirsten is in the bathroom at the end of the hotel corridor. She lets her tense shoulders drop. So long as she has some time to herself, the day will turn out okay.

With a sharp yank, she pulls the chain. The sound of rushing water echoes deafeningly through the pipes as the cistern empties. A single, persistent drip leaks from the faucet at the sink. Kirsten turns the rusty handle and the gurgling of wastewater in the drain stops with a final sigh.

At the Dependent Hotel, there's always drama; always someone getting on someone else's nerves. Day in and day out, a constant barrage of noise assaults her ears: laughter mixed with shrill arguments, petty bickering, and the crying of women. Kirsten is finding it increasingly irritating, and it has gotten to the point where she feels completely overwhelmed and at a loss for how to cope. In the bathroom, she lets her mask fall. Here, her state of constant alert takes a break.

She stares at her reflection, willing her thoughts to

narrow to which lipstick will complement her outfit. A moist film still coats her skin after the bath. Her toiletries balance on the edge of the sink. Kirsten swipes the condensation from the mirror then bends forward, carefully wrapping her damp hair in a soft towel. As she dresses, her clothes cling to her body.

"Here I come, world," the pouting mouth whispers to her in the mirror before she opens the bathroom door.

"Finally!"

Kirsten stares at the German girl. It's the one she can't stand.

The girl's eyes narrow, her mouth pursed. "You're always in the bathroom!"

"At least I don't parade my husband through the hotel and bring him to my room for some marital indiscretions in front of everyone to see," Kirsten retorts.

The woman's pupils widen. "What's the big deal?" She smacks her lips. "Might as well have some fun, since my husband hasn't left for America yet."

"The regulations clearly state that sleeping with a member of the opposite sex is strictly prohibited." Turning her back, Kirsten squares her shoulders, maintaining a position that allows her to keep the woman in view through the mirror's reflection as she meticulously checks her lipstick. The girl looks away. Kirsten tsks. "Running around in your nightgown, making a fool of yourself!"

She applies another coat of cherry-red lipstick, carefully blending the edges with her fingertip before closing the case and turning back to the woman. "Your noise levels are excessive, particularly during the night." With a sweeping glance that takes in the woman's entire figure, she snarls, "Given your German heritage, I would have expected a more pronounced inclination toward disciplined behavior and rigorous adherence to rules and regulations."

The woman lunges forward.

Kirsten raises an eyebrow. "I'd be careful if I were you. I know the colonel personally. With a snap of my fingers," she does so, an inch from the woman's face, "I could make sure you never embark on the USS General Harry Taylor, if you so much as lay a hand on me."

Red blotches spread across the woman's cheeks and down her neck.

Kirsten shakes her head. "You may have tricked your soldier, but you won't fool me." She twirls her skirt. "You can smear lipstick on a pig's face and dress it in a gown, but it's still a pig."

"You are the one smearing lipstick on a pig," The German girl snorts.

In a sudden, impulsive movement, Kirsten delivers a sharp, stinging slap to the girl's face. "All Germans are guilty. Every single one of you!"

The woman cries out. "I had no hand in it."

"Save it!" A surge of acrid, bitter saliva fills Kirsten's mouth. "Of course you knew what was going on!" She raises a finger to the woman's face. "The stench of corpses hung over Germany while you all held your noses."

The girl's lips tighten. Then she straightens her neck and meets Kirsten's gaze. "When you want to survive, you become more animal than human."

The air seeps out of Kirsten's lungs. "The bathroom will be yours in ten minutes," she says and closes the door, turning the key in the lock. Only then does she let herself cry.

How Long Must We Wait?
Kirsten

Kirsten wants to scream, but only a hoarse whisper escapes her throat. High waves pound the boat, showering it with spray as the vessel is tossed around by the relentless waves. Gasping for air, she desperately tries to keep herself away from the ship's sides to avoid being thrown into the dangerous waters below.

Then she wakes up.

The rhythmic creaking of a bed frame against the opposite wall jolts her awake in the hotel room. *Filth!* Kirsten thinks. She knows exactly what's going on in the next room. She scoots as far from the wall as she can. The muffled sounds of voices and laughter seep through.

"There's a man in there! I can hear them, even though they're trying to be quiet." Kirsten angrily turns to face Henny.

"They'll be done soon." Henny's voice carries a smile.

"I'm complaining to the colonel. This is against the regulations." Kirsten covers her head with her pillow, squeezing with both hands. The sounds fade, but the rocking vibrations still reach her bed. Getting up, she moves the bed away from the wall.

Henny props herself up with pillows and a blanket, then lights a cigarette. Smiling, she wiggles her toes "They seem to be enjoying themselves."

"They can enjoy themselves when they get to America!" Though Kirsten tries to remain angry, her voice softens as she gestures toward Henny's cigarette, "Give me one." She lights up and blows smoke out of her nose.

A long, low groan echoes from the next room. Laughter replaces the rhythmic thumping. A moment later: a creaking door and soft footsteps.

"She's terrorizing the hallway with her nighttime prowling!"

"Relax, Kirsten, they're finished."

Kirsten punches the wall.

"We'll get some too, soon." Henny winks at Kirsten. "I think you need it."

Kirsten glares at her friend but then bursts into laughter. "You're really something!"

"How much longer will we be stuck here?" Henny flicks ash off her blanket.

Kirsten gets up, finds an ashtray, and places it between the beds. "I chatted with a girl in the dining room who's been waiting for nine months!" She taps the ash from her cigarette and raises an eyebrow.

"I sure hope the kid is his."

"Henny!" Kirsten slaps her friend's bed frame.

Henny moves to the foot of Kirsten's bed where she sits and cradles Kirsten's feet in her hands. "It'll be our turn soon. In more ways than one, Kirsten-girl."

Bon Voyage, Ladies!
Kirsten

After weeks of waiting, the day has finally come. Today, Kirsten boards USS General Harry Taylor. Too nervous to eat, she skips the hotel's breakfast and heads for the reception area.

"Mrs. Sgt. Forest Edgar Rhodes, room fifty-six. I'd like to check out." She shows her passport and hands over her key. The receptionist's finger runs over the check-in list, crosses out Kirsten's name, writes the date, and finishes with a flourish. He then hands her a receipt and places the logbook back on its shelf.

The end of one chapter and the beginning of a new one, Kirsten thinks.

"Please leave your suitcase and trunk here, and I will arrange for a soldier to transport them to the bus." He consults his papers again. "You'll be on bus number five."

Outside, eight buses are waiting. Spotting number five, Kirsten greets the driver, who marks her off his list and tucks his pencil behind his ear.

"Could you make sure my suitcase is placed so it doesn't get scratched? The trunk doesn't matter as much."

Grumbling, the driver slowly gets out of his seat, locates the suitcase, and puts it where she wants.

Kirsten hurries on board and finds a seat. Eventually, without any sense of urgency and not a single wrinkle of anxiety on her forehead, Kirsten watches as Henny saunters from the hotel onto the bus.

"You certainly took your time, young lady!" Kirsten says, giving the seat next to her a pat.

"Some of us are more excited to see our men than others." Henny plops down next to Kirsten.

"We can't put off the inevitable much longer, I'm afraid."

"We can still delay it a little." With a wink, Henny bites into an apple, sending juice flying.

They sit in silence as the bus fills up. Kirsten can barely contain her excitement.

Then: "Ladies. All aboard," the driver says, and pulls away from the curb.

⁓

They drive along the boulevard, passing ruined block after ruined block in reverse order of her arrival to the hotel. Turning away from the window, Kirsten reclines in her seat. *Finally!* Thousands of women before her have followed their hearts and ambitions, left their fathers and mothers, sisters and brothers. Now it's her turn.

It has taken weeks for the office workers to review the paperwork, transferring documents through each stage of the process from desk to desk and obtaining the necessary approvals with each click-clacking stamp and signature. And after the final check, Kirsten's name has officially been approved. She is now listed among the passengers on the USS General Harry Taylor.

The bus turns off the main road and pulls into the port. Bringing the vehicle to a complete stop, the driver switches off the engine, turns in his seat, and says, "Safe travels, ladies!"

Port of Embarkation II
Kirsten

The port's thudding heartbeat, a deep, rhythmic pulse, settles like a gut-thrum in Kirsten's chest. The sign, *Bremerhaven Port of Embarkation*, draws her toward the building. Kirsten clutches her papers; the gateway to her new life. Hope and sorrow battle within her. And love. *America will be my new home,* she thinks, *escaping the war in Europe and a family that no longer accepts me.* She wipes her eyes with a frustrated swipe. *They're not worth the tears.* But looking at the ship, she feels a surge of fear. *Will I ever see them again?* she wonders. *Will I become someone else over there?* She shakes her head. *My future looks brighter and more promising than my past.*

Not far away, a group of American soldiers are whiling away the time playing cards. Kirsten's mind wanders to Forest. She pictures him: a cigarette dangling from his lips and a drink at his elbow. Is he counting the days until her arrival? Is his anticipation filled with joy or anxiety? Excitement or dread of the unknown? Has he given as much thought to their future as she has?

Kirsten's heels echo on the cobblestones as she and Henny head to the building. Inside, she walks up to the counter and hands over her documents. Without even glancing at her, the indifferent clerk takes them, his eyes fixed on the page before him, affixing the stamp with a swift motion. *Click.* Like a quick vaccination shot, barely felt.

"I never imagined my last hours in Europe would be marked by the sound of clamping." Kirsten shudders at the metallic noise. "If I hear one more stamp I'm jumping in the sea!" she mutters in Danish to Henny, and bows her head in thanks to the pen-pusher.

"Then you better get ready to take a dip, my dear Kirsten!" Henny gestures to the row of slouched backs waiting in the queue ahead; they have only just begun their stamp-clacking journey.

Inch by inch, Kirsten and Henny progress in line. Kirsten rolls onto the balls of her feet. She'd been up several times during the night, tossing and turning, a nagging feeling that she'd forgotten something plagued her mind. She shakes her head. Of course, everything was where it should be. The freshly pressed clothes and ready-to-wear dress hung on the chair. The travel documents, wrapped in brown cardboard. Kirsten sifts through the papers in her hands. Birth and marriage certificates, the health check-up, it's all there — paper, proof, and the fragile momentum of readiness.

Her gaze drifts toward the harbor. "I hope we don't hit a submarine or a mine!"

"Easy now, Kirsten."

Last night, Kirsten's thoughts spiraled down anxious paths. *What is the procedure for escaping onto a lifeboat if the USS General Harry Taylor capsizes? Will there be room for all of us, or will it be like the Titanic?*

"What about the stories of seasick women lying around on the deck, unable to control their vomiting?"

"Kirsten," Henny says, grasping her hand, "If that happens, we viking daughters will have a couple of boozy, smoky days in our cabin."

Kirsten nods. "I don't know what I'd do without you," she says, smiling gratefully at Henny. *I wonder how the bathroom facilities will be with so many people?* she thinks to herself. "What if we're not in the same cabin?" Exhaustion settles over Kirsten like a chill. "I miss Forest," she says, blinking away tears. "It'll be good to live together, even if it'll be with his mother."

"And here we thought we'd lack for nothing in God's own country!" Henny sighs.

"Housing shortage, they say."

"Maybe she'll become like a mother to you, Kirsten."

Kirsten feels a lump in her throat. "Sorry, Henny. I'm probably just a bit out of sorts."

They've reached the *Dependents Staging Area,* moving along in slow, uneven steps. *Here we go, like cattle, herded by procedure,* Kirsten thinks, fishing her cigarette case out of her bag.

"Not here, Kirsten. We're packed like sardines in a can."

Kirsten lets out a sigh. "I'll smoke if I feel like it."

The woman in front turns, giving her a disapproving look. "Watch out!"

All the fear, nervousness, and uncertainty she's been feeling for months seem to have coalesced into a tight knot of anxiety that threatens to overwhelm her at any moment. As Kirsten moves forward, she pushes the woman in front of her and flicks ashes onto her bag.

"Kirsten, drop it! You might not be allowed to board if you do that." Henny pokes Kirsten.

Henny is right, Kirsten muses, grinding out her cigarette on the case. Discovering some chocolate in her purse, she quickly pops it in her mouth.

"Maybe that'll keep you quiet?" Henny laughs.

As the sweetness slides down her throat, most of Kirsten's bitterness fades.

"One more question means one less question. Soon we'll be on our way: you to your Forest and me to my sorry excuse for a man." Henny makes a sweeping gesture with her arm toward the line of clerks. "Meanwhile, the bureaucrats stay behind, asking their tedious questions."

☽

AT LONG LAST, AFTER NAVIGATING THE NUMEROUS counters and enduring the endless document stamping process, they have finally completed the check-in procedure.

Now, they find themselves outside. A Red Cross nurse lifts a gaunt child out of a stroller and guides the emaciated pregnant mother, who is holding another child's hand, away from the line she's been standing in. Deep, dark circles shadow the woman's eyes. With her free hand, she adjusts her coarse scarf as the nurse leads her into the line for German women. Kirsten flicks the stub of her Lucky Strike onto the cobblestones and grinds it out.

A cacophony of foreign voices swirls fragments of exotic melodies from distant lands into the wind. Up on the deck, women and children wave. A streamer spirals down to the pier. A moment later, the space between those saying goodbye and those being bid farewell is filled with colorful paper garlands.

Turns out it was pointless for her to worry about the leather suitcase getting scratched on the bus. Now it's lying there on the dockside, all jumbled up with the others. A hoist mechanism carries the luggage-laden net and deposits it into a hole in the deck. A gust of cool November wind snatches Kirsten's ID tag and blows it against her face. She swats at it irritably.

☾

The ship unfurls from the pier like a curved petal. The steamer's bow looks powerful enough to smash through an iceberg. Kirsten imagines standing on the deck, looking out over the sea. What will it be like to be on a converted warship, where soldiers, gunpowder, and bullets have been replaced by refugees, war brides, and children? Because it's smaller than other war bride ships, she expects the steamer to rock heavily in open seas. She would much rather have sailed on the Queen Mary, which accommodates over two thousand passengers.

It's probably just as well that I'm going on this smaller vessel, Kirsten thinks. *The number of annoying people I can get in a fight with will be limited.* She hears a *swoosh* and sees a spray of foam striking the side of the hull, as if the ship is telling her it might well exceed her expectations. Tilting her head back, she scans the gangway from entrance to exit. It's like peering through a keyhole.

"You gonna stand there all day?"

Kirsten steps aside to let the woman pass. Following her with her eyes, she watches her take steady steps toward the ship. Kirsten looks at Henny. Then she grabs the railing. The thread to her family snaps as a rope of love pulls her forward.

"Goodbye," she whispers over her shoulder, and takes the first step.

USS GENERAL HARRY TAYLOR

Cabin 175
Kirsten

It smells stuffy in here. Salt, sugary decay and nicotine. Two bunks, four beds. Or five, since one of the lower bunks has a crib attached to its side. They had been informed that the women with children would be separated from those without. *That's disappointing.* Kirsten clicks her tongue. Good thing she's the first to arrive. She doesn't want the bunk above the crib — or the lower one opposite. If there's one thing she's learned, it's that a mother always needs help. Still, Kirsten was hoping to get a lower bunk. It would be convenient if she gets seasick. The upper bunk on the far side will have to do. At least it has a porthole.

Her suitcase is already here. Someone has also placed Henny's next to hers. Maybe the crib is a mistake? Did the crew forget to remove it after the last crossing?

Kirsten loosens her scarf and tosses it onto the bunk. Peering down the cabin's length, she notices a built-in door. Behind it, a bathroom reveals itself. What luxury! Shower, sink and toilet. The bar of soap on the sink smells of honey and jasmine.

The cabin has two closets. Blouses, scarves, underwear, and stockings go on one shelf, while dresses and skirts hang on the rod. Kirsten takes a clean scarf from the stack, folds it into a triangle, places it over her hair, and ties the ends under her chin.

"Peep, peep, the bird's nest is hidden away," she hums, standing in front of the mirror as she dabs lipstick on her cheeks. "There! Much better! Now you don't look like a corpse," she says to her reflection.

☽

SITTING ON HER BUNK, SHE LIGHTS A CIGARETTE. Stretches an arm out in front of her and studies her nails. "Ugh, you need some attention!" She runs her thumb over the chipped polish. The last few days have been filled with practical tasks, traveling, carrying luggage, and opening bags with zippers and buckles. Kirsten rests her head back against the wall, the nicotine makes her dizzy. She massages the tension at the back of her skull.

After smoking, she climbs down, rummages through her wash bag for nail polish and sets it on the desk. Beside it, she places her fountain pen, marking to her co-passengers, she intends to be the first at the table to write a letter.

The cabin door opens, and Henny appears. "You vanished!"

"There were so many people." Kirsten spreads out her arms. "Grab a bunk and make yourself at home."

Tossing her purse onto the bunk beneath Kirsten's, Henny walks over to the closets.

The door opens again. A woman with a child on her hip steps in. On her shoulder she carries a canvas bag. With one foot in the door, she turns and reaches for a suitcase with her free hand.

"And who might you be?" Kirsten makes an effort to look stern. "I hope he won't give us any trouble." She points her cigarette at the slumbering child.

"Ilse." The woman nods. "He's a good, quiet boy." She looks lovingly at the child.

Something about the woman's pronunciation, specifically the G's and vowels, catches Kirsten's attention. "You're German! No way am I sharing a cabin with you!" Kirsten steps towards her. "Aren't you supposed to be at the other end of the ship with your own kind?"

The woman flinches. Henny shoots Kirsten a nervous glance.

"I don't give a damn if it's only for ten days! I refuse to share a room with one of them!"

Ilse meets Kirsten's gaze. "They gave me this number."

A sudden tilt of the ship sends Ilse off balance for a moment. In a swift, protective move, Kirsten stops Ilse from falling. A look of gratitude passes between them before Kirsten quickly retreats. *She's just like me*, Kirsten thinks. *Just a young woman shaped by her country and family. There are bad people everywhere. And good ones.* Still, it's hard with the Germans, especially in group settings. But here in the cabin, one woman to another, compassion wins. Humanity wins.

After settling in, Ilse carefully places the child in the crib, puts her bag on the bunk, and goes to the closets.

"I'd be careful about turning my back if I were you." Kirsten says, hearing her voice harden. "You never know what people might do."

"Kirsten, let's check out the ship." Henny's voice is cheerful. "We've got time before dinner."

Out in the hallway, Henny stops. "Imagine if we were crammed together with forty women like the German girls are at the other end of the ship. You almost feel sorry for them."

"Honestly, Henny! There's a difference." Kirsten digs a piece of gum out of her purse. "Did you notice her teeth? Porous as sugar cubes." Despite her harsh words, Kirsten can't help but feel a pang of pity for Ilse. What a terrible ordeal that poor girl must have endured, judging by the state of her teeth. Kirsten feels the urge to turn around and apologize. Why does she have this habit of being so tough on the outside when her inner self feels so different?

Shaking off the thoughts, Kirsten instead focuses on the long hallway she's standing in. On each side, there are doors identical to theirs. She taps her temple with a finger. "Number one-seven-five."

"Write it on your inner wrist," Henny instructs.

"Like a KZ tattoo? No, thanks!"

I need a way to remember that number, Kirsten thinks. *One-seven-five. I'm all alone. That's number one. We were seven siblings in total. Only five remain. That comes to one-seven-five.* Kirsten shakes her head. *No, that's too depressing. Give it another shot. One-seven-five. I'm the number one, I have a good figure that resembles the number seven, and hopefully I'll soon be pregnant with a big, round belly that will make me look like the number five. Voila, one-seven-five!* Kirsten smiles. *That's a story I'll remember.*

"I'll remember it. One-seven-five."

"If not," Henny says with a playful wink, "I'm confident many crew members would happily escort a charming young Scandinavian woman back to her accommodations." With a flirtatious sway of her hips and a playful glance, Henny adds kissing noises and mimics a soldier's voice. "Howdy, ma'am," she says, touching her invisible cap. She gives Kirsten a nudge: "Don't you have eyes in your head? Look at all the lovely men we're surrounded by. We're going to have a swell time on this trip, Kirsten-mouse."

Breakfast
Kirsten

The next morning, Kirsten heads to the dining room for breakfast. The place is half-empty, but she assumes that's just the schedule making room for everyone.

"How did you sleep last night, ma'am?" A waiter stands ready by the breakfast buffet.

"Absolutely splendid. I took a nightcap before bed and slept like a rock through the foghorn and the swaying of the boat." Kirsten looks around. "Where is everybody?"

"Not everyone has had the same pleasant night as you."

Kirsten shakes her head. "I didn't realize how bad it was, although on the way here, I had to zigzag in between passengers. People are throwing up everywhere." Kirsten recalls seeing a woman vomit without any regard for the wind's direction.

"Unless you like children, I'd be careful not to tell anyone how strong your stomach is." He lowers his voice: "The Red Cross sisters usually advertise for babysitters for the worst-off mothers."

"Thanks for the heads-up." Kirsten looks at the buffet. Sweet and baked scents waft toward her. "There's a silver lining to every cloud." Pancakes, pastries, tarts, and bread are neatly arranged on platters. "That means more for the rest of us." Although she recognizes most of it, she makes a mental note to learn how to prepare an American breakfast.

One platter holds rows of small, thick, golden pancakes, each about the size of a saucer. Unlike large, flat European crepes, these are puffy. As Kirsten forks a pancake onto her plate, she wonders what makes them rise. She tears off a small piece and puts it into her mouth. Blueberries! A bittersweet flavor makes her mouth water and guides her gaze towards a pitcher beside the platter.

Henny's face has a look of mild confusion etched on it as she stands behind Kirsten, observing the buffet before her.

"That's some kind of sticky stuff," Kirsten says to Henny over her shoulder, nodding in the direction of the pitcher. Henny is busy piling bacon onto her plate. Golden drips stream down the side of the pitcher. "Want some of this on your bacon?" As Kirsten lifts the pitcher, a dark, sweet aroma hits her nose. Henny shakes her head. "A little splash of this and a piece of that white toast, and there won't be a dry eye in the house!"

"I don't think that's how Americans eat it."

Kirsten shrugs. "There's no right or wrong way to eat your food." A sign next to a plate of fried bread slices reads: *French toast*. "Forest loves that," Kirsten says, gesturing to the sign. "Bread dipped in a mixture of cinnamon, eggs, and milk, then fried in a pan with a pat of butter until golden."

"They look bone dry." Henny arches a skeptical eyebrow.

"That's why you need this." Kirsten waves the pitcher. "Don't judge a book by its cover." She points to the golden slices. "They taste a bit like a good old-fashioned Danish cinnamon roll."

Henny puts a couple of the squares on her plate and takes the maple syrup.

"Go easy, or you'll get a toothache," Kirsten grins.

Henny returns the pitcher to its place.

"No wonder Forest thinks our rye bread is sour when he's used to this." Kirsten takes a glass of juice, a few pieces of fruit, and a bowl of cornflakes. "It's like a party in my mouth when all I can hear is crunching and popping."

Henny laughs. "I thought you hated loud noises. Have you tried this?" Henny nods towards a bowl on the table. "It looks like dog poop, but it smells great."

Kirsten smiles. "It's peanut butter. It tastes much better than it looks." Spreading peanut butter thickly on toast, she adds banana slices, folds it, and takes a bite. Henny imitates her. "It tastes heavenly but it sticks to the roof of your mouth," Kirsten says with her mouth full. The flavor is rounder and nuttier than Danish walnuts and hazelnuts. "Finish it with a glass of milk." Kirsten wipes her mouth with the back of her hand. 'Give it a swish and use your tongue to check your teeth before you open your mouth."

Henny grimaces. "Next time I'll just have butter and jam."

"You just have to get used to it." Kirsten rolls her eyes.

"Good thing I don't get seasick." Henny makes a gagging sound.

"It probably won't be the last time you try something you don't like," says Kirsten, giving her hips a wiggle.

Information Meeting
Kirsten

The nurse looks at the attendees with a serious expression on her face. "More than twenty percent of the women on this ship are sick," she says somberly. "This is especially true of the German women, whose facilities differ from yours."

"As they should," Kirsten mumbles, fiddling with the sleeve of her cyclamen-colored dress suit.

"Many mothers have such severe seasickness that they are struggling to take care of their children."

"This place reeks!" a woman's voice rises above the crowd.

"We're knee-deep in yuck!" another woman chimes in.

The nurse gives them a long stare. "That's why we're asking for volunteers to take care of the sick mothers and their infants." She holds a clipboard with a pen attached to it. A wave of dissatisfied murmuring spreads.

Leaning toward Henny, Kirsten whispers, "I feel bad for the kids." Henny nods. "But I can't," Kirsten adds, "I wouldn't take care of a German women even if you paid me. Not after what their people did."

"We are overwhelmed," the nurse continues, "and risk having to delay continuing our trip to get assistance. If that happens, everyone will arrive in New York later than planned." She lets the message sink in. "We urgently appeal to your better selves."

"I don't have a better self. Not yet." Kirsten sighs in frustration. "But I want to get to Forest as quickly as possible."

"We'll contact everyone who signs up to volunteer." The nurse pins the sign-up sheet to the wall by the exit before leaving the room.

A Red Cross sister steps up to the podium. "We understand it's been a grueling day."

Kirsten glances at the other women. Many appear weary and drained. She prods Henny gently. "They look like they've had six meals today — three down and three up." Henny lets out a giggle.

"We thought a change of pace might do you good," The Red Cross sister says, "Tomorrow morning, you'll find the Taylor-Post with the day's schedule and some intriguing American facts."

Clapping and whistling erupt from the group of women.

"Each night in the cinema, under the supervision of our ship's chaplain, a new film will be shown." She smiles. "All are welcome — except children."

Thank God, Kirsten thinks.

"You'll find the program in that folder on the table." The Red Cross sister nods towards it. "Grab one after the meeting on your way out."

Kirsten straightens in her chair. Finally, something is happening beyond the scheduled monotony.

"And then there are the competitions," the sister continues, listing them off.

Henny nudges Kirsten. "Why don't you enter the 'best legs on the ship' contest, Kirsten?" she winks. Kirsten puts a finger to her lips. What the sister is saying is too important for her to joke around with Henny right now.

"In our experience, most of you don't know much about America. You're coming to a new country, with customs and habits you're not used to."

"I can't wait." Kirsten clicks her tongue impatiently.

"But how many of you know the names and capitals of the different states? How many of you know American history?"

Most of the women groan. "It's completely irrelevant," one says loudly, "so long as we can cook and bear children for our men!" The room fills with laughter.

"Listen to their stupid cackle!" Kirsten turns to give the woman a disdainful look.

The Red Cross nurse waits for the noise to subside. "You need to assimilate. Understand what your men are shaped by. Understanding a country's history and geography will teach you that."

Henny lets out a sigh. "I couldn't care less. As long as people can live peacefully side by side, they can do as they please."

"The lectures will discuss American democracy and the Constitution. It's vital to learn how the American voting system functions before you cast your first vote."

"I'll just vote however my husband tells me to," the woman from before pipes up again, this time earning applause from the room.

"Good grief, what a bunch of featherbrains." Kirsten feels a growing sense of irritation creep in.

"Come on, Kirsten." Henny squeezes Kirsten's arm. "I'm clueless about politics too."

"You could learn, though." Kirsten puts her purse in her lap and grabs her lipstick and mirror. "I can't wait to find out how Congress makes laws!"

"What does that have to do with me, Kirsten?"

"It has everything to do with you, you silly goose! Why do you think you're here?"

Henny raises a questioning eyebrow.

"Without the War Brides Act, we never could have come to America!" Kirsten thinks about the chaos that followed the war as thousands of wives found themselves stuck, unable to join their soldier husbands in America, until the quota laws were changed in 1945. But while the War Brides Act thrilled waiting wives and fiances, it angered soldiers who'd fought in Europe and now faced a delayed homecoming. With a click, Kirsten closes her purse. "It really does matter who's president and in Congress, even for us regular folks."

"Would you be able to answer these questions?" The sister gestures toward a chart.

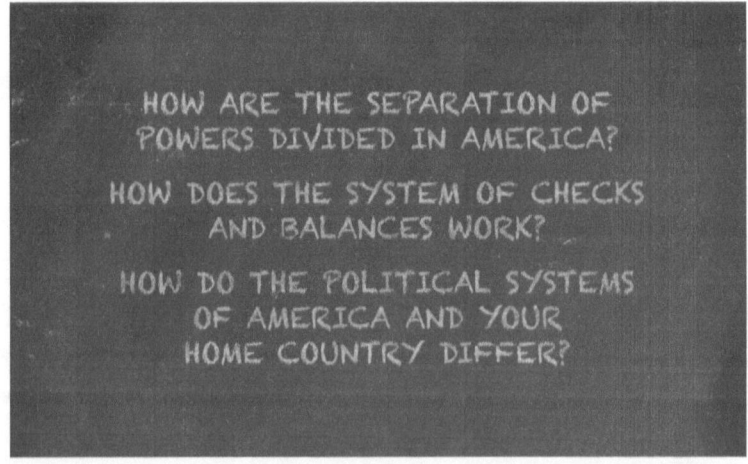

She scans the room. "I strongly encourage participation from those of you who don't know the answers." Pointing a lecturing finger, she continues, "It's your civic duty. The classes will be held in the Great Salon."

Just as Kirsten thinks the speech is over, the sister's stern gaze falls upon the group that seems least engaged. "There are forty-eight states in America, and on this voyage, you represent forty-five of them. The youngest of you is sixteen and has an eighteen-month-old daughter. The oldest is thirty-five. Just as each of you are different, so too are the areas you'll be living in America," the sister says. "So, for those of you with a songbird in your chest, we'll practice the American national anthem daily."

"*The Star-Spangled Banner*," Kirsten whispers. "I don't understand why Americans chose that one. It's so hard. Almost impossible to hit an honest note," she adds, humming a few notes to demonstrate her point to Henny.

"For those with children, one hour of childcare is available daily between five and six p.m. to allow parents some time to themselves. You can find the schedule displayed outside the nursery. If you can't find it, the ship's map clearly shows its location. This map will also appear in tomorrow's Taylor-Post."

The women are starting to shift in their seats.

"Just a few more logistical details," the sister says, smiling. "There's a playroom equipped with changing tables and facilities for sterilizing bottles."

Kirsten is growing bored, too.

"Lastly, there's a day of classes on how to make American food."

Several women groan again. Kirsten smiles. *Just the thought of food and they're about to faint.* She needs to learn how to make Kentucky fried chicken for Forest.

"Are there any questions?"

A woman raises her hand. "If you could offer just one piece of advice for our new life, what would it be?"

"Pay attention to your surroundings, be flexible, and embrace change."

Kirsten notes her words. *Maybe we really have no idea about what our future holds for us,* she thinks.

The sister sends a warm look across the sea of women. "You'll figure it out. Getting this far speaks volumes about your determination. Best of luck!"

᠊᠊᠊᠊᠊᠊᠊᠊᠊᠊

On her way out, Kirsten grabs a couple of brochures from the table. When she reaches the list of volunteer helpers for the Germans, she hesitates.

"Hey Kirsten, let's go!" Henny calls from the door.

Tearing her eyes from the list, Kirsten turns and follows.

Parker 51
Kirsten

Kirsten makes a brief stop at the ship's store. The shop sells a wide variety of items, from small perfumes and scarves to painkillers. But it's the display at the counter that draws Kirsten in.

The case gleams like gold. Kirsten trails her index finger along the pen. Its inscription reads: *Parker 51 Fountain Pen*. She taps her foot. It's within her budget. Writing ought to be an enjoyable experience. Her old fountain pen is temperamental; it only works when it wants to. Kirsten counts the cost on her fingers. There will be things she can't afford.

"Want to give it a try?" The man behind the counter hands her a piece of test paper.

Why did she agree? The ink flows smoothly in a long, beautiful stream. Her writing looks like elegant calligraphy:

Martha Pedersen

"Martha. Is that your name?" a deep voice sounds behind her.

Kirsten startles. The pen slips between her fingers and leaves an angry streak on the test paper. The aroma of Lucky Strikes and Old Spice envelops her. "Unfortunately, no."

"Maybe it could be for an evening?" His voice is soft and warm. Kirsten feels her heart race. *Stop it*, she scolds. *You mustn't let your body take over because of a man.* She admonishes herself and turns on the rational side of her brain. He's probably one of those guys they've been warned about. There are so many stories from the crossings about questionable behavior between brides and crew members.

"Sorry." He steps back. "Beautiful women make me nervous." He nods toward the pen in her hand. "Do you enjoy writing?"

"I'd like to write to my mother," Kirsten replies. What makes her say that? It's true that she wants to write home, but why didn't she seize the moment and tell him she'd write to her husband? "I need to tidy up before dinner," she says apologetically, trying to pass him.

"Ah yes. Protocols must be followed," he declares, making way for her.

Kirsten feels her tongue pressing against her cheek. Who does he believe she's doing this for? She returns the pen to the man at the counter. "I'll think about it until tomorrow."

☽

"Where's the fountain pen you had yesterday?" Kirsten asks the shopkeeper the next day.

"It's sold," he replies flatly.

Kirsten's jaw clenches in frustration, the disappointment so intense she feels like bursting into tears. "Then I'll take the dark pink lipstick and the matching nail polish."

The Scandinavian War Bride

Why did I buy this lipstick and nail polish? Kirsten muses. *I don't want either, really.* Disappointed by not getting the fountain pen she'd longed for, she felt compelled to buy something else; leaving empty-handed seemed wrong.

Back in the cabin, she feels a ringing in her ears and a growing restlessness. She picks up her nail file. As she climbs up onto the bunk, her hands tremble. She files her nails, the flakes fall in a rhythmic flow making Kirsten smile as she hums in her head, *Like the dance of a violinist's bow across the strings,* she thinks, filing away. *I'll have no nails left if I continue this.*

Tossing the nail file aside, Kirsten leaps from the bunk, snatches her coat, and slams the cabin door shut behind her.

Standing at the railing, she turns her face toward the wind and cools her cheeks. In her pocket lies her old fountain pen, the confirmation gift from her parents. That same day, Martha gave her a fish's skin holder. Kirsten takes out the fountain pen and holds it up. Almost of its own accord, it slips through her fingers. Deep below, she watches the boat's wake ripple the water's surface.

"If you want something, you should never let the chance slip away."

Beside her stands the man she'd seen the day before. Kirsten's heart skips. Again, she has the feeling that he's snuck up on her.

"I didn't hear you." Stepping back, she avoids his eyes. "I hope you're happy." She hardens her voice. "I assume it was you who bought the fountain pen?" She gives him a sharp look. "Are you a prolific writer?"

He chuckles softly before replying, "My mother would probably say no. But I didn't buy it for myself." He reaches into his pocket. "It belongs with you," he says, holding out the case.

Hesitantly, she reaches for it. What is she to do? Martha's words echo in her memory: *You never get something for nothing.* "I can't accept it."

"Of course you can." He searches her eyes. "You just don't want to."

Kirsten considers him. He is very attractive. Tall, with nice teeth and big hands. Stepping closer, she glances around. The ship is constantly filled with rumors and hushed conversations, speculating about the crew and passengers. "Can we do this somewhere else?" she whispers.

"Of course. The gossip hounds… I understand."

She catches his scent as he shifts. It's a pleasant smell; something unique to him, mixed with cologne. She wants to take his arm. But of course, that's not possible here, where everyone is watching one another.

They move away from the railing, positioning themselves closer to the ship's hull. He steps closer to her. "So, now we're hiding here." His coat grazes her cheek.

"I wouldn't call it that." Kirsten steps back. How should she respond if he makes a move? Maybe she wants him to make a move? An urge to lean against him, press herself into him, rushes over her. She takes a deep breath. A moment later, he takes another step closer. As he lifts his left arm and rests it near her face, his coat opens. That's how Forest stood that evening by the barrack wall. Kirsten feels metal pressing against her back. This can't happen. And yet, she turns her face upward. Kind, golden eyes. Her gaze travels slowly down his shirt buttons, lingering on his belt, and finally settling on the zipper of his pants. Suddenly, she envisions him spinning her around, gripping her waist tightly; imagines instinctively pushing her hips back, feeling the pressure of his lower body against hers, her face nestled under his chin as she surrenders to the moment and he smoothly enters her. She closes her eyes, but when she opens them again, the images won't disappear. Visions of him squeezing one of her breasts fill her head. She feels the warmth of it and wants to drive a fist into her crotch. She wants the impact to be forceful, like a hammer blow, like a deep pain. Like a physical void that must be filled — now!

Reality crashes back as the foghorn blares and the ship's door opens.

No! She must think of Forest and what awaits. Kirsten pushes the man away from her tense body and steps sideways. Straightening, she says. "You're giving me the fountain pen, then?" She fixes her eyes on him. Clearing her throat, she steadies her trembling voice. "What's in it for you?"

"Your companionship would be a comfort during the journey."

Kirsten smooths her coat. What kind of companionship is he thinking of? "If you're in civilian clothes," she says, her tone flat, "the regulations are different. That might work."

"Oh, that nonsense about you ladies not being allowed to talk to soldiers. No one can see you playing cards with an officer when I'm in my slacks."

"And the fountain pen?"

"Why don't you write me when you arrive in America?" He brushes his finger gently against her cheek. "I think we have a lot in common."

Kirsten blinks. "I'm not sure that's appropriate for a married woman."

"Look," he says, reaching into his pocket. "Let me give you my address." He suddenly looks serious. "You seem like a clever girl. I'm sure you can memorize it." Then he smiles at her. "In the meantime, we'll meet here on the ship in the evenings and get to know each other better."

Kirsten watches her fingers curl around the case.

"When we dock, I'll go home to California," he says. "Every day I'll go to my mailbox and hope there's a letter from you."

"You're putting me in a rather awkward position." Kirsten nervously bites her lip.

"You seem to have a strong will." He hands her a slip of paper, his hand lingering over hers.

"Deal," Kirsten says, pulling her hand away. She wants to leave. This game is dangerous. If she violates any regulations, she risks being denied entry to New York and forced to remain on the ship when it heads back to Europe.

"I'll look forward to it." He searches her gaze.

Those eyes! Kirsten feels the pull in her stomach again. Breaking free, she gives a nod, hand on the door handle, before slipping inside and hurrying to her cabin.

Her room is empty; the beds made with military precision, as they have been taught to do.

꽃

PERHAPS HENNY AND ILSE ARE ATTENDING THE informational meeting. No, tonight's regular program is canceled because of problems with the German girls. It has been reported that some female passengers broke the ship's rules by engaging in sexual activity with crew members. Ilse and her fellow countrywomen are in a disciplinary meeting, and all other nationalities have been strictly prohibited from attending. Only God knows where Henny is. They should both be here any minute.

Kirsten pulls the note out from under her fountain pen.

> You Know Who
> 155 52nd Street
> Los Angeles
> California

Settling into her bunk, she opens her book. *Men!* "No, stick to Forest," she whispers to herself. Looking back at the address, she knows it is now stored in her memory. Piece by piece, she tears the note into smaller and smaller fragments, creating a little heap on the book before scooping them up and popping them in her mouth, chewing with determination. After a while, she feels a hard lump form between her molars. Prying the paper lump free with her tongue, she swallows.

She examines her new fountain pen. It resists her grip for a moment before yielding as she pulls it from its holder. She flips to the first page of her book and writes:

This book belongs to Mrs. Sgt. Forest Edgar Rhodes.

Drill
Kirsten

Bubbly sea spray coats the deck before vanishing into its cracks and crevices. As instructed, the women stand in rows. From inside the ship, the sound of children crying can be heard. The rain lashes down. Skirts hug legs; scarves rip free and vanish into the sea.

Sheltered from the rain, the captain stands on a raised platform. His uniform sleeves, adorned with eagles, appear to survey the women, their eyes looking left and right. A row of gleaming golden buttons shines on his dark blue uniform. His face is stern, and his gray-blue eyes sweep over the assembled crowd as he declares, "Your ship is one of thirty carrying wives to American servicemen." He pauses, drawing out the moment. "Notwithstanding our present distance from the continental United States, your current location is under American authority." He casts another glance over the women. "In a few days, you will set foot on American soil. While not yet in America, this vessel remains under American jurisdiction."

"Gosh," muses Kirsten, "He's military to the core."

"Aboard this vessel, United States military law is in effect. Consequently, you are now subject to American laws." His upright stance and commanding presence give the impression of someone unaccustomed to being questioned.

"That sounds serious, Herr Captain." The German woman elicits laughter from her countrywomen.

A massive American flag flutters behind the captain. "You bear a striking resemblance to a group of soaked, heavily pregnant mice." He wrinkles his nose.

Every woman wears a life belt around her waist. A wave of discontent sweeps through the crowd. "Here we stand, soaked like herring in a barrel," a voice says angrily, "Can't the old sea dog just finish so I can get into something warm and dry?" A murmur of agreement from the group.

"God knows what I've done to be punished with this task." The captain looks to the sky as if searching for an answer. A crew member at his side smiles slyly. "As you are aware, this vessel was not designed for women and children." With a shake of his head, the captain shows his displeasure. "The USS General Harry Taylor has a distinguished record of service in naval operations. Global stability currently requires her aid, and she is providing it. That's why you are here. Consequently, this lifeboat drill is being conducted to ensure the safe arrival of all passengers in New York."

Although none of us shivering women wear medals or uniforms, Kirsten thinks, *we've all played, or will play, our part.*

"It might be assumed that compliance from women is easily obtained, however, my experience suggests the contrary." He lets out a loud sigh. "Given the choice, I would always prefer to have a group of energetic young men with high testosterone levels on board my ship."

Shifting her weight, Kirsten feels a growing irritation.

"But I assure you," the captain says, "this exercise is being conducted with the utmost seriousness. Should difficulties arise during our voyage, it is imperative that you understand the proper deployment of the lifeboats."

"He's talking down to us like we're dumb chickens destined for the pot," Kirsten whispers to Henny.

In the same lecturing tone, the captain continues, "Knowing what *not* to do is also crucial. Every year, many fatalities occur among healthy young males attempting to deploy lifeboats."

Another murmur ripples through the crowd.

"How, then, are a bunch of young ladies like yourselves supposed to manage it?" He lets his gaze sweep over the women.

As she glances at the ship's lifeboats, Kirsten's hand glides over the life vest tied around her waist. *Thank God I know how to swim,* she thinks. *I'm more worried about staying balanced in a crowded lifeboat.* She feels a nervous flutter in her stomach. While the lifeboats' wide shape allows them to accommodate many passengers, the low sides necessitate perfectly calm seas to prevent the vessel from capsizing.

"The USS General Harry Taylor will execute her mission, fulfilling her national duty." There is a high-pitched tone in the captain's voice now. "Please bear this in mind while aboard my ship."

With a roll of her eyes, Henny whispers, "Such a military man."

꜠

ALL THE RAISED FINGERS AND SCOLDING AIMED AT WOMEN — IT'S A *constant barrage,* Kirsten thinks to herself, distracted. Straightening up, she turns to Henny. "We keep hearing it's our responsibility to help our soldiers transition back to civilian life after the war," she whispers. "I'm starting to wonder what that's all about."

Henny nods. "You're fortunate to have your Forest."

Kirsten averts her eyes. "He has his weaknesses too."

At the podium, a crew member demonstrates the proper operation of the hoist and correct rope-handling techniques.

The captain's voice echoes, refocusing Kirsten's attention on the deck: "Adherence to discipline and procedure is crucial for error prevention." Again, that piercing gaze, flanked by the two eagles. "Take note of that. In all aspects of life. Don't expect smooth sailing like this when things get serious."

Kirsten stares at the horizon. The rain has stopped, the wind has died down, and the water now lies still, reflecting the sky like an ice-blue mirror, its surface undisturbed. She imagines something from below breaking the surface, causing the smooth plane to rise into dark, foaming, meter-high peaks.

Sighing, she looks at Henny. "After this, I'm getting a soda from the vending machine. Or an ice cream," she says. "All this talk of disasters makes you crave sweets."

A girl a few rows ahead giggles. *At least women can still have a good laugh when confronted with this kind of authority*, Kirsten thinks, following her eyeline. But the girl isn't paying attention to the captain's words. Parker 51 is standing there, winking at the giggling girl!

Kirsten feels a tingling in her cheeks; the kind that comes right before tears well up. How could she think his attention was undivided? She almost threw it all away for him! "Damn you, Parker 51!"

His look of surprise quickly turns to a smile. Tipping his cap, he vanishes into the crowd.

"The vessel will soon make port in the English Channel, at which time shore leave will be granted to all. For your safety, it is recommended that you remain in groups and use your time judiciously." The captain pats his pocket. "Don't spend all your money on unnecessary knick-knacks."

Emergency Meeting
Kirsten

The churning of the water and the howling wind fills the deck. The women have been summoned to an emergency meeting; no one yet knows why. With a stoic demeanor, the captain mounts the podium once more and addresses the assembled crowd. It's plain to see that his news isn't good. Kirsten's heart pounds and sweat breaks out beneath her armpits.

"Some of you have been 'entertaining' the officers in the dining room and the lounge." Using his index and middle fingers, the captain emphasizes the word. "This is highly irregular. Consequently, access to the deck will be prohibited from the commencement of dinner until breakfast the following morning."

A collective gasp rises from the crowd.

"These newly implemented regulations do not pertain to women traveling with children. Their six-to-twenty-two schedule remains in effect." A stern look sweeps across his face as his eyes scan the women on deck. Some giggle, adjusting their hair with telling gestures. "I must express my concern regarding the moral failings of you German women." He looks to the area where the German war brides are gathered. "You ought to be ashamed of yourselves," he says, baring his teeth in a mocking smile, "considering your country's standing."

Why do they insist on causing problems, making it tough for the rest of us who abide by the rules? Kirsten thinks. *Given a chance at a new life, why wouldn't they take it and better themselves?*

"As a result, the planned disembarkation at Dover is canceled."

There's a low grumble of discontent from the women.

The captain waits until the noise subsides. "It's probably for the best. Getting women back on the ship is usually quite troublesome. God knows how many times we've had to search for ladies who couldn't — or didn't want to — find their way back." He glances at his watch. "Not to mention how quarrelsome women can be."

Maybe he should stick to the point and not lump us all together? Kirsten thinks.

"I also want to impress upon you German women the importance of being prepared to behave in a completely different moral manner when you arrive in America."

In protest, the German group collectively turns their backs, creating a unified wall of defiance.

In a commanding tone, the captain's voice cuts through the gathering: "I must ask all non-Germans to vacate the deck." A flinty expression is on his face as he regards Kirsten. "What I have to say does not concern you. It is solely intended for the ears of the German passengers."

"Damn strict, this rule against us going ashore because of their ridiculous antics!" Kirsten's palms tingle.

Henny nods, but then takes Kirsten's hand. "Let's find a cozy spot until the dinner gong sounds."

The Rat
Kirsten

Kirsten sits in the lounge, impatiently tapping her foot. She is finding it hard to concentrate on her letter to her mother.

"Easy, Kirsten," Henny says, looking up. "You're like an angry bull."

Kirsten's hands shake. Little spurts of ash fall onto the table and her letter, leaving streaks as she brushes it away. *I need something to calm my nerves*, she thinks. *Why's it so loud in here?* She looks around. Music, smoke, and the clinking of drinks fill the room around her. *To make matters worse, our planned adventure has been canceled. I should have been enjoying a leisurely stroll in Dover.* She looks at Henny, who is hunched over her letter. "I long so terribly to feel solid ground beneath my feet."

Henny nods.

"Now we're missing out on everything I was looking forward to, " Kirsten continues: "The English Channel, Dover, a portrait photo, a little souvenir as a memento."

Henny's engrossed in her letter and doesn't react.

"It's all been ruined because of them."

Finally, Henny looks up. "Good thing we got our portraits taken in Bremerhaven."

"Why are you always such a chirpy little optimist? It's enough to make one feel guilty!" Rising from her seat, Kirsten gives Henny a nudge, causing a small blob of ink to drip onto her letter. "This trip is taking forever, zigzagging around all those mines and subs!"

"At least it's only four of us crammed in that cabin." A look of regret crosses Henny's face as she looks at the letter.

"I long to be with my husband, to feel his hand in mine, and to begin a new life!" Kirsten crosses her arms. "I'm out of cigarettes, bored with cards, and done with afternoon naps."

Henny folds the letter and licks the seal on the envelope. "I'm fine with the journey taking a little longer. I'm so glad to have extra time with you, Kirsten."

A pang of guilt surges through Kirsten.

"My journey is only just beginning," Henny says, tapping her letter with a red nail. "Following this, I'll take the train from New York to the West Coast, then sail on to Hawaii."

Henny is right, Kirsten thinks. *I always want to push forward, that's my nature. Why can't I just be in the moment, enjoying exactly where I am, instead of worrying what's next? Always moving on, never satisfied, believing that tomorrow is better than today.*

She places her hand on Henny's arm. "Come on! I know how we can get revenge on those stupid Huns."

☾

KIRSTEN LEADS HENNY TO THE REAR OF THE VESSEL where the German women and children sleep. They slip into a room with wall-mounted changing tables.

"Now let's hear them squeal and scream like the rats they are." Kirsten grimaces as she fishes a soggy, brownish-yellow cloth diaper from the laundry hamper. Running into the sleeping quarters, she pulls aside a blanket and smears the contents over the sheet. "Straighten the blanket so they won't know we were here."

Henny does what Kirsten says. "I'd love to see their reaction when they crawl into bed tonight," she laughs.

Back in the changing room, Kirsten tosses the cloth in the hamper. As she's washing her hands, she hears Henny at the door.

"Look, what I found." A dead rat lies at Henny's feet.

"You didn't touch it, did you? They're crawling with bugs."

"I'm not that stupid." Using the toe of her shoe, Henny nudges the rodent. Grabbing a clean cloth from the stack, she says, "I'll hold it by the tail with this."

Rushing back to the sleeping quarters, Kirsten pulls back a blanket on a cot in the far corner so Henny can put the rat at the foot of the bed. Using her fingertips, Henny neatly folds the blanket over the mattress. "No one will notice in the dark."

"Hey, Henny, don't you think this is a bit much?" Kirsten is filled with an adrenaline rush, but at the same time feels a sense of responsibility for the situation — the way bullies prey on the most vulnerable students and nobody intervenes.

"They reap what they sow." Taking Kirsten by the arm, Henny guides her from the sleeping quarters, past a line of baby clothes drying on a pipe.

BACK IN THE LOUNGE, KIRSTEN TRIES TO CALM HER racing heart. Henny pretends nothing has happened as they both swirl the contents of their drinks. Occasionally, they catch each other's eyes and toast without words. *Beat softly, little heart*, Kirsten thinks. Henny gives her a look and bursts into laughter.

"I really don't understand what's so funny," Kirsten smiles. "I must finish this letter to Mom," she mutters, leaning down over her stationery.

UTILITIES
KIRSTEN

The mere thought of touching the ship's railings and handles makes Kirsten nauseous. *All those germs!*

Amused, Henny rolls her eyes. "Relax!" she says.

With a sigh, Kirsten grabs the railing. A shiver runs through her body. The floor feels spongy under her feet. The thought of dirt and scabies disgusts her. Perhaps it's all in her head, but the idea is hard to ignore once it's been planted. She misses the inner calm that washes over her as she wipes down countertops; the satisfying weight of straightening a bedspread. She misses the simple comfort of resting her elbows on a clean, smooth table, instead of the sticky, greasy surfaces on the boat.

A door down the hall says: *Utilities*. Kirsten opens it with her shoulder. The sounds change. A rhythmic humming comes from the machines along the wall. Labels on each of the three large, round-topped, metal cylinders read: *Kenmore Wringer Washer*.

"Look at them! Imagine having one of these in your

home!" A radiant smile lights Kirsten's face as she looks around the room.

"Do you know how to run a machine like that?" Henny looks at the units.

"It can't be that complicated." Kirsten goes to one of the appliances. The round button says: *low*. It has a milkmaid-style lid, but it's easier to open. Small whirlpools of water churn with a gentle hiss, pushing grayish foam right up to the edge. A wave of warmth and the fresh scent of clean laundry envelopes her face.

"I could easily spend all day in this place." Kirsten closes the lid and inspects the roller and folding section.

"Hearing you talk about cleaning and laundry that way is concerning." Henny smiles crookedly.

"I'll gladly press your clean, wrinkly laundry for you, my dear Henny." Kirsten walks out, Henny right behind her. The fire door slams shut with a hollow, metallic clang.

༄

ON THE DECK, THE RHYTHMIC ROCKING OF THE ship causes them to heel forward as it tilts. In several places, women sit pale-faced against the railing and bulkhead. Some are smeared with vomit, their hair clinging to their foreheads.

Kirsten is cautious about where she walks. In her mind's eye, she sees herself balancing as if she were a sea lion on a circus ball. In a dance with gravity, she gracefully extends her arms like a ballerina. "Can you taste the salt spray in the wind?" she asks Henny. Two sailors glance at them as they pass by.

A little later, they encounter a Red Cross nurse. "We're serving dinner in an hour." Her Southern accent reveals a hint of weariness. "Make sure you know your cabin number to queue correctly." Kirsten and Henny nod and the nurse continues, "And don't forget about the information meeting later." Her gaze is tired, yet stern.

In unison, Kirsten and Henny reply, "Yes, sister!"

They check the bulletin board for the day's schedule. Henny runs a pink fingernail down the list. "Knitting club. I'll have to look into that."

Kirsten rolls her eyes. "Good Lord! I'll play some card games. I hope they serve drinks and cigarettes there." She glances at the schedule again. "Bingo and table tennis aren't my thing, but check the schedule for the next few days." Kirsten tries to catch Henny's attention. "I love the evening classes where we learn about America." Scanning the offerings, she reads:

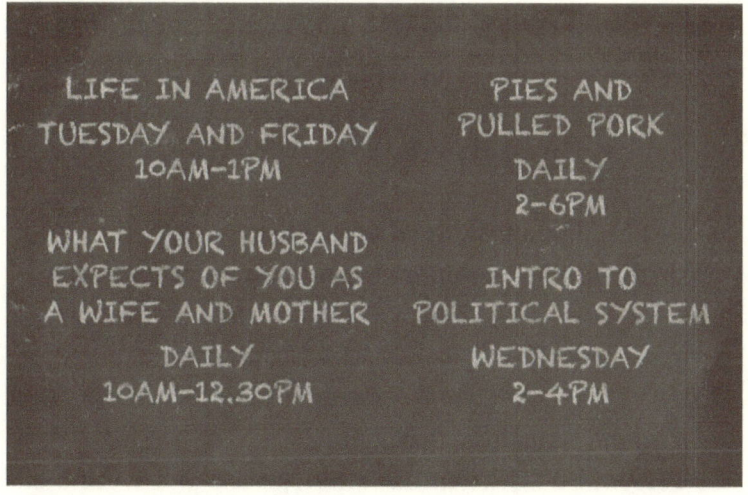

LIFE IN AMERICA
TUESDAY AND FRIDAY
10AM–1PM

WHAT YOUR HUSBAND
EXPECTS OF YOU AS
A WIFE AND MOTHER
DAILY
10AM–12.30PM

PIES AND
PULLED PORK
DAILY
2–6PM

INTRO TO
POLITICAL SYSTEM
WEDNESDAY
2–4PM

"There's so much to learn," Kirsten says, her voice bright.

"Kirsten, it's really not that exciting," Henny sighs.

"It's the perfect thing for us!" Kirsten nudges her friend a little harder than intended. "It's in The Great Salon, but I always get lost trying to find it." Kirsten examines the ship's map.

"Are there no parties on this dinghy? I'm going stir-crazy, pacing the deck." Henny glares irritably out over the water. "Not to mention our cramped little cabin. I feel like a lion in a cage! I've heard most of the others' stories. It's time for something to happen."

"Don't pout, Henny," Kirsten says, "Use your eyes! A big party is scheduled for the night before we arrive in New York." Her stomach growls. "Dinner time!"

Henny sighs. "Have you forgotten? 'Women must change for dinner every evening. Only skirts or dresses are acceptable.'" She snorts. "I've already exhausted my supply of suitable outfits."

"I'll lend you something." Kirsten squeezes Henny's arm. "That will also save us an hour of listening to the whining kids in the nursery." She smiles, "Have you seen tonight's menu?"

CREAMY ASPARAGUS SOUP.

Crispy-skinned whole fish served with steamed cauliflower and hollandaise sauce.

"I wonder if it'll come with Danish new potatoes." Kirsten can almost taste the sweet and buttery flavor of the small, round Scandinavian delight.

"Less will do, Kirsten. Let's hurry back to the cabin and change," Henny urges, pulling her along.

The Star-Spangled Banner
Kirsten

As Kirsten adjusts her hair, she pictures herself arriving in New York: the Statue of Liberty looming behind; her future stretching out before her. What does the future hold for her? Is Forest picking her up at the dock? Will his love for her match the love he had for Martha? Or will she have to return to Denmark a failure, cap in hand? *Calm down, Kirsten,* she thinks. *Fretting won't change a thing. The decision has been made and worrying won't ease my anxiety.*

Practical tasks, like the repetitive motions of cleaning, have always helped her focus. The problem is, there are not many chores to tackle here. Instead, she tries to stay busy to keep her mind occupied. She concentrates on the podium before her.

"Upon your arrival, you will be greeted by your new families. Photographers and journalists will be present as well," a Red Cross nurse explains.

Kirsten takes notes, focusing on keeping her attention in the room.

"Americans, especially now, after the war, take great pride

in their nation. Your priority is showing your appreciation and making it clear that America is your new homeland."

I will, Kirsten thinks. *But I refuse to abandon my Danish heritage.*

"One of the ways you can do this is by learning the American national anthem, *The Star-Spangled Banner*. Singing it makes a good impression."

The Red Cross sister hands a stack of papers to a woman in the front row, who passes the song sheets around.

Kirsten skims the page. Four long verses. "So much of this is gibberish," she admits to an equally bewildered Henny. "I usually manage to understand even the most demanding official letters, but the abstract imagery and archaic words are a bit too complicated for me."

"Do we have to learn all of it?" asks a woman.

"No, we'll do like the Americans and only sing the first verse," the Red Cross nurse says. "Please stand."

There's a clatter. The Red Cross sister nods to the pianist to begin.

"Place your right hand over your heart." Then, with a wink, she adds, "It's on the left side, for those who might not know." Laying a hand on her chest, she straightens her back.

Kirsten feels a nervous tug in her stomach as she does the same. "I feel like a traitor," she whispers to Henny, who nods in agreement.

> O say, can you see,
> By the dawn's early light,
> What so proudly we hailed
> At the twilight's last gleaming?
> Whose broad stripes and bright stars,
> Through the perilous fight,
> O'er the ramparts we watch'd,
> Were so gallantly streaming?
> And the rockets' red glare,
> The bombs bursting in air,
> Gave proof through the night
> That our flag was still there.

While the Red Cross nurse sings, Kirsten watches the other women. Several seem filled with a similar mix of conflicting feelings, but the atmosphere crackles with pride, a palpable energy filling the room. Then, as the sister reaches the final few lines, slowing her tempo, her voice resonates with a powerful force:

> O say, does that star-spangled banner
> Yet wave o'er the land of the free
> And the home of the brave?

Kirsten lowers her gaze to get a hold of her emotions. Setting aside the song's 'hail', which reminds her of her aversion to anything reminiscent of the German occupation — particularly the outstretched arms of the Nazi salute — the fundamental truth remains: America is the nation that has bestowed freedom upon the world. America is the land of the brave. *Forest was brave, the American soldiers were brave, and maybe I am, too,* Kirsten thinks to herself.

There's a connection between songs and emotions. During her time at the air force base, she found herself captivated as the delicate melodies at Red Cross functions washed over her. At Martha's funeral, the hymns filled the air as Kirsten's grief overwhelmed her. Here on the ship, her feelings are different. Still, a recognizable pattern emerges between music and emotion: a mix of anticipation, hope, and elation, overshadowed by the sadness, fear, and apprehension of parting. All of it amplified by the Red Cross sister's singing voice. Euphoria and purpose fill Kirsten, making her body vibrate. She'll learn the anthem — prove to Forest, everyone at the dock, and herself that she's committed to her husband and her new country. She needs to conceal her Danish identity. For now, anyway.

"Damn, these lyrics are tough!" Next to her, the woman's eyes are red.

"We can do this!" Kirsten smiles at the woman, then quickly wipes under her own eyes.

The applause fades and the sister curtsies. "There you go." She smiles as she looks around. "Let's start from the top and go line by line."

Arrival
Kirsten

Nothing about the end of her journey and arrival in New York feels as Kirsten had imagined.

When the USS General Harry Taylor departed Bremerhaven, the cries of gulls pierced the air, mingling with the whimpers of frightened children and the sobs of women. A shrill wind whistled past their ears, carrying the sounds of masts groaning, the rhythmic clang of the industrious harbor, snatches of songs, and well wishes shouted from the dock.

"Gute Reise!" the Germans called out to their loved ones.

"Au revoir!" the French parents waved as they wished their children a safe crossing.

On the dock, families tearfully bid farewell, dreaming of brighter futures for their daughters and sisters. On board, the women wept at their parting, but were also joyful at the prospect of rejoining their husbands across the Atlantic. Goodbyes are hard, but the ones left behind experience it more severely than the one who is leaving.

Only one thing about the arrival in New York feels similar to when they set sail: the tempo. It takes just as long to be towed into the harbor in New York as it did to be towed out of the harbor in Germany. When the tugboat pulled the ship out of Bremerhaven, the women turned inward; here it's the opposite. Feet shuffle and stand on tiptoes. Torsos lean forward. Dreams, anxiety, and restlessness fill the air. They've agreed to sing *The Star-Spangled Banner* as soon as the Statue of Liberty comes into view.

"She stands on Liberty Island," the Red Cross sister told them at one meeting, "and not, as one might think, on Ellis Island, where immigrants have been processed on their arrival in America since January 1892." It sounded like she was reading from a book.

"Was-it-a-gift-from-France?" The Frenchwoman's question was a single, long, nasal, guttural sound.

It annoys Kirsten when people ask questions they already know the answers to. Had the French not suffered so terribly during the war, she might have mentioned their cooperation with Nazi orders to round up and hand over their Jewish people.

"Yes," the Red Cross sister agreed, "The Statue of Liberty represents freedom and new beginnings in America."

"That's the quick, touristy explanation," Kirsten murmured to Henny, "It represents national independence and human rights."

Maybe we even resemble her, standing alone on that island, she mused.

NOW SHE STANDS HERE ON THE DECK, BUT THE Statue of Liberty is nowhere in sight. Icy raindrops on a cold wind snap Kirsten back to reality. *We are like wet mice huddled together, just like the captain said,* she thinks, pulling her shoulders up to her ears.

The crossing's complicated system of rotating deck access schedules has been entirely abandoned. In a chaotic scene of jostling bodies, women, children, and people of English, Danish, Dutch, and German descent all vie for the best position to witness the sight of their new homeland for the very first time.

Kirsten's gaze sweeps over the powdered cheeks and bobbed hair. The air is filled with the sweet scent of vanilla. Everyone has been up since before sunrise getting ready. The scented air reminds Kirsten of Ingrid. *I'll send you the best of America,* she thinks. *Feathered hats, form-fitting clothes, leather shoes, and handbags. You'll find a brand-new wardrobe waiting for you when you wake up. And once you're better, we'll have you come to Texas.*

A broad-shouldered woman interrupts Kirsten's thoughts, cutting in line.

"Stop it!" Kirsten cries out, pushing the woman back, only to be shoved by a scratchy woolen shoulder. A heel stomps down on her foot and the scent of damp wool, smoker's breath, and sweaty underarms assaults her nostrils. A light touch on her arm prevents Kirsten's anger from erupting; Henny silently slides in beside her.

"Where did you come from?" Kirsten gratefully leans her head on her friend's shoulder.

☽

What if it doesn't work out between us? We barely know each other. Am I going to be happy in this place?

Swallowing hard, Kirsten leans toward Henny. Without words, they stand together, a silent exchange passing between them as they contemplate the uncertain paths ahead, the weight of their decisions pressing down. *Will I have the same connection and closeness to Forest?* Kirsten thinks, then straightens up. *Unless you take risks, you won't get anywhere.*

"Where's everything I wanted to see in New York — the Statue of Liberty, the tall buildings, and all the rest?" Kirsten looks questioningly at Henny, who responds with a shrug.

Thick fog shrouds the ship, limiting visibility to just a few feet. The first impressions are overwhelming, but not in the way Kirsten had imagined. She lowers her gaze to compose herself. The harbor water is murky gray.

Like a single organism, the women sway to the right as the ship turns. *What's going on?* The women exchange confused glances. As the boat straightens up, the sharp November wind lashes their faces. Kirsten's eyes well. *We needn't have bothered with our hair.* She considers brushing the stray strands from her cheek, but what would be the point?

When Henny suddenly moves her hand toward her face, Kirsten instinctively jerks her head backward, only realizing afterward that her friend was trying to fix her scarf, which had slipped from her hair. Shame trickles through her. Normally, she manages to stop her body's automatic defense mechanisms.

"Sorry, Henny, I got startled." Kirsten looks away, biting her lower lip. "It was just a reflex."

"I know that feeling."

Placing her hands on the railing, Kirsten looks toward the dock she knows must be close. "Now life begins."

Henny's voice is tinged with sadness, "I'm going to be utterly lonely on that island. He's so unpredictable." Though she attempts a smile, her tone betrays her unease.

"It's a new beginning," Kirsten says, stroking Henny's wet face. *For all of us.*`

How can something be so close and yet so far away? There's still an hour before the steamer docks at the Brooklyn Navy Yard, the world's largest harbor in the world's largest city. The iconic symbol of freedom and opportunity, eagerly anticipated by everyone, remains hidden from view, as the weather conspires to keep it shrouded. Confusion spreads. Suppressed tears make the women's voices thick.

"Won't we be passing by the Statue of Liberty?" Kirsten grabs Henny's arm. It's as if all the scars that were healing are breaking open again. "I'm cold and soaked, and I'm so disappointed I could cry!" *With her torch held high, the Statue of Liberty was supposed to give us her blessing, to show us that everything will be all right,* Kirsten thinks.

"It's just a statue. Remember why we're here." Henny pats Kirsten's hand.

Unconcerned with her appearance, Kirsten allows the snot and tears to flow freely, smudging her make-up; the rain plastering her hair to her head.

Her vision was of a cheerful crowd, filled with billowing flags, the waving of children, and a crisp fall sun shining down. She fantasized about an orchestra offering a warm welcome, journalists eager to learn all about her, and dockworkers tipping their caps. Instead, there's no grandeur — only industry. Harbor cranes protrude from the fog. As the boat slowly pulls the women through the mist, skyscrapers, cars, and machinery emerge from the haze. Five musicians play their instruments discordantly. Kirsten's eyes search for land.

A few dockworkers glance up, then resume their work. A line of buses is parked by the pier, a welcome hall situated behind them. Kirsten scans the faces, carefully examining each one. Forest is nowhere to be seen.

A CRACKLE OF STATIC FROM THE LOUDSPEAKERS IS punctuated by orders barked in German and English: "Disembark... ID cards... luggage... reception..."

A woman spontaneously starts singing the national anthem and more voices join in. But it never becomes more than a hiccupping whisper, far from the upbeat mood in the rehearsal room. It's as if they're already failing the test that will determine if they're good enough to belong. The singing from the deck and fragments of notes from the orchestra on the pier blend together.

A gust of wind blows Kirsten's ID card into her face. The lining feels like the same material as her mother's dishrag. She allows the knot of grief, fear, and expectations to unravel.

"Ladies!" the captain's voice calls out across the deck, "Welcome to America, the land of freedom and democracy. May you find warm hearts and kindness, peace and happiness in your new, distant land. May it become the new beginning you dream of. Carry out your duties as wives to honor both your old and new homelands. "

Thank You

This book would never have found its way into your hands without the love, patience, and generosity of the people around me.

My deepest gratitude belongs to the love of my life, Andreas. He has read every version of this manuscript, believed in me when I doubted myself, and supported me in countless quiet ways — cooking dinner for our family, placing coffee or a glass of wine beside my keyboard, and surrounding me with steady love and care. *You and me, baby. Always.*

While I was writing *The Scandinavian War Bride*, my children, Lina and Ingmar, somehow grew into teenagers. I've lost track of how many times I said, "in a minute," or "not now, I'm working." Please know that my love for you reaches far beyond the stars, even when my mind wandered deep into the world of writing.

Although Kirsten is not my grandmother, her life — and the lives of the women who came before me — planted the seed for this story. I am deeply grateful for their quiet strength, resilience, and courage, which continue to guide me.

'Indian' Stig saw my artistic soul before I did. His thoughtful readings, encouragement, and unwavering belief have meant more to me than he knows, and I am profoundly thankful for his presence in my life.

I am grateful to Ph.D. Katherine Hanson, who brought wit, humor, and exceptional competence to her reading of the English manuscript. Since we became colleagues in 2010 at the Scandinavian Studies Department at the University of Washington in Seattle, I have cherished her kindness, knowledge, and warm, generous spirit.

In the UK, award-winning novelist, poet, playwright, screenwriter, and short fiction writer Jo Gatford offered invaluable insight, edits, and encouragement to the English version of the manuscript, for which I am sincerely thankful.

My thanks also go to designer Kerry Ellis, who worked with me on the cover, logo, and interior of *The Scandinavian War Bride*. I deeply appreciate your creativity, professionalism, and patience.

Thank you to Paul Davis of Hazy Bay Recording Studio and to Nick Biscardi for post-production. I am grateful to Mary Kae Irvin of Cedar House Audio Production, whose talent gave life to the audiobook.

My dear friend Jerene opened not only her beautiful Pacific Northwest cabin but also her heart to me. During both the Danish and English writing phases, her tranquil retreat — surrounded by towering pines — gave me the peace, space, and stillness I needed to write and reflect. Thank you, my dear friend, for opening your heart and your home to me.

Finally, I extend my heartfelt thanks to the publishing house Byens Forlag for believing in this project and for publishing the Danish edition of *The Scandinavian War Bride*.

www.ingramcontent.com/pod-product-compliance
Lightning Source LLC
LaVergne TN
LVHW091704070526
838199LV00050B/2282